THE ORIGIN OF EVIL

THE ORIGIN OF EVIL

ELLERY QUEEN

HarperPerennial

A Division of HarperCollins*Publishers*

Reprinted by arrangement with The Ellery Queen (Manfred B. Lee and Frederic Dannay) Trusts and Scott Meredith Literary Agency, Inc. Originally published by Little Brown & Company in 1951.

HarperCollins books may be purchased for educational, business, or sales promotional use. For information, please call or write: Special Markets Department, HarperCollins Publishers, Inc., 10 East 53rd Street, New York, NY 10022. Telephone: (212) 207-7528; Fax: (212) 207-7222.

First HarperPerennial edition published 1992.

Library of Congress Cataloging-in-Publication Data

Queen, Ellery.
    The origin of evil / by Ellery Queen. — 1st HarperPerennial ed.
        p. cm.
    ISBN 0-06-097439-7 (paper)
    I. Title.
PS3533.U4075   1992
813' .52—dc20   91-50533

92 93 94 95 96 MB 10 9 8 7 6 5 4 3 2 1

1

Ellery was spread over the pony-skin chair before the picture window, *huarachos* crossed on the typewriter table, a ten-inch frosted glass in his hand, and the corpse at his feet. He was studying the victim between sips and making not too much out of her. However, he was not concerned. It was early in the investigation, she was of unusual proportions, and the *ron* consoled.

He took another sip.

It was a curious case. The victim still squirmed; from where he sat he could make out signs of life. Back in New York they had warned him that these were an illusion, reflexes following the death-rattle. Why, you won't believe it, they had said, but corruption's set in already and anyone who can tell a stinkweed from a camellia will testify to it. Ellery had been sceptical. He had known deceased in her heyday—a tumid wench, every man's daydream, and the laughing target of curses and longing. It was hard to believe that such vitality could be exterminated.

On the scene of the crime—or rather above it, for the little house he had taken was high over the city, a bird's nest perched on the twig-tip of an upper branch of the hills—Ellery still doubted. There she lay under a thin blanket of smog, stirring a little, and they said she was dead.

Fair Hollywood.

Murdered, ran the post-mortem, by Television.

He squinted down at the city, sipping his rum and enjoying his nakedness. It was a blue-white day. The hill ran green and flowered to the twinkled plain, simmering in the sun.

There had been no technical reason for choosing Hollywood as the setting for his new novel. Mystery stories operate under special laws of growth; their beginnings may lie in the look in a faceless woman's eye glimpsed in a crowd for exactly the duration of one heartbeat, or in the small type on page five of a life-insurance policy; generally the writer has the atlas to pick from. Ellery had had only the gauziest idea of where he was going; at that stage of the game it could as well have been Joplin, Missouri or the kitchens of the Kremlin. In fact, his plot was in such a cloudy state that when he heard about the murder of Hollywood he took it as a sign from the heavens and made immediate arrangements to be present at the autopsy. His trade being violent death, a city with a knife in its back seemed just the place to take his empty sample cases.

Well, there was life in the old girl yet. Of course, theatres with *MOVIES ARE BETTER THAN EVER* on their marquees had crossbars over their portals saying *CLOSED*; you could now get a table at *The Brown Derby* without waiting more than twenty minutes; that eminent haberdasher of the Strip, Mickey Cohen, was out of business; movie stars were cutting their prices for radio; radio actors were auditioning tensely for television as they redesigned their belts or put their houses up for sale; shopkeepers were complaining that how could anybody find money for yard goods or nail files when the family budget was mortgaged to Hoppy labels, the new car, and the television set; teen-age gangs, solemnly christened "wolf-packs" by the Los Angeles newspapers, cruised the streets beating up strangers, high-school boys were regularly caught selling marijuana, and "Chicken!" was the favourite highway sport of the hot-rodders; and you could throttle a tourist on Hollywood Boulevard

2

between Vine and La Brea any night after 10.30 and feel reasonably secure against interruption.

But out in the San Fernando Valley mobs of little cheap stuccos and redwood fronts were beginning to elbow the pained hills, paint-fresh signal lights at intersections were stopping cars which had previously known only the carefree California conscience, and a great concrete ditch labelled "Flood Control Project" was making its way across the sandy valley like an opening zipper.

On the ocean side of the Santa Monica Mountains, from Beverly Glen to Topanga Canyon, lordlier mansions were going up which called themselves "estates"—disdaining the outmoded "ranch" or "rancho," which more and more out-of-State ex-innocents were learning was a four-or-five-and-den on a 50 × 100 lot containing three callow apricot-trees. Beverly Hills might be biting its perfect fingernails, but Glendale and Encino were booming, and Ellery could detect no moans from the direction of Brentwood, Flintridge, Sunland, or Eagle Rock. New schools were assembling, more oldsters were chugging in from Iowa and Michigan, flexing their arthritic fingers and practising old age pension-check-taking, and to drive a car in downtown Los Angeles at noontime the four blocks from 3rd to 7th along Broadway, Spring, Hill, or Main now took thirty minutes instead of fifteen. Ellery heard tell of huge factories moving in; of thousands of migrants swarming into Southern California through Blythe and Indio on 60 and Needles and Barstow on 66—latter-day pioneers to whom the movies still represented Life and Love and "television" remained a high-falutin word, like "antibiotic." The car-hops were more beautiful and numerous than ever; more twenty-foot ice-cream cones punctuated the skyline; Tchaikovsky under the stars continued to fill Hollywood Bowl with brave-bottomed music-lovers; Grand Openings of hardware stores now used two giant searchlights instead of one; the Farmers' Market on Fairfax and 3rd chittered and heaved like an Egyptian bazaar in the tourist season; Madman Muntz had apparently taken permanent possession of the skies, his name in mile-high letters drifting expensively away daily; and the newspapers offered an even more tempting line of cheese-cake than in the old days—Ellery actually saw one photograph of the routine well-stacked cutie in a Bikini bathing-suit perched zippily on a long flower-decked box inscribed *Miss National Casket Week*. And in three days or so, according to the reports, the Imperial Potentate would lead a six-hour safari of thirteen thousand red-fezzed, capering, elderly Penrods, accompanied by fifty-one bands, assorted camels, clowns, and floats, along Figueroa Street to the Memorial Coliseum to convene the seventy-umpth Imperial Session of the Ancient Arabic Order of the Nobles of the Mystic Shrine—a civic event guaranteed to rouse even the dead.

It became plain in his first few days in Hollywood and environs that what the crape-hangers back East were erroneously bewailing was not the death of the angelic city but its exuberant rebirth in another shape. The old order changeth. The new organism was exciting, but it was a little out of his line; and Ellery almost packed up and flew back East. But then he thought, It's all hassle and hurly-burly, everybody snarling or making hay; and there's still the twitching nucleus of the old Hollywood bunch—stick around, old boy, the atmosphere is murderous and it may well inspire a collector's item or two for the circulating library shelves.

Also, there had been the press and its agents. Ellery had thought to slip into town by dropping off at the Lockheed field in Burbank rather than the International Airport in Inglewood. But he touched Southern California soil to a bazooka fire of questions and lenses, and the next day his picture was on the front page of all the papers. They had even got his address in the hills straight, although his pal the real estate man later swore by the beard of Nature Boy that he'd had nothing to do with the leak. It had been that way for Ellery ever since the publicity explosion over the Cat case. The newspaper boys were convinced that, having saved Manhattan from a fate equivalent to

4

death, Ellery was in Los Angeles on a mission at least equally large and torrid. When he plaintively explained that he had come to write a book they all laughed, and their printed explanations ascribed his visit to everything from a top-secret appointment by the Mayor as Special Investigator to Clean Up Greater L.A. to the turning of his peculiar talents upon the perennial problem of the Black Dahlia.

How could he run out?

At this point Ellery noticed that his glass was as empty as his typewriter.

He got up from the pony-skin chair, and found himself face to face with a pretty girl.

As he jumped nudely for the bedroom doorway Ellery thought, The *huarachos* must look ridiculous. Then he thought, Why didn't I put on those ten pounds Barney prescribed? Then he got angry and poked his head around the door to whine, "I told Mrs. Williams I wasn't seeing anybody today, not even her. How did you get in?"

"Through the garden," said the girl. "Climbed up from the road below. I tried not to trample your marigolds. I hope you don't mind."

"I do mind. Go away."

"But I've got to see you."

"Everybody's got to see me. But I don't have to see everybody. Especially when I look like this."

"You are sort of pale, aren't you? And your ribs stick out, Ellery." She sounded like a debunked sister. Ellery suddenly remembered that in Hollywood dress is a matter of free enterprise. You could don a parka and drive a team of Siberian huskies from Schwab's Drug Store at the foot of Laurel Canyon to NBC at Sunset and Vine and never turn a head. Fur stoles over slacks are acceptable if not *de rigueur*, the exposed navel is considered conservative, and at least one man dressed in nothing but Waikiki trunks may be found poking sullenly among the avocados at any vegetable stand. "You ought to put on some weight, Ellery. And get out in the sun."

"Thank you," Ellery heard himself saying.

His Garden of Eden costume meant absolutely nothing to her. And she was even prettier than he had thought. Hollywood prettiness, he thought sulkily; they all look alike. Probably Miss Universe of Pasadena. She was dressed in zebra-striped culottes and bolero over a bra-like doodad of bright green suède. Green open-toed sandals on her tiny feet. A matching suède jockey cap on her cinnamon hair. Skin toast-coloured where it was showing, and *no* ribs. A small and slender number, but three-dimensional where it counted. About nineteen years old. For no reason at all she reminded him of Meg in Thorne Smith's *The Night Life of the Gods,* and he pulled his head back and banged the door.

When he came out safe and suave in slacks, shantung shirt, and burgundy corduroy jacket, she was curled up in his pony-skin chair smoking a cigarette.

"I've fixed your drink," she said.

"Kind of you. I suppose that means I must offer you one." No point in being too friendly.

"Thanks. I don't drink before five." She was thinking of something else.

Ellery leaned against the picture window and looked down at her with hostility. "It's not that I'm a prude, Miss—"

"Hill. Laurel Hill."

"—Miss Laurel Hill, but when I receive strange young things *au naturel* in Hollywood I like to be sure no confederate with a camera and an offer to do business is skulking behind my drapes. Why do you think you have to see me?"

"Because the police are dummies."

"Ah, the police. They won't listen to you?"

"They listen, all right. But then they laugh. I don't think there's anything funny in a dead dog, do you?"

"In a what?"

6

"A dead dog."

Ellery sighed, rolling the frosty glass along his brow. "Your pooch was poisoned, of course?"

"Guess again," said the set-faced intruder. "He wasn't my pooch, and I don't know what caused his death. What's more, dog-lover though I am, I don't care a curse.... They said it was somebody's idea of a rib, and I know they're talking through their big feet. I don't know what it meant, but it was no rib."

Ellery had set the glass down. She stared back. Finally he shook his head, smiling. "The tactics are primitive, Laurel. E for Effort. But no dice."

"No tactics," she said impatiently. "Let me tell you—"

"Who sent you to me?"

"Not a soul. You were all over the papers. It solved my problem."

"It doesn't solve mine, Laurel. My problem is to find the background of peaceful isolation which passeth the understanding of the mere, dear reader. I'm here to do a book, Laurel—a poor thing in a state of arrested development, but writing is a habit writers get into, and my time has come. So, you see, I can't take any cases."

"You won't even listen." Her mouth was in trouble. She got up and started across the room. He watched the brown flesh below the bolero. Not his type, but nice.

"Dogs die all the time," Ellery said in a kindly voice.

"It wasn't the dog, I tell you. It was the way it happened." She did not turn at the front door.

"The way he died?" Sucker.

"The way we found him." The girl suddenly leaned against the door, sidewise to him, staring down at her cigarette. "He was on our doorstep. Did you ever have a cat who insisted on leaving tidily dead mice on your mat to go with your breakfast eggs? He was a ... gift." She looked round for an ashtray, went over to the fireplace. "And it killed my father."

A dead dog killing anybody struck Ellery as worth a tentative glance. And there was something about the girl—a remote, hardened purpose—that interested him.

"Sit down again."

She betrayed herself by the quick way in which she came back to the pony-skin chair, by the way she folded her tense hands and waited.

"How exactly, Laurel, did a dead dog 'kill' your father?"

"It murdered him."

He didn't like the way she sat there. He said deliberately, "Don't build it up for me. This isn't a suspense programme. A strange dead hound is left on your doorstep, and your father dies. What's the connection?"

"It frightened him to death!"

"And what did the death certificate say?" He now understood the official hilarity.

"Coronary something. I don't care what it said. Getting the dog did it."

"Let's go back." Ellery offered her one of his cigarettes, but she shook her head and took a pack of Dunhills from her green pouch bag. He held a match for her; the cigarette between her lips was shaking. "Your name is Laurel Hill. You had a father. Who was he? Where do you live? What did he do for a living? And so on." She looked surprised, as if it had not occurred to her that such trivia could be of any interest to him. "I'm not necessarily taking it, Laurel. But I promise not to laugh."

"Thank you.... Leander Hill. Hill & Priam, Wholesale Jewellers."

"Yes." He had never heard of the firm. "Los Angeles?"

"The main office is here, though Dad and Roger have—I mean had ..." She laughed. "What tense *do* I use?... branch offices in New York, Amsterdam, South Africa."

"Who is Roger?"

"Roger Priam. Dad's partner. We live off Outpost, not far from here. Twelve acres of lop-sided woods. Formal gardens, with

8

mathematical eucalyptus and royal palms, and plenty of bougainvillea, bird-of-paradise, poinsettia—all the stuff that curls up and dies at a touch of frost, which we get regularly every winter and which everybody says can't possibly happen again, not in Southern California. But dad liked it. Made him feel like a Caribbean pirate, he used to say. Three in help in the house, a gardener who comes in every day, and the Priams have the adjoining property." From the carefully scrubbed way in which she produced the name Priam it might have been Hatfield. "Daddy had a bad heart, and we should have lived on level ground. But he liked hills and wouldn't hear of moving."

"Mother alive?" He knew she was not. Laurel had the motherless look. The self-made female. A man's girl, and there were times when she would insist on being a man's man. Not Miss Universe of Pasadena or anywhere else, he thought. He began to like her. "She isn't?" he said, when Laurel was silent.

"I don't know." A sore spot. "If I ever knew my mother, I've forgotten."

"Foster-mother, then?"

"He never married. I was brought up by a nurse, who died when I was fifteen—four years ago. I never liked her, and I think she got pneumonia just to make me feel guilty. I'm—I was his daughter by adoption." She looked around for an ashtray, and Ellery brought her one. She said steadily as she crushed the cigarette, "But really his daughter. None of that fake pal stuff, you understand, that covers contempt on one side and being unsure on the other. I loved and respected him, and—as he used to say—I was the only woman in his life. Dad was a little on the old-school side. Held my chair for me. That sort of thing. He was ... solid." And now, Ellery thought, it's jelly and you're hanging on to the stuff with your hard little fingers. "It happened," Laurel Hill went on in the same toneless way, "two weeks ago. June third. We were just finishing breakfast. Simeon, our chauffeur, came in to tell daddy he'd just brought the car around and there was something 'funny' at the front door. We all went out, and there it was—a dead dog lying on the doorstep with an ordinary shipping tag attached to its collar. Dad's name was printed on it in pencil: *Leander Hill*."

"Any address?"

"Just the name."

"Did the printing look familiar? Did you recognize it?"

"I didn't really look at it. I just saw one line of pencil-marks as dad bent over the dog. He said in a surprised way, 'Why, it's addressed to me.' Then he opened the little casket."

"Casket?"

"There was a tiny silver box—about the size of a pill-box—attached to the collar. Dad opened it and found a wad of thin paper inside, folded over enough times so it would fit into the box. He unfolded it, and it was covered with writing or printing—it might even have been typewriting; I couldn't really see because he half-turned away as he read it.

"By the time he'd finished reading his face was the colour of bread-dough, and his lips looked bluish. I started to ask him who'd sent it to him and what was wrong, when he crushed the paper in a sort of spasm and gave a choked cry and fell. I'd seen it happen before. It was a heart attack."

She stared out the picture window at Hollywood.

"How about a drink, Laurel?"

"No, thanks. Simeon and—"

"What kind of dog was it?"

"Some sort of hunting dog, I think."

"Was there a licence-tag on his collar?"

"I don't remember seeing any."

"An anti-rabies tag?"

"I saw no tag except the paper one with dad's name on it."

"Anything special about the dog-collar?"

"It couldn't have cost more than seventy-five cents."

"Just a collar." Ellery dragged over a chartreuse latticed blond chair and straddled it. "Go on, Laurel."

"Simeon and Ichiro, our houseman, carried him up to his bedroom while I ran for the brandy, and Mrs. Monk, our housekeeper, phoned the doctor. He lives on Castilian Drive and he was over in a few minutes. Daddy didn't die—that time."

"Oh, I see," said Ellery. "And what did the paper in the silver box on the dead dog's collar say, Laurel?"

"That's what I don't know."

"Oh, come."

"When he fell unconscious the paper was still in his hand, crumpled into a ball. I was too busy to try to open his fist, and by the time Dr. Voluta came, I'd forgotten it. But I remembered it that night, and the first chance I got—the next morning—I asked dad about it. The minute I mentioned it he got pale, mumbled, 'It was nothing, nothing,' and I changed the subject fast. But when Dr. Voluta dropped in, I took him aside and asked him if he'd seen the note. He said he had opened daddy's hand and put the wad of paper on the night table beside the bed without reading it. I asked Simeon, Ichiro, and the housekeeper if they had taken the paper, but none of them had seen it. Daddy must have spotted it when he came to, and when he was alone he took it back."

"Have you looked for it since?"

"Yes, but I haven't found it. I assume he destroyed it."

Ellery did not comment on such assumptions. "Well, then, the dog, the collar, the little box. Have you done anything about them?"

"I was too excited over whether daddy was going to live or die to think about the dog. I recall telling Itchie or Sim to get it out of the way. I only meant for them to get it off the doorstep, but the next day when I went looking for it, Mrs. Monk told me she had called the Pound Department or some place and it had been picked up and carted away."

"Up the flue," said Ellery, tapping his teeth with a fingernail. "Although the collar and box … You're sure your father didn't react to the mere sight of the dead dog? He wasn't afraid of dogs? Or," he added suddenly, "of dying?"

11

"He adored dogs. So much so that when Sarah, our Chesapeake bitch, died of old age last year he refused to get another dog. He said it was too hard losing them. As far as dying is concerned, I don't think the prospect of death as such bothered daddy very much. Certainly not so much as the suffering. He hated the idea of a lingering illness with a lot of pain, and he always hoped that when his time came he'd pass away in his sleep. But that's all. Does that answer your question?"

"Yes," said Ellery, "and no. Was he superstitious?"

"Not especially. Why?"

"You said he was frightened to death. I'm groping."

Laurel was silent. Then she said, "But he was. I mean frightened to death. It wasn't the dog—at first." She gripped her ankles, staring ahead. "I got the feeling that the dog didn't mean anything till he read the note. Maybe it didn't mean anything to him even then. But whatever was in that note terrified him. It came as a tremendous shock to him. I'd never seen him look *afraid* before. I mean the real thing. And I could have sworn he died on the way down. He looked really dead lying there.... That note did something devastating." She turned to Ellery. Her eyes were greenish, with brown flecks in them; they were a little bulgy. "Something he'd forgotten, maybe. Something so important it made Roger come out of his shell for the first time in fifteen years."

"What?" said Ellery. "What was that again?"

"I told you—Roger Priam, Dad's business partner. His oldest friend. Roger left his house."

"For the first time in fifteen years?" exclaimed Ellery.

"Fifteen years ago Roger became partly paralyzed. He's lived in a wheel-chair ever since, and ever since he's refused to leave the Priam premises. All vanity; he was a large hunk of man in his day, I understand, proud of his build, his physical strength; he can't stand the thought of having people see him helpless, and it's turned him into something pretty unpleasant.

"Through it all Roger pretends he's as good as ever and he

brags that running the biggest jewellery business on the West coast from a wheel-chair in the hills proves it. Of course, he doesn't do any such thing. Daddy ran it all, though to keep peace he played along with Roger and pretended with him—gave Roger special jobs to do that he could handle over the phone, never took an important step without consulting him, and so on. Why, some of the people at the office and showrooms downtown have been with the firm for years and have never even laid eyes on Roger. The employees hate him. They call him 'the invisible God,'" Laurel said with a smile. Ellery did not care for the smile. "Of course—being employees—they're scared to death of him."

"A fear which you don't share?"

"I can't stand him." It came out calmly enough, but when Ellery kept looking at her she glanced elsewhere.

"You're afraid of him, too."

"I just dislike him."

"Go on."

"I'd notified the Priams of Dad's heart attack the first chance I got, which was the evening of the day it happened. I spoke to Roger myself on the phone. He seemed very curious about the circumstances and kept insisting he had to talk to daddy. I refused—Dr. Voluta had forbidden excitement of any kind. The next morning Roger phoned twice, and dad seemed just as anxious to talk to *him*. In fact, he was getting so upset I let him phone. There's a private line between his bedroom and the Priam house. But after I got Roger on the phone dad asked me to leave the room."

Laurel jumped up, but immediately she sat down again, fumbling for another Dunhill. Ellery let her strike her own match; she failed to notice.

She puffed rapidly. "Nobody knows what he said to Roger. Whatever it was, it took only a few minutes, and it brought Roger right over. He'd been lifted, wheel-chair and all, into the back of the Priams' station wagon, and Delia—Roger's wife—

drove him over herself." And Laurel's voice stabbed at the name of Mrs. Priam. So another Hatfield went with this McCoy. "When he was carried up to dad's bedroom in his chair, Roger locked the door. They talked for three hours."

"Discussing the dead dog and the note?"

"There's no other possibility. It couldn't have been business—Roger had never felt the necessity of coming over before on business, and daddy had had two previous heart attacks. It was about the dog and note, all right. And if I had any doubts, the look on Roger Priam's face when he wheeled himself out of the bedroom killed them. He was as frightened as daddy had been the day before, and for the same reason.

"And that was something to see," said Laurel softly. "If you were to meet Roger Priam, you'd know what I mean. Frightened looks don't go with his face. If there's any fright around, he's usually dishing it out.... He even talked to me, something he rarely bothers to do. 'You take good care of your father,' he said to me. I pleaded with him to tell me what was wrong, and he pretended not to have heard me. Simeon and Itchie lifted him into the station wagon, and Delia drove off with him.

"A week ago—during the night of June tenth—daddy got his wish. He died in his sleep. Dr. Voluta says that last shock to his heart did it. He was cremated, and his ashes are in a bronze drawer fifteen feet from the floor at Forest Lawn. But that's what he wanted, and that's where he is. The sixty-four-dollar question, Ellery, is: Who murdered him? And I want it answered."

Ellery rang for Mrs. Williams. When she did not appear, he excused himself and went downstairs to the miniature lower level to find a note from his housekeeper describing minutely her plan to shop at the supermarket on North Highland. A pot of fresh coffee on the range and a deep dish of whipped avocado and bacon bits surrounded by crackers told him that Mrs. Williams had overheard all, so he took them upstairs.

Laurel said, surprised, "How nice of you," as if niceness these days were a quality that called for surprise. She refused the crackers just as nicely, but then she changed her mind and ate ten of them without pausing, and she drank three cups of coffee. "I remembered I hadn't eaten anything today."

"That's what I thought."

She was frowning now, which he regarded as an improvement over the stone face she had been wearing. "I've tried to talk to Roger Priam half a dozen times since then, but he won't even admit he and dad discussed anything unusual. I told him in words of one syllable where I thought his obligations lay—certainly his debt to their lifelong friendship and partnership—and I explained my belief that daddy was murdered by somebody who knew how bad his heart was and deliberately shocked him into a heart attack. And I asked for the letter. He said innocently, 'What letter?' and I realized I'd never get a thing out of him. Roger's either over his scare or he's being his usual Napoleonic self. There's a big secret behind all this and he means to keep it."

"Do you think," asked Ellery, "that he's confided in Mrs. Priam?"

"Roger doesn't confide in anybody," replied Laurel grimly. "And if he did, the last person in the world he'd tell anything to would be Delia."

"Oh, the Priams don't get along?"

"I didn't say they don't get along."

"They do get along?"

"Let's change the subject, shall we?"

"Why, Laurel?"

"Because Roger's relationship with Delia has nothing to do with any of this." Laurel sounded earnest. But she was hiding something just the same. "I'm interested in only one thing—finding out who wrote that note to my father."

"Still," said Ellery, "what was your father's relationship with Delia Priam?"

"Oh!" Laurel laughed. "Of course you couldn't know. No, they weren't having an affair. Not possibly. Besides, I told you Daddy said I was the only woman in his life."

"Then they were hostile to each other?"

15

"Why do you keep on the subject of Delia?" she asked, a snap in her voice.

"Why do you keep off it?"

"Dad got along with Delia fine. He got along with everybody."

"Not everybody, Laurel," said Ellery.

She looked at him sharply.

"That is, if your theory that someone deliberately scared him to death is sound. You can't blame the police, Laurel, for being fright-shy. Fright is a dangerous weapon that doesn't show up under the microscope. It takes no finger-prints and it's the most unsatisfactory kind of legal evidence. Now the letter ... if you had the letter, that would be different. But you don't have it."

"You're laughing at me." Laurel prepared to rise.

"Not at all. The smooth stories are usually as slick as their surface. I like a good rough story. You can scrape away at the uneven places, and the dust tells you things. Now I know there's something about Delia and Roger Priam. What is it?"

"Why must you know?"

"Because you're so reluctant to tell me."

"I'm not. I just don't want to waste any time, and to talk about Delia and Roger is wasting time. Their relationship has nothing to do with my father."

Their eyes locked.

Finally, with a smile, Ellery wavered.

"No, I don't have the letter. And that's what the police said. Without the letter, or some evidence to go on, they can't come into it. I've asked Roger to tell them what he knows—knowing that what he knows *would* be enough for them to go on—and he laughed and recommended Arrowhead or Palm Springs as a cure for my 'pipe dream,' as he called it. The police point to the autopsy report and dad's cardiac history and send me politely away. Are you going to do the same?"

Ellery turned to the window. To get into a live murder case was the last thing in the world he had bargained for. But the

16

dead dog fascinated him. Why a dead dog as a messenger of bad news? It smacked of symbolism. And murderers with metaphoric minds he had never been able to resist. If, of course, there was a murder. Hollywood was a playful place. People produced practical jokes on the colossal scale. A dead dog was nothing compared with some of the elaborations of record. One he knew of personally involved a race-horse in a bathroom, another the employment for two days of seventy-six extras. Some wit had sent a cardiac jeweller a recently deceased canine and a fake Mafia note, and before common sense could set in the victim of the dog-play had a heart attack. Learning the unexpected snapper of his joke, the joker would not unnaturally turn shy. The victim, ill and shaken, summoned his oldest friend and business partner to a conference. Perhaps the note threatened Sicilian tortures unless the crown jewels were deposited in the oily crypt of the pterodactyl pit in Hancock Park by midnight of the following day. For three hours the partners discussed the note, Hill nervously insisting it might be legitimate, Priam reasonably poohing and boshing the very notion. In the end Priam came away, and what Laurel Hill had taken to be fear was probably annoyance at Hill's womanish obduracy. Hill was immobilized by his partner's irritation, and before he could rouse himself his heart gave out altogether. End of mystery. Of course, there were a few dangling ends.... But you could sympathize with the police. It was a lot likelier than a wild detective-story theory dreamed up by deceased's daughter. They had undoubtedly dismissed her as either a neurotic girl tipped over by grief or a publicity hound with a yen for a starlet contract. She was determined enough to be either.

Ellery turned about. She was leaning forward, the forgotten cigarette sending up question marks.

"I suppose," said Ellery, "your father had a closetful of bony enemies?"

"Not to my knowledge."

This astonished him. To run true to form she should have

come prepared with names, dates, and vital statistics.

"He was an easy, comfortable sort of man. He liked people, and people liked him. Dad's personality was one of the big assets of Hill & Priam. He'd have his moments like everybody else, but I never knew anyone who could stay mad at him. Not even Roger."

"Then you haven't the smoggiest notion who could be behind this ... fright murder?"

"Now you *are* laughing." Laurel Hill got to her feet and dropped her cigarette definitely into the ashtray. "Sorry I've taken up so much of your time."

"You might try a reliable agency. I'll be glad to—"

"I've decided," she smiled at him, "to go into the racket personally. Thanks for the avocado—"

"Why, Laurel."

Laurel turned quickly.

A tall woman stood in the doorway.

"Hello, Delia," said Laurel.

2

Nothing in Laurel Hill's carefully edited remarks had prepared him for Delia Priam. Through his only available windows—the narrow eyes of Laurel's youth—he had seen Delia's husband as a pompous and tyrannical old cock, crippled but rampant, ruling his roost with a beak of iron; and from this it followed that the wife must be a grey-feathered hennypenny, preening herself emptily in corners, one of Bullock's elderly barnyard trade ... a dumpy, nervous, insignificant old biddy.

But the woman in his doorway was no helpless fowl, to be plucked, swallowed, and forgotten. Delia Priam was of a far different species, higher in the ranks of the animal kingdom, and she would linger on the palate.

She was so much younger than his mental sketch of her that only much later was Ellery to recognize this as one of her routine illusions, among the easiest of the magic tricks she performed as professionally as she carried her breasts. At that time he was to discover that she was forty-four, but the knowledge remained as physically meaningless as—the figure leaped into his mind—learning the chronological age of Ayesha. The romantic nonsense of this metaphor was to persist. He would even be appalled to find that he was identifying himself in his fantasy with that hero of his adolescence, Allan Quatermain, who had been privileged to witness the immortal strip-tease of She-Who-Must-Be-Obeyed behind her curtain of living flame. It was the most naked juvenility, and Ellery was duly amused at himself. But there she was, a glowing end in herself; it took only imagination, a commodity with which he was plentifully provided, to supply the veils.

Delia Priam was big game; one glance told him that. His doorway framed the most superbly proportioned woman he had ever seen. She was dressed in a tawny peasant blouse of some sheer material and a California print skirt of bold colours. Her heavy black hair was massed to one side of her head, sleekly, in the Polynesian fashion; she wore plain broad hoops of gold in her ears. Head, shoulders, bust, hips—he could not decide which pleased him more. She stood there not so much in an attitude as in an atmosphere—an atmosphere of intense repose, watchful and disquieting.

By Hollywood standards she was not beautiful: her eyes were too deep and light-tinted, her eyebrows too lush; her mouth was too full, her colouring too high, her figure too heroic. But it was this very excessiveness that excited—a tropical quality, humid, brilliant, still, and overpowering. Seeing her for the first time was like stepping into a jungle. She seized and held the senses; everything was leashed, lovely, and dangerous. He found his ears trying to recapture her voice, the sleepy growl of something heard from a thicket.

Ellery's first sensible thought was, *Roger, old cock, you can have her.* His second was, *But how do you keep her?* He was on his third when he saw the chilly smile on Laurel Hill's lips.

Ellery pulled himself together. This was evidently an old story to Laurel.

"Then Laurel's ... mentioned me." A dot-dot-dot talker. It had always annoyed him. But it prolonged the sound of that bitch-in-a-thicket voice.

20

"I answered Mr. Queen's questions," said Laurel in a warm, friendly voice. "Delia, you don't seem surprised to see me."

"I left my surprise outside with your car." Those lazy throat-tones were warm and friendly, too. "I could say … the same to you, Laurel."

"Darling, you never surprise me."

They smiled at each other.

Laurel turned suddenly and reached for another cigarette.

"Don't bother, Ellery. Delia always makes a man forget there's another woman in the room."

"Now, Laurel." She was indulgent. Laurel slashed the match across the packet.

"Won't you come in and sit down, Mrs. Priam?"

"If I'd had any idea Laurel was coming here …"

Laurel said abruptly, "I came to see the man about the dog, Delia. *And* the note. Did you follow me?"

"What a ridiculous thing to say."

"Did you?"

"Certainly not, dear. I read about Mr. Queen in the papers and it coincided with something that's been bothering me."

"I'm sorry, Delia. I've been upset."

"I'll come back, Mr. Queen."

"Mrs. Priam, does it concern Miss Hill's father's death?"

"I don't know. It may."

"Then Miss Hill won't mind your sitting in. I repeat my invitation."

She had a trick of moving slowly, as if she were pushing against something. As he brought the chartreuse chair around he watched her obliquely. When she sat down she was close enough so that he could have touched her bare back with a very slight movement of his finger. He almost moved it.

She did not seem to have taken him in at all. And yet she had looked him over; up and down, as if he had been a gown in a dress shop. Perhaps he didn't interest her. As a gown, that is.

"Drink, Mrs. Priam?"

21

"Delia doesn't drink," said Laurel in the same warm, friendly voice. Two jets spurted from her nostrils.

"Thank you, darling. It goes to my head, Mr. Queen."

And you wouldn't let anything go to your head, wherefore it stands to reason, thought Ellery, that one way to get at you is to pour a few extra-dry Martinis down that red gullet.... He was surprised at himself. A married woman, obviously a lady, and her husband was a cripple. But that wading walk was something to see.

"Laurel was about to leave. The facts interest me, but I'm in Hollywood to do a book...."

The shirring of her blouse rose and fell. He moved off to the picture window, making her turn her head.

"If, however, you have something to contribute, Mrs. Priam ..."

He suspected there would be no book for some time.

Delia Priam's story penetrated imperfectly. Ellery found it hard to concentrate. He tended to lose himself in details. The curves of her blouse. The promise of her skirt, which moulded her strongly below the waist. Her large, shapely hands rested precisely in the middle of her lap, like compass points. *"Mistresses with great smooth marbly limbs...."* Right out of Browning's Renaissance. She would have brought joy to the dying Bishop of Saint Praxed's.

"Mr. Queen?"

Ellery said guiltily, "You mean, Mrs. Priam, the same day Leander Hill received the dead dog?"

"The same morning. It was a sort of gift. I don't know what else you'd call it."

Laurel's cigarette hung in the air. "Delia, you didn't tell me Roger had got something, too!"

"He told me not to say anything, Laurel. But you've forced my hand, dear. Kicking up such a fuss about that poor dog. First the police, now Mr. Queen."

"Then you did follow me."

"I didn't have to." The woman smiled. "I saw you looking at Mr. Queen's photo in the paper."

"Delia, you're wonderful."

"Thank you, darling." She sat peaceful as a lady tiger, smiling over secrets.... Here, Brother Q!

"Oh. Oh, yes, Mrs. Priam. Mr. Priam's been frightened—"

"Ever since the day he got the box. He won't admit it, but when a man keeps roaring that he won't be intimidated it's pretty clear that he is. He's broken things, too, some of his own things. That's not like Roger. Usually they're mine."

Delightful. What a pity.

"What was in the box, Mrs. Priam?"

"I haven't any idea."

"A dead dog," said Laurel. "Another dead dog!" Laurel looked something like a little dog herself, nose up, testing the air. It was remarkable how meaningless she was across from Delia Priam. As sexless as a child.

"It would have to have been an awfully small one, Laurel. The box wasn't more than a foot square, of cardboard."

"Unmarked?" asked Ellery.

"Yes. But there was a shipping tag attached to the string that was tied around the box. 'Roger Priam' was printed on it in crayon." The beautiful woman paused. "Mr. Queen, are you listening?"

"In crayon. Yes, certainly, Mrs. Priam. Colour?" What the devil difference did the colour make?

"Black, I think."

"No address?"

"No. Nothing but the name."

"And you don't know what was in it. No idea."

"No. But whatever it was, it hit Roger hard. One of the servants found the box at the front door and gave it to Alfred—"

"Alfred?"

"Roger's ... secretary."

23

"Wouldn't you call him more of a … companion, Delia?" asked Laurel, blowing a smoke-ring.

"I suppose so, dear. Companion, nurse, handyman, secretary—what-have-you. My husband, you know, Mr. Queen, is an invalid."

"Laurel's told me. All things to one man, eh, Mrs. Priam? I mean Alfred. We now have the versatile Alfred with the mysterious box. He takes it to Mr. Priam's room. And then?" Why was Laurel laughing? Not outwardly. But she was. Delia Priam seemed not to notice.

"I happened to be in Roger's room when Alfred came in. We didn't know then about … Leander and *his* gift, of course. Alfred gave Roger the box, and Roger lifted a corner of the lid and looked inside. He looked angry, then puzzled. He slammed the lid down and told me to get out. Alfred went out with me, and I heard Roger lock his door. And that's the last … I've seen of the box or its contents. Roger won't tell me what was in it or what he's done with it. Won't talk about it at all."

"When did your husband begin to show fear, Mrs. Priam?"

"After he talked to Leander in the Hill house the next day. On the way back home he didn't say a word, just stared out the window of the station wagon. Shaking. He's been shaking … ever since. It was especially bad a week later when Leander died …"

Then what was in Roger Priam's box had little significance for him until he compared gifts with Leander Hill, perhaps until he read the note Hill had found in the collar of the dog. Unless there had been a note in Priam's box as well. But then …

Ellery fidgeted before the picture window, sending up a smoke-screen. It was ridiculous, at his age … pretending to be interested in a case because a respectable married woman had the misfortune to evoke the jungle. Still, he thought, what a waste.

He became conscious of the two women's eyes and expelled a mouthful of smoke, trying to appear professional. "Leander Hill received a queer gift, and he died. Are you afraid, Mrs. Priam,

24

that your husband's life is in danger, too?"

Now he was more than a piece of merchandise; he was a piece of merchandise that interested her. Her eyes were so empty of colour that in the sunlight coming through the window she looked eyeless; it was like being looked over by a statue. He felt himself reddening and it seemed to him she was amused. He immediately bristled. She could take her precious husband and her fears elsewhere.

"Laurel darling," Delia Priam was saying with an apologetic glance, "would you mind terribly if I spoke to Mr. Queen ... alone?"

Laurel got up. "I'll wait in the garden," she said, and she tossed her cigarette into the tray and walked out.

Roger Priam's wife waited until Laurel's slim figure appeared beyond the picture window, among the shaggy asters. Laurel's head was turned away. She was switching her thigh with her cap.

"Laurel's sweet," said Delia Priam. "But so young, don't you think? Right now she's on a crusade and she's feeling ever so knightly. She'll get over it.... Why, about your question, Mr. Queen. I'm going to be perfectly frank with you. I haven't the slightest interest in my husband. I'm not afraid that he may die. If anything, it's the other way around."

Ellery stared. For a moment her eyes slanted to the sun and they sparkled in a mineral way. But her features were without guile. The next instant she was eyeless again.

"You're honest, Mrs. Priam. Brutally so."

"I've had a rather broad education in brutality, Mr. Queen."

So there was that, too. Ellery sighed.

"I'll be even franker," she went on. "I don't know whether Laurel told you specifically.... Did she say what kind of invalid my husband is?"

"She said he's partly paralyzed."

"She didn't say what part?"

"What part?" said Ellery.

25

"Then she didn't. Why, Mr. Queen, my husband is paralyzed," said Delia Priam with a smile, "from the waist down."

You had to admire the way she said that. The brave smile. The
smile that said *Don't pity me.*

"I'm very sorry," he said.

"I've had fifteen years of it."

Ellery was silent. She rested her head against the back of the
chair. Her eyes were almost closed and her throat was strong
and defenceless.

"You're wondering why I told you that."

Ellery nodded.

"I told you because you can't understand why I've come to
you unless you understand that first. Weren't you wondering?"

"All right. Why have you come to me?"

"For appearance's sake."

Ellery stared. "You ask me to investigate a possible threat
against your husband's life, Mrs. Priam, for appearance's sake?"

"You don't believe me."

"I do believe you. Nobody would invent such a reason!" Seating himself beside her, he took one of her hands. It was cool and
secretive, and it remained perfectly lax in his. "You haven't had
much of a life."

"What do you mean?"

"You've never done any work with these hands."

"Is that bad?"

"It could be." Ellery put her hand back in her lap. "A woman
like you has no right to remain tied to a man who's half-dead. If
he were some saintly character, if there were love between you,
I'd understand it. But I gather he's a brute and that you loathe
him. Then why haven't you done something with your life?
Why haven't you divorced him? Is there a religious reason?"

"There might have been when I was young. Now ..." She
shook her head. "Now it's the way it would look. You see, I'm
stripping myself quite bare."

Ellery looked pained.

26

"You're very gallant to an old woman." She laughed. "No, I'm serious, Mr. Queen. I come from one of the old California families. Formal upbringing. Convent-trained. Duennas in the old fashion. A pride of caste and tradition. I could never take it as seriously as they did....

"My mother had married a heretic from New England. They ostracized her, and it killed her when I was a little girl. I'd have got away from them completely, except that when my mother died they talked my father into giving me into their custody. I was brought up by an aunt who wore a *mantilla*. I married the first man who came along just to get away from them. He wasn't their choice—he was an 'American,' like my father. I didn't love him, but he had money, we were very poor, and I wanted to escape. It cut me off from my family, my church, and my world. I have a ninety-year-old grandmother who lives only three miles from this spot. I haven't seen her for eighteen years. She considers me dead."

Her head rolled. "Harvey died when we'd been married three years, leaving me with a child. Then I met Roger Priam. I couldn't go back to my mother's family, my father was off on one of his jaunts, and Roger attracted me. I would have followed him to hell." She laughed again. "And that's exactly where he led me.

"When I found out what Roger really was, and then when he became crippled and I lost even that, there was nothing left. I've filled the vacuum by trying to go back where I came from.

"It hasn't been easy," murmured Delia Priam. "They don't forget such things, and they never forgive. But the younger generation is softer-bottomed and corrupted by modern ways. Their men, of course, have helped.... Now it's the only thing I have to hang on to."

Her face showed a passion not to be shared or relished. Ellery was glad when the moment passed. "The life I lead in Roger Priam's house isn't even suspected by these people. If they knew the truth, I'd be dropped and there'd be no return. And if I left

Roger, they'd say I deserted my husband. Upper-caste women of the old California society don't do that sort of thing, Mr. Queen; it doesn't matter what the husband is. So ... I don't do it.

"Now something is happening, I don't know what. If Laurel had kept her mouth shut, I wouldn't have lifted a finger. But by going about insisting that Leander Hill was murdered, Laurel's created an atmosphere of suspicion that threatens my position. Sooner or later the papers will get hold of it—it's a wonder they haven't already—and the fact that Roger is apparently in the same danger might come out. I can't sit by and wait for that. My people will expect me to be the loyal wife. So that's what I'm being. Mr. Queen, I ask you to proceed as if I'm terribly concerned about my husband's safety." Delia Priam shrugged. "Or is this all too involved for you?"

"It would seem to me far simpler," said Ellery, "to clear out and start over again somewhere else."

"This is where I was born." She looked out at Hollywood. Laurel had moved over to a corner of the garden. "I don't mean all that popcorn and false front down there. I mean the hills, the orchards, the old missions. But there's another reason, and it has nothing to do with me, or my people, or Southern California."

"What's that, Mrs. Priam?"

"Roger wouldn't let me go. He's a man of violence, Mr. Queen. You don't—you can't—know his furious possessiveness, his pride, his compulsion to dominate, his ... depravity. Sometimes I think I'm married to a maniac."

She closed her eyes. The room was still. From below Ellery heard Mrs. Williams's Louisiana-bred tones complaining to the gold parakeet she kept in a cage above the kitchen sink about the scandalous price of coffee. An invisible finger was writing in the sky above the Wilshire district: MUNTZ TV. The empty typewriter nudged his elbow.

But there she sat, the jungle in batiste and coloured cotton. His slick and characterless Hollywood house would never be the same again. It was exciting just to be able to look at her lying in the silly chair. It was dismaying to imagine the chair empty.

"Mrs. Priam."

"Yes?"

"Why," asked Ellery, trying not to think of Roger Priam, "didn't you want Laurel Hill to hear what you just told me?"

The woman opened her eyes. "I don't mind undressing before a man," she said, "but I do draw the line at a woman."

She said it lightly, but something ran up Ellery's spine.

He jumped to his feet. "Take me to your husband."

3

When they came out of Ellery's house Laurel said pleasantly, "Has a contract been drawn up, Ellery? And if so, with which one of us? Or is the question incompetent and none of my business?"

"No contract," said Ellery testily. "No contract, Laurel. I'm just going to take a look around."

"Starting at the *Priam* house, of course."

"Yes."

"In that case, since we're all in this together—aren't we, Delia?—I suppose there's no objection if I trail along?"

"Of course not, darling," said Delia. "But do try not to antagonize Roger. He always takes it out on me afterwards."

"What do you think he's going to say when he finds out you've brought a detective around?"

"Oh, dear," said Delia. Then she brightened. "Why, darling, *you're* bringing Mr. Queen around, don't you see? Do you mind very much? I know it's yellow, but I have to live with him. And you did get to Mr. Queen first."

"All right," said Laurel with a shrug. "We'll give you a head start, Delia. You take Franklin and Outpost, and I'll go around

30

the long way, over Cahuenga and Mulholland. Where have you been? Shopping?"

Delia Priam laughed. She got into her car, a new cream Cadillac convertible, and drove off down the hill.

"Hardly a substitute," said Laurel after a moment. Ellery started. Laurel was holding open the door of her car, a tiny green Austin. "Either car *or* driver. Can you see Delia in an Austin? Like the Queen of Sheba in a rowboat. Get in."

"Unusual type," remarked Ellery absently, as the little car shot off.

"The adjective, yes. But as to the noun," said Laurel, "there is only one Delia Priam."

"She seems remarkably frank and honest."

"Does she?"

"I thought so. Don't you?"

"It doesn't matter what I think."

"By which you tell me what you think."

"No, you don't! But if you must know.... You never get to the bottom of Delia. She doesn't lie, but she doesn't tell the truth, either—I mean the whole truth. She always keeps something in reserve that you dig out much, much later, if you're lucky to dig it out at all. Now I'm not going to say anything more about Delia, because whatever I say you'll hold, not against her, but against me. Delia bowls over big shots especially.... I suppose it's no use asking you what she wanted to talk to you alone about?"

"Take—it—easy," said Ellery, holding his hat. "Another bounce like that and my knees will stab me to death."

"Nice try, Laurel," said Laurel; and she darted into the freeway-bound traffic on North Highland with a savage flip of her exhaust.

After a while Ellery remarked to Laurel's profile: "You said something about Roger Priam's 'never' leaving his wheel-chair. You didn't mean that literally, by any chance?"

"Yes. Not ever. Didn't Delia tell you about the chair?"

"No."

"It's fabulous. After Roger became paralyzed he had an ordinary wheel-chair for a time, which meant he had to be lifted into and out of it. Daddy told me about it. It seems Roger the Lion-Hearted couldn't take that. It made him too dependent on others. So he designed a special chair for himself."

"What does it do, boost him in and out of bed on mechanical arms?"

"It does away with a bed altogether."

Ellery stared.

"That's right. He sleeps in it, eats in it, does his work in it—everything. A combination office, study, living-room, dining-room, bedroom and bathroom on wheels. It's quite a production. From one of the arms of the chair hangs a small shelf which he can swing around to the front and raise; he eats on that, mixes drinks, and so on. Under the shelf are compartments for cutlery, napkins, cocktail things, and liquor. There's a similar shelf on the other arm of the chair which holds his typewriter, screwed on, of course, so it won't fall off when it's swung aside. And under that shelf are places for paper, carbon, pencils, and Lord knows what else. The chair is equipped with two phones of the plug-in type—the regular line and a private wire to our house—and with an intercom system to Wallace's room."

"Who's Wallace?"

"Alfred Wallace, his secretary-companion. Then—let's see." Laurel frowned. "Oh, he's got compartments and cubbyholes all around the chair for just about everything imaginable—magazines, cigars, his reading glasses, his toothbrush; everything he could possibly need. The chair's built so that it can be lowered and the front raised, making a bed out of it for daytime napping or sleeping at night. Of course, he needs Alfred to help him sponge-bathe and dress and undress and so on, but he's made himself as self-sufficient as possible—hates help of any kind, even the most essential. When I was there yesterday his typewriter had just been sent into Hollywood to be repaired and he had to dictate business memoranda to Alfred instead of doing them himself, and he was in such a foul mood because of it that even Alfred got mad. Roger in a foul mood can be awfully foul.... I'm sorry, I thought you wanted to know."

"What?"

"You're not listening."

"I am, though not with both ears." They were on Mulholland Drive now, and Ellery was clutching the side of the Austin to avoid being thrown clear as Laurel zoomed the little car around the hairpin curves. "Tell me, Laurel. Who inherits your father's estate? I mean besides yourself?"

"Nobody. There isn't anyone else."

"He didn't leave anything to Priam?"

"Why should he? Roger and Daddy were equal partners. There are some small cash bequests to people in the firm and to the household help. Everything else goes to me. So you see, Ellery," said Laurel, soaring over a rise, "I'm your big suspect."

"Yes," said Ellery, "and you're also Roger Priam's new partner. Or are you?"

"My status isn't clear. The lawyers are working on that now. Of course I don't know anything about the jewellery business and I'm not sure I want to. Roger can't chisel me out of anything, if that's what's in your mind. One of the biggest law firms in Los Angeles is protecting my interests. I must say Roger's been surprisingly decent about that end of it—for Roger, I mean. Maybe Daddy's death hit him harder than he expected—made him realize how important Dad was to the business and how unimportant *he* is. Actually, he hasn't much to worry about. Dad trained a very good man to run things, a Mr. Foss, in case anything happened to him.... Anyway, there's one item on my agenda that takes priority over everything else. And if you won't clear it up for me, I'll do it myself."

"Because you loved Leander Hill very much?"

33

"Yes!"

"And because, of course," remarked Ellery, "you *are* the big suspect?"

Laurel's little hands tightened on the wheel. Then they relaxed. "That's the stuff, Ellery," she laughed. "Just keep firing away at the whites of our eyes. I love it. There's the Priam place."

The Priam place stood on a private road, a house of dark round stones and blackish wood wedged into a fold of the hills and kept in forest gloom by a thick growth of overhanging sycamore, elm, and eucalyptus. Ellery's first thought was that the grounds were neglected, but then he saw evidences of both old and recent pruning on the sides away from the house and he realized that nature had been coaxed into the role she was playing. The hopeless matting of leaves and boughs was deliberate; the secretive gloom was wanted. Priam had dug into the hill and pulled the trees over him. Who was it who had defied the sun?

It was more like an isolated hunting lodge than a Hollywood house. Most of it was hidden from the view of passers-by on the main road, and by its character it transformed a suburban section of ordinary Southern California canyon into a wild Scottish glen. Laurel told Ellery that the Priam property extended up and along the hill for four or five acres and that it was all like the area about the house.

"Jungle," said Ellery as Laurel parked the car in the driveway. There was no sign of the cream Cadillac.

"Well, he's a wild animal. Like the deer you flush occasionally up behind the Bowl."

"He's paying for the privilege. His electric bills must be enormous."

"I'm sure they are. There isn't a sunny room in the house. When he wants—you can't say more *light*—when he wants less gloom, and air that isn't so stale, he wheels himself out on that terrace there." To one side of the house there was a large terrace, half of it screened and roofed, the other open not to the sky but to a high arch of bare gum eucalyptus leaves and branches which the sun did not penetrate. "His den—den is the word—is directly off the terrace, past those French and screen doors. We'd better go in the front way; Roger doesn't like people barging in on his sacred preserves. In the Priam house you're announced."

"Doesn't Delia Priam have anything to say about the way her house is run?"

"Who said it's her house?" said Laurel.

A uniformed maid with a tic admitted them. "Oh, Miss Hill," she said nervously. "I don't think Mr. Priam … He's dictatin' to Mr. Wallace. I better not…."

"Is Mrs. Priam in, Muggs?"

"She just got in from shoppin', Miss Hill. She's upstairs in her room. Said she was tired and was not to be disturbed."

"Poor Delia," said Laurel calmly. "I know Mr. Queen is terribly disappointed. Tell Mr. Priam I want to see him."

"But, Miss Hill—"

A muffled roar of rage stopped her instantly. She glanced over her shoulder in a panic.

"It's all right, Muggsy. I'll take the rap. *Vamos*, Ellery."

"I wonder why she—" Ellery began in a mumble as Laurel led him up the hall.

"Yours not to, where Delia is concerned."

The house was even grimmer than he had expected. They passed shrouded rooms with dark panelling, heavy and humourless drapes, massive uncomfortable-looking furniture. It was a house for secrets and for violence.

The roar was a bass snarl now. "I don't give a damn what Mr. *Hill* wanted to do about the Newman-Arco account, Foss! Mr. *Hill*'s locked in a drawer in Forest Lawn and he ain't in any condition to give us the benefit of his advice…. No, I won't wait a minute, Foss! I'm running this—business, and you'll either handle things my way or get the hell out!"

Laurel's lips thinned. She raised her fist and hammered on the door.

"Whoever that is, Alfred—! Foss, you still there?"

A man opened the heavy door and slipped into the hall, pulling the door to and keeping his hand on the knob behind him.

"You picked a fine time, Laurel. He's on the phone to the office."

"So I hear," said Laurel. "Mr. Queen, Mr. Wallace. His other name ought to be Job, but it's Alfred. The perfect man, I call him. Super-efficient. Discreet as all get-out. Never slips. One side, Alfred. I've got business with my partner."

"Better let me set him up," said Wallace with a smile. As he slipped back into the room, his eyes flicked over Ellery. Then the door was shut again, and Ellery waved his right hand tenderly. It still tingled from Wallace's grip.

"Surprised?" murmured Laurel.

Ellery was. He had expected a Milquetoast character. Instead Alfred Wallace was a towering, powerfully assembled man with even, rather sharp features, thick white hair, a tan, and an air of lean distinction. His voice was strong and thoughtful, with the merest touch of ... superiority? Whatever it was, it was barely enough to impress, not quite enough to annoy. Wallace might have stepped out of a set on the MGM lot labelled *High Society Drawing Room;* and, in fact, "well-preserved actor" had been Ellery's impulsive characterization—Hollywood leading-men types with Athletic Club tans were turning up these days in the most unexpected places, swallowing their pride in order to be able to swallow at all. But a moment later Ellery was not so sure. Wallace's shoulders did not look as if they came off with his coat. His physique, even his elegance, seemed home-grown.

"I should think you'd be smitten, Laurel," said Ellery as they waited. "That's a virile character. Perfectly disciplined, and dashing as the devil."

"A little too old," said Laurel. "For me, that is."

"He can't be much more than fifty-five. And he doesn't look forty-five, white hair notwithstanding."

"Alfred would be too old for me if he were twenty.—Oh. Well? Do I have to get Mr. Queen to brush you aside, Alfred, or is the Grand Vizier going to play gracious this morning?"

Alfred Wallace smiled and let them pass.

The man who slammed the phone down and spun the steel chair about as if it were a studio production of balsa wood was a creature of immensities. He was all bulge, spread, and thickness. Bull eyes blazed above iron cheekbones; the nose was a massive snout; a tremendous black beard fell to his chest. The hands which gripped the wheels of the chair were enormous; forearms and biceps strained his coat sleeves. And the whole powerful mechanism was in continuous movement, as if even that great frame was unable to contain his energy. Something by Wolf Larsen out of Captain Teach, on a restless quarter-deck. Beside that immense torso Alfred Wallace's strong figure looked frail. And Ellery felt like an underfed boy.

But below the waist Roger Priam was dead. His bulk sat on a withered base, an underpinning of skeletal flesh and atrophied muscle. He was trousered and shod—and Ellery tried not to imagine the labour that went into that operation twice daily—but his ankles were visible, two shrivelled bones, and his knees were twisted projections, like girders struck by lightning. The whole shrunken substructure of his body hung, useless.

It was all explicable, Ellery thought, on ordinary grounds: the torso over-developed by the extraordinary exertions required for the simplest movements; the beard grown to eliminate one of the irksome processes of his daily toilet; the savage manner an expression of his hatred of the fate that had played such a trick on him; and the restlessness a sign of the agony he endured to maintain a sitting position. Those were the reasons; still, they left something unexplained.... Ferocity—fierce strength, fierce emotions, fierce reaction to pain and people—ferocity seemed his centre. Take everything else away, and Ellery suspected it would still be there. He must have been fierce in his mother's womb, a wild beast by nature. What had happened to him merely brought it into play.

"What d'ye want, Laurel? Who's this?" His voice was a coarse, threatening bass, rumbling up from his chest like live lava. He was still furious from his telephone conversation with the hapless Foss; his eyes were filled with hate. "What are you looking at? Why don't you open your mouth?"

"This is Ellery Queen."

"Who?"

Laurel repeated it.

"Never heard of him. What's he want?" The feral glance turned on Ellery. "What d'ye want? Hey?"

"Mr. Priam," said the beautiful voice of Alfred Wallace from the doorway, "Ellery Queen is a famous writer."

"Writer?"

"And detective, Mr. Priam."

Priam's lips pushed out, dragging his beard forward. The great hands on the wheel became clamps.

"I told you I wasn't going to let go, Roger," said Laurel evenly. "My father was murdered. There must have been a reason. And whatever it was, you were mixed up in it as well as daddy. I've asked Ellery Queen to investigate, and he wants to talk to you."

"He does, does he?" The rumble was distant; the fiery eyes gave out heat. "Go ahead, Mister. Talk away."

"In the first place, Mr. Priam," said Ellery, "I'd like to know—"

"The answer is no," said Roger Priam, his teeth showing through his beard. "What's in the second place?"

"Mr. Priam," Ellery began again, patiently.

"No good, Mister. I don't like your questions. Now you listen to me, Laurel." His right fist crashed on the arm of the chair. "You're a damn busybody. This ain't your business. It's mine. I'll tend to it. I'll do it my way, and I'll do it myself. Can you get that through your head?"

"You're afraid, Roger," said Laurel Hill.

38

Priam half-raised his bulk, his eyes boiling. The lava burst with a roar.

"Me afraid? Afraid of what? A *ghost?* What d'ye think I am, another Leander Hill? The snivellin' dirt! Shaking in his shoes—looking over his shoulder—creeping on his face! He was born a—yellow-belly, and he died the same—"

Laurel hit him on the cheek with her fist. His left arm came up impatiently and brushed her aside. She staggered backward half-way across the room into Alfred Wallace's arms.

"Let go of me," she whispered. "Let go!"

"Laurel," said Ellery.

She stopped, breathing from her diaphragm. Wallace silently released her.

Laurel walked out of the room.

"*Afraid!*" A spot swelled on Priam's cheekbone. "You think so?" he bellowed after her. "Well, a certain somebody's gonna find out that *my* pump don't go to pieces at the first blow! Afraid, am I? I'm ready for the goddam—! Any hour of the day or night, understand? Any time he wants to show his scummy hand! He'll find out I got a pretty good pair myself!" And he opened and closed his murderous hands, and Ellery thought again of Wolf Larsen.

"Roger. What's the matter?"

And there she was in the doorway. She had changed to a hostess gown of golden silk which clung as if it loved her. It was slit to the knee. She was glancing coolly from her husband to Ellery.

Wallace's eyes were on her. They seemed amused.

"Who is this man?"

"Nobody. Nothing, Delia. It don't concern you." Priam glared at Ellery. "You. Get out!"

She had come downstairs just to establish the fact that she didn't know him. As a point in character, it should have interested him. Instead, it annoyed him. Why, he could not quite make out. What was he to Hecuba? Although she was making clear enough what Hecuba was to *him*. He felt chagrined and challenged, and at the same time he wondered if she affected other men the same way.... Wallace was enjoying himself discreetly, like a playgoer who has caught a point which escaped the rest of the audience and is too polite to laugh aloud.... Her attitude towards her husband was calm, without fear or any other visible emotion.

"What are you waiting for? You ain't wanted, Mister. Get out!"

"I've been trying to make up my mind, Mr. Priam," said Ellery, "whether you're a bag of wind or a damned fool."

Priam's bearded lips did a little dance. His rage, apparently always in shallow water, was surfacing again. Ellery braced himself for the splash. Priam *was* afraid. Wallace—silent, amused, attentive Wallace—Wallace saw it. And Delia Priam saw it; she was smiling.

"Alfred, if this fella shows up again, break his—back!"

Ellery looked down at his arm. Wallace's hand was on it.

"I'm afraid, Mr. Queen," murmured Wallace, "that I'm man enough to do it, too."

The man's grip was paralyzing. Priam was grinning, a yellow hairy grin that jarred him. And the woman—that animate piece of jungle—watching. To his amazement, Ellery felt himself going blind-mad. When he came to, Alfred Wallace was sitting on the floor chafing his wrist and staring up at Ellery. He did not seem angry; just surprised.

"That's a good trick," Wallace said. "I'll remember it."

Ellery fumbled for a cigarette, decided against it. "I've made up my mind, Mr. Priam. You're a bag of wind and a damned fool."

The doorway was empty....

He was furious with himself. Never lose your temper. Rule One in the book; he had learned it on his father's lap. Just the same, she must have seen it. Wallace flying through the air. And the gape on Priam's ugly face. Probably set her up for the week....

40

He found himself searching for her out of the corners of his eyes as he strode down the hall. The place was over-crowded with shadows; she was certainly waiting in one of them. With the shades of her eyes pulled down, but everything else showing....

The hall was empty, too....

Slit to the knee! That one was older than the pyramids. And how old was his stupidity? It probably went back to the primordial slime.

Then he remembered that Delia Priam was a lady and that he was behaving exactly like a frustrated college boy, and he slammed the front door.

Laurel was waiting for him in the Austin. She was still white; smoking with energy. Ellery jumped in beside her and growled, "Well, what are we waiting for?"

"He's cracking," said Laurel tensely. "He's going to pieces, Ellery. I've seen him yell and push his weight around before, but today was something special. I'm glad I brought you. What do you want to do now?"

"Go home. Or get me a cab."

She was bewildered. "Aren't you taking the case?"

"I can't waste my time on idiots."

"Meaning me?"

"Not meaning you."

"But we found out something," she said eagerly. "He admitted it. You heard him. A 'ghost,' he said. A 'certain somebody'— I heard that on my way out. I wasn't being delirious, Ellery. Roger thinks daddy was deliberately shocked to death, too. And, what's more, he knows what the dog meant—"

"Not necessarily," grunted Ellery. "That's the trouble with you amateurs. Always jumping to conclusions. Anyway, it's too impossible. You can't get anywhere without Priam, and Priam isn't budging."

"It's Delia," said Laurel, "isn't it?"

41

"Delia? You mean Mrs. Priam? Rubbish."

"Don't tell me about Delia," said Laurel. "Or about men, either. She's catnip for anything in pants."

"Oh, I admit her charms," muttered Ellery. "But they're a bit obvious, don't you think?" He was trying not to look up at the second-storey windows, where her bedroom undoubtedly was. "Laurel, we can't park here in the driveway like a couple of adenoidal tourists—" He had to see her again. Just to see her.

Laurel gave him an odd look and drove off. She turned left at the road, driving slowly.

Ellery sat embracing his knees. He had the emptiest feeling that he was losing something with each spin of the Austin's wheels. And there was Laurel, seeing the road ahead and something else, too. Sturdy little customer. And she must be feeling pretty much alone. Ellery suddenly felt himself weakening.

"What do you intend to do, Laurel?"

"Keep poking around."

"You're determined to go through with this?"

"Don't feel sorry for me. I'll make out."

"Laurel, I'll tell you what I'll do."

She looked at him.

"I'll go as far as that note with you; I mean, give you a head start, anyway. If, of course, it's possible."

"What are you talking about?" She stopped the car with a bump.

"The note your father found in that silver box on the dog's collar. You thought he must have destroyed it."

"I told you I looked for it and it wasn't there."

"Suppose I do the looking."

Laurel stared. Then she laughed and the Austin jumped.

The Hill house spread itself high on one of the canyon walls, cheerfully exposing its red tiles to the sun. It was a two-storey Spanish house, beautifully bleached, with black wrought-iron tracery, arched and balconied and patioed and covered with pyracantha. It was set in two acres of flowers, flowering shrubs, and trees—palm and fruit and nut and bird-of-paradise. Around the lower perimeter ran the woods.

"Our property line runs down the hill," Laurel said as they got out of the car, "over towards the Priams. A little over nine additional acres meeting the Priam woods. Through the woods it's no distance at all."

"It's a very great distance," mumbled Ellery. "About as far as from an eagle's nest to an undersea cave. True Spanish, I notice, like the missions, not the modern fakes so common out here. It must be a punishment to Delia Priam—born to this and condemned to *that*."

"Oh, she's told you about that," murmured Laurel; then she took him into her house.

It was cool with black Spanish tile underfoot and the touch of iron. There was a sunken living-room forty feet long, a great fireplace set with Goya tiles, books and music and paintings and ceramics and huge jars of flowers everywhere. A tall Japanese in a white jacket came in smiling and took Ellery's hat.

"Ichiro Sotowa," said Laurel. "Itchie's been with us for ages. This is Mr. Queen, Itchie. He's interested in the way daddy died, too."

The houseman's smile faded. "Bad—bad," he said, shaking his head. "Heart no good. You like a drink, sir?"

"Not just now, thanks," said Ellery. "Just how long did you work for Mr. Hill, Ichiro?"

"Sixteen year, sir."

"Oh, then you don't go back to the time of ... What about that chauffeur—Simon, was it?"

"Shimmie shopping with Mis' Monk."

"I meant how long Simeon's been employed here."

"About ten years," said Laurel. "Mrs. Monk came around the same time."

"That's that, then. All right, Laurel, let's begin."

"Where?"

"From the time your father had his last heart attack—the day the dog came—until his death, did he leave his bedroom?"

"No. Itchie and I took turns nursing him. Night and day the entire week."

"Bedroom indicated. Lead the way."

An hour and a half later, Ellery opened the door of Leander Hill's room. Laurel was curled up in a window niche on the landing, head resting against the wall.

"I suppose you think I'm an awful sissy," she said, without turning. "But all I can see when I'm in there is his marbly face and blue lips and the crooked way his mouth hung open ... not my daddy at all. Nothing, I suppose."

"Come here, Laurel."

She jerked about. Then she jumped off the ledge and ran to him. Ellery shut the bedroom door.

Laurel's eyes hunted wildly. But aside from the four-poster bed, which was disarranged, she could see nothing unusual. The spread, sheets, and quilt were peeled back, revealing the side walls of the box-spring and mattress.

"What—?"

"The note you saw him remove from the dog's collar," Ellery said. "It was on thin paper, didn't you tell me?"

"Very. A sort of flimsy, or onion skin."

"White?"

"White."

Ellery nodded. He went over to the exposed mattress. "He was in this room for a week, Laurel, between his attack and death. During that week did he have many visitors?"

"The Priam household. Some people from the office. A few friends."

"Some time during that week," said Ellery, "your father decided that the note he had received was in danger of being stolen or destroyed. So he took out insurance." His finger traced on the side wall of the mattress one of the perpendicular blue lines of the ticking. "He had no tool but a dull penknife from the

44

night table there. And I suppose he was in a hurry, afraid he might be caught at it. So the job had to be crude." Half his finger suddenly vanished. "He simply made a slit here, where the blue line meets the undyed ticking. And he slipped the paper into it, where I found it."

"The note," breathed Laurel. "You've found the note. Let me see!"

Ellery put his hand in his pocket. But just as he was about to withdraw it, he stopped. His eyes were on one of the windows.

Some ten yards away there was an old walnut tree.

"Yes?" Laurel was confused. "What's the matter?"

"Get off the bed, yawn, smile at me if you can, and then stroll over to the door. Go out on the landing. Leave the door open."

Her eyes widened.

She got off the bed, yawned, stretched, showed her teeth, and went to the door. Ellery moved a little as she moved, so that he remained between her and the window.

When she had disappeared, he casually followed. Smiling in profile at her, he shut the bedroom door.

And sprang for the staircase.

"Ellery—"

"Stay here!"

He scrambled down the black-tiled stairs, leaving Laurel with her lips parted.

A man had been roosting high in the walnut tree, peering in at them through Leander Hill's bedroom window from behind a screen of leaves. But the sun had been on the tree, and Ellery could have sworn the fellow was mother-naked.

45

4

The naked man was gone. Ellery thrashed about among the fruit and nut trees feeling like Robinson Crusoe. From the flagged piazza Ichiro gaped at him, and a chunky fellow with a florid face and a chauffeur's cap, carrying a carton of groceries, was gaping with him.

Ellery found a large footprint at the margin of the orchard, splayed and deep-toed, indicating running or jumping, and it pointed directly to the woods. He darted into the underbrush, and in a moment he was nosing past trees and scrub on a twisting but clear trail. There were numerous specimens of the naked print on the trail, both coming and going.

"He's made a habit of this," Ellery mumbled. It was hot in the woods and he was soon drenched, uncomfortable, and out of temper.

The trail ended unceremoniously in the middle of a clearing. No other footprints anywhere. The trunk of the nearest tree, an ancient, oakish-looking monster, was yards away. There were no vines.

Ellery looked around, swabbing his neck. Then he looked up. The giant limbs of the trees covered the clearing with a thick fabric of small spiny leaves, but the lowest branch was thirty feet from the ground.

The creature must have flapped his arms and taken off.

Ellery sat down on a corrupting log and wiped his face, reflecting on this latest wonder. Not that anything in Southern California ever really surprised him. But this was a little out of even God's country's class. Flying nudes!

"Lost?"

Ellery leaped. A little old man in khaki shorts, woollen socks, and a T-shirt was smiling at him from a bush. He wore a paper topee on his head and he carried a butterfly net; a bright red case of some sort was slung over one skinny shoulder. His skin was a shrivelled brown and his hands were like the bark of the big tree, but his eyes were a bright young blue and they seemed keen.

"I'm not lost," said Ellery irritably. "I'm looking for a man."

"I don't like the way you say that," said the old man, stepping into the clearing. "You're on the wrong track, young fellow. People mean trouble. Know anything about the Lepidoptera?"

"Not a thing. Have you seen—?"

"You catch 'em with this ding-bat. I just bought the kit yesterday—passed a toy-shop on Hollywood Boulevard and there it was, all new and shiny, in the window. I've caught four beauties so far." The butterfly hunter began to trot down the trail, waving his net menacingly.

"Wait! Have you seen anyone running through these woods?"

"Running? Well, now, depends."

"Depends? My dear sir, it doesn't depend on a thing! Either you saw somebody or you didn't."

"Not necessarily," replied the little man earnestly, trotting back. "It depends on whether it's going to get him—or you—in trouble. There's too much trouble in this world, young man. What's this runner look like?"

"I can't give you a description," snapped Ellery, "inasmuch as I didn't see enough of him to be able to. Or rather, I saw the wrong parts.—Hell. He's naked."

47

"Ah," said the hunter, making an unsuccessful pass at a large, paint-splashed butterfly. "Naked, hm?"

"And there was a lot of him."

"There was. You wouldn't start any trouble?"

"No, no, I won't hurt him. Just tell me which way he went."

"I'm not worried about your hurting him. He's much more likely to hurt you. Powerful build, that boy. Once knew a stoker built like him—could bend a coal-shovel. That was in the old *Susie Belle*, beating up to Alaska—"

"You sound as if you know him."

"Know him? I darned well ought to. He's my grandson. There he is!" cried the hunter.

"Where?"

But it was only the fifth butterfly, and the little old man hopped between two bushes and was gone.

Ellery was morosely studying the last footprint in the trail when Laurel poked her head cautiously into the clearing.

"There you are," she said with relief. "You scared the buttermilk out of me. What happened?"

"Character spying on us from the walnut tree outside the bedroom window. I trailed him here—"

"What did he look like?" frowned Laurel.

"No clothes on."

"Why, the lying mugwump!" she said angrily. "He promised on his honour he wouldn't do that any more. It's got so I have to undress in the dark."

"So you know him, too," growled Ellery. "I thought California had a drive on these sex cases."

"Oh, he's no sex case. He just throws gravel at my window and tries to get me to talk drool to him. I can't waste my time on somebody who's preparing for Armageddon at the age of twenty-three. Ellery, let's see that note."

"Whose grandson is he?"

"Grandson? Mr. Collier's."

"Mr. Collier wouldn't be a little skinny old gent with a face like a sun-dried fig?"

48

"That's right."

"And who is Mr. Collier?"

"Delia Priam's father. He lives with the Priams."

"Her *father*." You couldn't keep her out of anything. "But if this Peeping Tom is Delia Priam's father's grandson, then he must be—"

"Didn't Delia tell you," asked Laurel with a *soupçon* of malice, "that she has a twenty-three-year-old son? His name is Crowe Macgowan. Delia's child by her first husband. Roger's stepson. But let's not waste any time on him—"

"How does he disappear into thin air? He pulled that miracle right here."

"Oh, that." Laurel looked straight up. So Ellery looked straight up, too. But all he could see was a leafy ceiling where the great oak branched ten yards over his head.

"Mac!" said Laurel sharply. "Show your face."

To Ellery's amazement, a large young male face appeared in the middle of the green mass thirty feet from the ground. On the face there was a formidable scowl.

"Laurel, who is this guy?"

"You come down here."

"Is he a reporter?"

"Heavens, no," said Laurel disgustedly. "He's Ellery Queen."

"Who?"

"Ellery Queen."

"You're kidding!"

"I wouldn't have time."

"Say, I'll be right down."

The face vanished. At once something materialized where it had been and hurtled to the ground, missing Ellery's nose by inches. It was a rope ladder. A massive male leg broke the green ceiling, then another, then a whole young man, and in a moment the tree man was standing on the ground on the exact spot where the trail of naked footprints ended.

"I'm certainly thrilled to meet you!"

Ellery's hand was seized and the bones broken before he

could cry out. At least, they felt broken. It was a bad day for the Master's self-respect: he could not decide which had the most powerful hands, Roger Priam, Alfred Wallace, or the awesome brute trying to pulverize him. Delia's son towered six inches above him, a handsome giant with an impossible spread of shoulder, an unbelievable minimum of waist, the muscular development of Mr. America, the skin of a Hawaiian—all of which was on view except a negligible area covered by a brown loincloth—and a grin that made Ellery feel positively aged.

"I thought you were a news-hound, Mr. Queen. Can't stand those guys—they've made my life miserable. But what are we standing here for? Come on up to the house."

"Some other time, Mac," said Laurel coldly, taking Ellery's arm.

"Oh, that murder foolitchness. Why don't you relax, Laur?"

"I don't think I'd be exactly welcome at your stepfather's, Mac," said Ellery.

"You've already had the pleasure? But I meant come up to *my* house."

"He really means 'up,' Ellery," sighed Laurel. "All right, let's get it over with. You wouldn't believe it second-hand."

"House? Up?" Feebly Ellery glanced aloft; and to his horror the young giant nodded and sprang up the rope ladder, beckoning them hospitably to follow.

It really was a house, high in the tree. A one-room house, to be sure, and not commodious, but it had four walls and a thatched roof, a sound floor, a beamed ceiling, two windows, and a platform from which the ladder dangled—this dangerous-looking perch young Macgowan referred to cheerfully as his "porch," and perfectly safe if you didn't fall off.

The tree, he explained, was *Quercus Agrifolia*, with a bole circumference of eighteen feet, and "watch those leaves, Mr. Queen, they bite." Ellery, who was gingerly digging several of

50

the spiny little devils out of his shirt, nodded sourly. But the structure was built on a foundation of foot-thick boughs and seemed solid enough underfoot.

He poked his head indoors at his host's invitation and gaped like a tourist. Every foot of wall- and floor-space was occupied by—it was the only phrase Ellery could muster—aids to tree-living.

"Sorry I can't entertain you inside," said the young man, "but three of us would bug it out a bit. We'd better sit on the porch. Anybody like a drink? Bourbon? Scotch?" Without waiting for a reply Macgowan bent double and slithered into his house. Various liquid sounds followed.

"Laurel, why don't they put the poor kid away?" whispered Ellery.

"You have to have grounds."

"What do you call this?" cried Ellery. "Sanity?"

"Don't blame you, Mr. Queen," said the big fellow amiably, appearing with two chilled glasses. "Appearances are against me. But that's because you people live in a world of fantasy." He thrust a long arm into the house and it came out with another glass.

"Fantasy. We." Ellery gulped a third of the contents of his glass. "You, of course, live in a world of reality?"

"Do we have to?" asked Laurel wearily. "If he gets started on this, Ellery, we'll be here till sundown. That note—"

"I'm the only realist I know," said the giant, lying down at the edge of his porch and kicking his powerful legs in space. "Because, look. What are you people doing? Living in the same old houses, reading the same old newspapers, going to the same old movies or looking at the same old television, walking on the same old sidewalks, riding in the same old new cars. That's a dream world, don't you realize it? What price business-as-usual? What price, well sky-writing, Jacques Fath, Double-Crostics, murder? Do you get my point?"

"Can't say it's entirely clear, Mac," said Ellery, swallowing the second third. He realized for the first time that his glass contained bourbon, which he loathed. However.

"We are living," said young Mr. Macgowan, "in the crisis of the disease commonly called human history. You mess around with your piddling murders while mankind is being set up for the biggest homicide since the Flood. The atom bomb is already fuddy-duddy. Now it's hydrogen bombs, guaranteed to make the nuclear chain reaction—or whatever the hell it is—look like a Fourth of July firecracker. Stuff that can poison all the drinking-water on a continent. Nerve gases that paralyze and kill. Germs there's no protection against. And only God knows what else. They won't use it? My friend, those words constitute the epitaph of Man. Somebody'll pull the cork in a place like Yugoslavia or Iran or Korea and, whoosh! that'll be that.

"It's all going to go," said Macgowan, waving his glass at the invisible world below. "Cities uninhabitable. Crop soil poisoned for a hundred years. Domestic animals going wild. Insects multiplying. Balance of nature upset. Ruins and plagues and millions of square miles radioactive and maybe most of the earth's atmosphere. The roads crack, the lines sag, the machines rust, the libraries mildew, the buzzards fatten, and the forest primeval creeps over Hollywood and Vine, which maybe isn't such a bad idea. But there you'll have it. Thirty thousand years of primate development knocked over like a sleeping duck. Civilization atomized and annihilated. Yes, there'll be some survivors—I'm going to be one of them. But what are we going to have to do? Why, go back where we came from, brother—to the trees. That's logic, isn't it? So here I am. All ready for it."

"Now let's have the note," said Laurel.

"In a moment." Ellery polished off the last third, shuddering. "Very logical, Mac, except for one or two items."

"Such as?" said Crowe Macgowan courteously. "Here, let me give you a refill."

"No, thanks, not just now. Why, such as these." Ellery pointed to a network of cables winging from some hidden spot to the roof of Macgowan's tree house. "For a chap who's written off thirty thousand years of primate development you don't seem to mind tapping the main powerline for such things as"—he craned, surveying the interior—"electric lights, a small electric range and refrigerator, and similar primitive devices; not to mention"—he indicated a maze of pipes—"running water, a compact little privy connected with—I assume—a septic tank buried somewhere below, and so on. These things—forgive me, Mac—blow bugs through your logic. The only essential differences between your house and your stepfather's are that yours is smaller and thirty feet in the air."

"Just being practical," shrugged the giant. "It's my opinion it'll happen any day now. But I can be wrong—it may not come till next year. I'm just taking advantage of the civilized comforts while they're still available. But you'll notice I have a .22 rifle hanging there, a couple of .45s, and when my ammunition runs out or I can't rustle any more there's a bow that'll bring down any deer that survives the party. I practise daily. And I'm getting pretty good running around these tree-tops—"

"Which reminds me," said Laurel. "Use your own trees after this, will you, Mac? I'm no prude, but a girl likes her privacy sometimes. Really, Ellery—"

"Macgowan," said Ellery, eyeing their host, "what's the pitch?"

"Pitch? I've just told you."

"I know what you've just told me, and it's already out the other ear. What character are you playing? And in what script by whom?" Ellery set the glass down and got to his feet. The effect he was trying to achieve was slightly spoiled, as he almost fell off the porch. He jumped to the side of the house, a little green. "I've been to Hollywood before."

"Go ahead and sneer," said the brown giant without rancour. "I promise to give you a decent burial if I can find the component parts."

53

Ellery eyed the wide back for a moment. It was perfectly calm. He shrugged. Every time he came to Hollywood something fantastic happened. This was the screwiest yet. He was well out of it.

But then he remembered that he was still in it.

He put his hand in his pocket.

"Laurel," he said meaningly, "shall we go?"

"If it's about that piece of paper I saw you find in Leander's mattress," said young Macgowan, "I wouldn't mind knowing myself what's in it."

"It's all right, Ellery," said Laurel with an exasperated laugh. "Crowe is a lot more interested in the petty affairs of us dreamers than he lets on. And in a perverted sort of way I trust him. May I *please* see that note?"

"It isn't the note you saw your father take from the collar of the dog," said Ellery, eyeing Macgowan disapprovingly as he took a sheet of paper from his pocket. "It's a copy. The original is gone." The sheet was folded over once. He unfolded it. It was a stiff vellum paper, tinted green-grey, with an embossed green monogram.

"Daddy's personal stationery."

"From his night table. Where I also found this bicoloured pencil." Ellery fished an automatic pencil from his pocket. "The blue lead is snapped. The note starts in blue and ends in red. Evidently the blue ran out half-way through his copying and he finished writing with the red. So the pencil places the copying in his bedroom, too." Ellery held out the sheet. "Is this your father's handwriting?"

"Yes."

"No doubt about it?"

"No."

In a rather peculiar voice, Ellery said, "All right, Laurel. Read it."

"But it's not signed." Laurel sounded as if she wanted to punch somebody.

"Read it."

Macgowan knelt behind her, nuzzling her shoulder with his big chin. Laurel paid no attention to him; she read the note with a set face.

> You believed me dead. Killed, murdered. For over a score of years I have looked for you—for you and for him. And now I have found you. Can you guess my plan? You'll die. Quickly? No, very slowly. And so pay me back for my long years of searching and dreaming of revenge. Slow dying ... unavoidable dying. For you and for him. Slow and sure—dying in mind and in body. And for each pace forward a warning ... a warning of special meaning for you—and for him. Meanings for pondering and puzzling. Here is warning number one.

Laurel stared at the notepaper.

"That," said Crowe Macgowan, taking the sheet, "is the unfunniest gag of the century." He frowned over it.

"Not just that." Laurel shook her head. "Warning number one. Murder. Revenge. Special meanings.... It—it has a long curly moustache on it. Next week *Uncle Tom's Cabin*." She looked around with a laugh. "Even in Hollywood."

"Why'd the old scout take it seriously?" Crowe watched Laurel a little anxiously.

Ellery took the sheet from him and folded it carefully. "Melodrama is a matter of atmosphere and expression. Pick up any Los Angeles newspaper and you'll find three new stories running serially, and one of which would make this one look like a work by Einstein. But they're real because they're couched in everyday terms. What makes this note incredible is not the contents. It's the wording."

"The wording?"

"It's painful. Actually archaic in spots. As if it were composed by someone who wears a ruff, or a tricorn. Someone who speaks a different kind of English. Or writes it. It has a ... bouquet, an archive smell. A something that would never have been put into it purely for deception, for instance ... like the ransom-note writers who deliberately misspell words and mix their tenses to give the impression of illiteracy. And yet—I don't know." Ellery slipped the note into his pocket. "It's the strangest mixture of genuineness and contrivance. I don't understand it."

"Maybe," suggested the young man, putting his arm carelessly around Laurel's shoulders, "maybe it's the work of some psycho foreigner. It reads like somebody translating from another language."

"Possible." Ellery sucked his lower lip. Then he shrugged. "Anyway, Laurel, there's something to go on. Are you sure you wouldn't rather discuss this—?"

"You mean because it involves Roger?" Laurel laughed again, removing Macgowan's paw. "Mac isn't one of Roger's more ardent admirers, Ellery. It's all right."

"What did he do now?" growled Roger Priam's stepson.

"He said he wasn't going to be scared by any 'ghost,' Mac. Or rather roared it. And here's a clue to someone from his past and, apparently, Leander Hill's. 'For you and for him....' Laurel, what do you know of your father's background?"

"Not much. He'd led an adventurous life, I think, but whenever I used to ask him questions about it—especially when I was little—he'd laugh, slap me on the bottom, and send me off to Mad'moiselle."

"What about his family?"

"Family?" said Laurel vaguely.

"Brothers, sisters, uncle, cousins—family. Where did he come from? Laurel, I'm fishing. We need some facts."

"I'm no help there. Daddy never talked about himself. I always felt I couldn't pry. I can't remember his ever having any contact with relatives. I don't even know if any exist."

"When did he and Priam go into business together?"

"It must have been around twenty, twenty-five years ago."

"Before Delia and he got married," said Crowe. "Delia—that's my mother, Mr. Queen."

"I know," said Ellery, a bit stiffly. "Had Priam and Hill known each other well before they started the jewellery business, Macgowan?"

"I don't know." The giant put his arm about Laurel's waist.

"I suppose they did. They must have," Laurel said in a helpless way, absently removing the arm. "I realize now how little I know about dad's past."

"Or I about Roger's," said Crowe, marching two fingers up Laurel's back. She wriggled and said, "Oh, stop it, Mac." He got up. "Neither of them ever talked about it." He went over to the other end of the platform and stretched out again.

"Apparently with reason. Leander Hill and Roger Priam had a common enemy in the old days, someone they thought was dead. *He* says they tried to put him out of the way, and he's spent over twenty years tracking them down."

Ellery began to walk about, avoiding Crowe Macgowan's arms.

"Dad tried to murder somebody?" Laurel bit her thumb.

"When you yell bloody murder, Laurel," said Ellery, "you've got to be prepared for a certain echo of nastiness. This kind of murder," he said, lighting a cigarette and placing it between her lips, "is never nice. It's usually rooted in pretty mucky soil. Priam means nothing to you, and your father is dead. Do you still want to go through with this? *You're* my client, you know, not Mrs. Priam. At her own suggestion."

"Did Mother come to you?" exclaimed Macgowan.

"Yes, but we're keeping it confidential."

"I didn't know she cared," muttered the giant.

Ellery lit a cigarette for himself.

Laurel was wrinkling her nose and looking a little sick.

Ellery tossed the match overside. "Whoever composed that note is on a delayed murder spree. He wants revenge badly enough to have nursed it for over twenty years. A quick killing doesn't suit him at all. He wants the men who injured him to suffer, presumably, as he's suffered. To accomplish this he starts a private war of nerves. His strategy is all plotted. Working from the dark, he makes his first tactical move ... the warning, the first of the 'special meanings' he promises. Number one is—of all things—a dead pooch, number two whatever was in the box to Roger Priam—I wonder what it was, by the way! You wouldn't know, Mac, would you?"

"I wouldn't know *anything* about my mother's husband," replied Macgowan.

"And he means to send other warnings with other 'gifts' which have special meanings. To Priam exclusively now—Hill foxed him by dying at once. He's a man with a fixed idea, Laurel, and an obsessive sense of injury. I really think you ought to keep out of his way. Let Priam defy him. It's his skin, and if he needs help he knows where he can apply for it."

Laurel threw herself back on the platform, blowing smoke to the appliquéd sky.

"Don't you feel you have to act like the heroine of a magazine serial?"

Laurel did not reply.

"Laurel, drop it. Now."

She rolled her head. "I don't care what daddy did. People make mistakes, even commit crimes, who are decent and nice. Sometimes events force you, or other people. I knew him—as a human being—better than anyone in creation. If he and Roger Priam got into a mess, it was Roger who thought up the dirty work.... The fact that he wasn't my real father makes it even more important. I owe him everything." She sat up suddenly. "I'm not going to stay out of this, Ellery. I can't."

"You'll find, Queen," scowled young Macgowan in the silence that followed, "that this is a very tough number."

"Tough she may be, my Tarzanian friend," grumbled Ellery, "but this sort of thing is a business, not an endurance contest. It takes know-how and connections and a technique. And experience. None of which Miss Strongheart has." He crushed his cigarette out on the platform vindictively. "Not to mention the personal danger.... Well, I'll root around a little, Laurel. Do some checking back. It shouldn't be too much of a job to get a line on those two and find out what they were up to in the Twenties. And who got caught in the meat-grinder.... You driving me back to the world of fantasy?"

5

The next morning Ellery called the Los Angeles Police Department and asked to speak to the officer in charge of the Public Relations Department.

"Sergeant Lordetti."

"Sergeant, this is Ellery Queen.... Yes, how do you do. Sergeant, I'm in town to write a Hollywood novel—oh, you've seen that ... no, I can't make the newspapers believe it and, frankly, I've given up trying. Sergeant Lordetti, I need some expert advice for background on my book. Is there anyone in, say, the Hollywood Division who could give me a couple hours of his time? Some trouble-shooter with lots of experience in murder investigation and enough drag in the Department so I could call on him from time to time?... Exposé? So you fell for that, too, haha! Me, the son of a cop? No, no, Sergeant, nothing like that, believe me.... Who?... K-e-a-t-s. Thanks a lot.... Not at all, Sergeant. If you can make a little item out of it, you're entirely welcome."

Ellery called the Hollywood Division on Wilcox below Sunset and asked to speak to Lieutenant Keats. Informed that Lieutenant Keats was on another phone, Ellery left his telephone number and name with the request that Lieutenant Keats call back as soon as he was free.

Twenty minutes later a car drew up to his house and a big lean man in a comfortable-looking business suit got out and rang the bell, glancing around curiously at Ellery's pint-sized garden. Hiding behind a drape, Ellery decided he was not a salesman, for he carried nothing and his interest had something amused in it. Possibly a reporter, although he seemed too carefully dressed for that. He might have been a sports announcer or a veteran airline pilot off duty.

"It's a policeman, Mr. Queen," reported Mrs. Williams nervously. "You done something?"

"I'll keep you out of it, Mrs. Williams. Lieutenant Keats? The service staggers me. I merely left a message for you to phone back."

"Sergeant Lordetti phoned and told me about it," said the Hollywood detective, filling the doorway. "Thought I'd take the short-cut. No, thanks, don't drink when I'm working."

"Working—? Oh, Mrs. Williams, close the door, will you?... Working, Lieutenant? But I explained to Lordetti—"

"He told me." Keats placed his hat neatly on the chartreuse chair. "You want expert advice for a mystery novel. Such as what, Mr. Queen? How a homicide is reported in Los Angeles? That was for the benefit of the *Mirror* and *News*. What's really on your mind?"

Ellery stared. Then they both grinned, shook hands, and sat down like old friends.

Keats was a sandy-haired man of thirty-eight or forty with clear, rather distant grey eyes below reddish brows. His hands were big and well-kept, with a reliable look to them; there was a gold band on the fourth finger of the left. His eyes were intelligent and his jaw had been developed by adversity. His manner was slightly standoffish. A smart cop, Ellery decided, and a rugged one.

"Let me light that for you, Lieutenant."

"The nail?" Keats laughed, taking a shredded cigarette from between his lips. It was unlit. "I'm a dry smoker, Mr. Queen. Given up smoking." He put the ruin on an ashtray and fingered a fresh cigarette, settling back. "Some case you're interested in? Something you don't want to get around?"

"It came my way yesterday morning. Do you know anything about the death of a wholesale jeweller named Leander Hill?"

"So she got to you." Keats lipped the unlit cigarette. "It passed through our Division. The girl made a pest of herself. Something about a dead dog and a note that scared her father to death. But no note. An awfully fancy yarn. More in your line than ours."

Ellery handed Keats the sheet of Leander Hill's stationery.

Keats read it slowly. Then he examined the notepaper, front and back.

"That's Hill's handwriting, by the way. Obviously a copy he made. I found it in a slit in his mattress."

"Where's the original of this, Mr. Queen?"

"Probably destroyed."

"Even if this were the McCoy"—Keats put the sheet down— "there's nothing here that legally connects Hill's death with a murder plot. Of course, the revenge business ..."

"I know, Lieutenant. It's the kind of case that gives you fellows a hard ache. Every indication of a psycho, and a possible victim who won't co-operate."

"Who's that?"

"The 'him' of the note." Ellery told Keats about Roger Priam's mysterious box, and of what Priam had let slip during Ellery's visit. "There's something more than a gangrenous imagination behind this, Lieutenant. Even though no one's going to get anywhere with Priam, still ... it ought to be looked into, don't you agree?"

The detective pulled at his unlit cigarette.

"I'm not sure I want any part of it myself," Ellery said, glancing at his typewriter and thinking of Delia Priam. "I'd like a little more to go on before I commit myself. It seemed to me that if we could find something in Hill's past, and Priam's, that takes this note out of the ordinary crack-pot class ..."

"On the q.t.?"

"Yes. Could you swing it?"

For a moment Keats did not reply. He picked up the note and read it over again.

"I'd like to have this."

"Of course. But I want it back."

"I'll have it photostatted. Tell you what I'll do, Mr. Queen." Lieutenant Keats rose. "I'll talk to the Chief, and if he thinks it's worth my time, I'll see what I can dig up."

"Oh, Keats."

"Yes, sir?"

"While you're digging ... do a little spade work on a man who calls himself Alfred Wallace. Roger Priam's secretary-general."

Delia Priam phoned that afternoon. "I'm surprised you're in."

"Where did you think I'd be, Mrs. Priam?" The moment he heard her throaty purr his blood began stewing. Damn her, she was like the first cocktail after a hard day....

"Out detecting, or whatever it is detectives do."

"I haven't taken the case." He was careful to keep his voice good-humoured. "I haven't made up my mind."

"You're angry with me about yesterday."

"Angry? Mrs. Priam!"

"Sorry. I thought you were." Oh, were you? "I'm afraid I'm allergic to messes. I usually take the line of least resistance."

"In everything?"

"Give me an example." Her laugh was soft.

He wanted to say, *I'd be glad to specify if you'd drop in on me, say, this afternoon.* Instead, he said innocuously, "Who's questioning whom?"

"You're such a careful man, Mr. Queen."

"Well, I haven't taken the case—yet, Mrs. Priam."

"Do you suppose I could help you make up your mind?"

There's the nibble. Reel 'er in....

"You know, Mrs. Priam, that might be a perilous offer.... Mrs. Priam?... Hello!"

She said in a low voice, quickly, "I must stop," and the line went dead.

Ellery hung up perspiring. He was so annoyed with himself that he went upstairs and took a shower.

Laurel Hill dropped in on him twice in the next twenty-four hours. The first time she was "just passing by" and thought she would report that nothing was happening, nothing at all. Priam wouldn't see her, and as far as she could tell he was being his old bullying, beastly self. Delia had tried to pump her about Ellery and what he was doing, and as a matter of fact she couldn't help wondering herself if ...

Ellery's glance kept going to his typewriter, and after a few moments Laurel left abruptly.

She was back the next morning, recklessly hostile.

"Are you taking this case, or aren't you?"

"I don't know, Laurel."

"I've talked to my lawyers. The estate isn't settled, but I can get the money together to give you a retainer of five thousand dollars."

"It isn't the money, Laurel."

"If you don't want to bother, say so and I'll get someone else."

"That's always the alternative, of course."

"But you're just sitting here!"

"I'm making a few preliminary inquiries," he said patiently.

"From this—this ivory tower?"

"Stucco. What I'll do, Laurel, depends entirely on what I find out."

"You've sold out to Delia, that's what you've done," Laurel cried. "She doesn't really want this investigated at all. She only followed me the other day to see what I was up to—the rest was malarkey! She *wants* Roger murdered! And that's all right with me, you understand—all I'm interested in is the case of Leander Hill. But if Delia's standing in the way—"

"You're being nineteen, Laurel." He tried not to let his anger show.

"I'll admit I can't offer you what *she* can—"

"Delia Priam hasn't offered me a thing, Laurel. We haven't even discussed my fee."

"And I *don't* mean money!" She was close to tears.

"Now you're hysterical." His voice came out sharp, not what he had intended at all. "Have a little patience, Laurel. Right now there's nothing to do but wait."

She strode out.

The next morning Ellery spread his newspaper behind a late breakfast tray to find Roger Priam, Leander Hill, and Crowe Macgowan glaring back at him. Mac was glaring from a tree.

$$$aire Denies Murder Threat;
Says Partner Not Slain

Denying that he has received a threat against his life, Roger Priam, wealthy wholesale gem merchant of L.A., barred himself behind the doors of his secluded home above Hollywood Bowl this morning when reporters investigated a tip that he is the intended victim of a murder plot which allegedly took the life of his business partner, Leander Hill, last week....

Mr. Priam, it appeared, after ousting reporters had issued a brief statement through his secretary, Alfred Wallace, repeating his denial and adding that the cause of Hill's death was "a matter of official record."

Detectives at the Hollywood Division of the L.A.P.D. admitted this morning that Hill's daughter, Laurel, had charged her father was "frightened to death," but said that they had found no evidence to support the charge, which they termed "fantastic."

Miss Hill, interviewed at her home adjoining the Priam property, said: "If Roger Priam wants to bury his head in the sand, it's his head." She intimated that she "had reason to believe" both her father and Priam were slated to be murdered "by some enemy out of their past."

The story concluded with the reminder that "Mr. Priam is the stepfather of twenty-three-year-old Crowe Macgowan, the Atomic Age Tree Boy, who broke into print in a big way recently by taking off his clothes and bedding down in a tree house on his stepfather's estate in preparation for the end of the world."

Observing to himself that Los Angeles journalism was continuing to maintain its usual standards, Ellery went to the phone and called the Hill home.

"Laurel? I didn't expect you'd be answering the phone in person this morning."

"I've got nothing to hide." Laurel laid the slightest stress on her pronoun. Also, she was cold, very cold.

"One question. Did you tip off the papers about Priam?"

"No."

"Cross your heart and—?"

"I said no!" There was a definite *snick*!

It was puzzling, and Ellery puzzled over it all through breakfast, which Mrs. Williams with obvious disapproval persisted in calling lunch. He was just putting down his second cup of coffee when Keats walked in with a paper in his pocket.

"I was hoping you'd drop around," said Ellery, as Mrs. Williams set another place. "Thanks, Mrs. W., I'll do the rest.... Not knowing exactly what is leaking where, Keats, I decided not to risk a phone call. So far I've been kept out of it."

"Then you didn't feed the kitty?" asked Keats. "Thanks. No cream or sugar."

"Of course not. I was wondering if it was you."

"Not me. Must have been the Hill girl."

"Not she. I've asked her."

"Funny."

"Very. How was the tip tipped?"

"By phone call to the city room. Disguised voice, and they couldn't trace it."

"Male or female?"

"They said male, but they admitted it was pitched in a queer way and might have been female. With all the actors floating around this town you never know." Keats automatically struck a match, but then he shook his head and put it out. "You know, Mr. Queen," he said, scowling at his cigarette, "if there's anything to this thing, that tip might have come ... I know it sounds screwy ..."

"From the writer of the note? I've been dandling that notion myself, Lieutenant."

"Pressure, say."

"In the war on Priam's nerves."

"If he's got an iron nerve himself." Keats rose. "Well, this isn't getting us anywhere."

"Anything yet on Hill and Priam?"

"Not yet." Keats slowly crumpled his cigarette. "It might be a toughie, Mr. Queen. So far I haven't got to first base."

"What's holding you up?"

"I don't know yet. Give me another few days."

"What about Wallace?"

"I'll let you know."

Late that afternoon—it was the twenty-first, the day after the Shriners parade—Ellery looked around from his typewriter to see the creamy nose of Delia Priam's convertible in profile against his front window.

He deliberately forced himself to wait until Mrs. Williams answered the door.

As he ran his hand over his hair, Mrs. Williams said: "It's a naked man. You in?"

Macgowan was alone. He was in his Tree Boy costume—one

loincloth, flame-coloured this time. He shook Ellery's hand limply and accepted a Scotch on the Rocks, settling himself on the sofa with his bare heels on the sill of the picture window.

"I thought I recognized the car," said Ellery.

"It's my mother's. Mine was out of gas. Am I inconvenient?" The giant glanced at the typewriter. "How do you knock that stuff out? But I had to see you." He seemed uneasy.

"What about, Mac?"

"Well ... I thought maybe the reason you hadn't made up your mind to take the case was that there wasn't enough money in it for you."

"Did you?"

"Look. Maybe I could put enough more in the pot to make it worth your while."

"You mean *you* want to hire me, too, Mac?"

"That's it." He seemed relieved that it was out. "I got to thinking ... that note, and then whatever it was Roger got in that box the morning old man Hill got the dead dog.... I mean, maybe there's something in it, after all, Mr. Queen."

"Suppose there is." Ellery studied him with curiosity. "Why are you interested enough to want to put money into an investigation?"

"Roger's my mother's husband, isn't he?"

"Touching, Mac. When did you two fall in love?"

Young Macgowan's brown skin turned mahogany. "I mean ... It's true Roger and I never got along. He's always tried to dominate me as well as everybody else. But he means well, and—"

"And that's why," smiled Ellery, "you call yourself Crowe Macgowan instead of Crowe Priam."

Crowe laughed. "Okay, I detest his lazy colon. We've always fought like a couple of wild dogs. When Delia married him he wouldn't adopt me legally; the idea was to keep me dependent on him. I was a kid, and it made me hate him. So I kept my father's name and I refused to take any money from Roger. I wasn't altogether a hero—I had a small income from a trust fund

68

my father left for me. You can imagine how that set with Mr. Priam." He laughed again. But then he finished lamely, "The last few years I've grown up, I guess. I tolerate him for Mother's sake. That's it," he added, brightening, "Mother's sake. That's why I'd like to get to the bottom of this. You see, Mr. Queen?"

"Your mother loves Priam?"

"She's married to him, isn't she?"

"Come off it, Mac. I intimated to you myself the other day, in your tree, that your mother had already offered to engage my services. Not to mention Laurel. What's this all about?"

Macgowan got up angrily. "What difference does my reason make? It's an honest offer. All I want is this damned business cleaned up. Name your fee and get going on it!"

"As they say in the textbooks, Mac," said Ellery, "I'll leave you now. It's the best I can do."

"What are you waiting for!"

"Warning number two. If this business is on the level, Mac, there will be a warning number two, and I can't do a thing till it comes. With Priam being pig-headed, you and your mother can be most useful by simply keeping your eyes open. I'll decide then."

"What do we watch for," sneered the young man, "another mysterious box?"

"I've no idea. But whatever it turns out to be—and it may not be a thing, Mac, but an event—whatever happens out of the ordinary, no matter how silly or trivial it may seem to you—let me know about it right away. You," and Ellery added, as if in afterthought, "or your mother."

The phone was ringing. He opened his eyes, conscious that it had been ringing for some time.

He switched on the light, blinking at his wrist-watch.

4.35. He hadn't got to bed until 1.30.

"Hello?" he mumbled.

"Mr. Queen—"

Delia Priam.

"Yes?" He had never felt so wakeful.

"My son Crowe said to call you if—" She sounded far away, a little frightened.

"Yes? Yes?"

"It's probably nothing at all. But you told Crowe—"

"Delia, what's happened?"

"Roger's sick, Ellery. Dr. Voluta is here. He says it's ptomaine poisoning. But—"

"I'll be right over!"

Dr. Voluta was a floppy man with jowls and a dirty eye, and it was a case of hate at first sight. The doctor was in a bright blue yachting jacket over a yellow silk undershirt and his greasy brown hair stuck up all over his head. He wore carpet slippers. Twice Ellery caught himself about to address him as Captain Bligh, and it would not have surprised him if, in his own improvised costume of soiled white ducks and turtle-neck sweater, he had inspired Priam's doctor to address him in turn as Mr. Christian.

"The trouble with you fellows," Dr. Voluta was saying as he scraped an evil mess from a rumpled bedsheet into a specimen vial, "is that you really enjoy murder. Otherwise you wouldn't see it in every belly-ache."

"Quite a belly-ache," said Ellery. "The stopper's right there over the sink, Doctor."

"Thank you. Priam is a damn pig. He eats too much for even a well man. His alimentary apparatus is a medical problem in itself. I've warned him for years to lay off bedtime snacks, especially spicy fish."

"I'm told he's fond of spicy fish."

"I'm fond of spicy blondes, Mr. Queen," snapped Dr. Voluta, "but I keep my appetite within bounds."

"I thought you said there's something wrong with the tuna."

"Certainly there's something wrong with it. I tasted it myself.

70

But that's not the point. The point is that if he'd followed my orders he wouldn't have eaten any in the first place."

They were in the butler's pantry, and Dr. Voluta was looking irritably about for something to cover a plastic dish into which he had dumped the remains of the tuna.

"Then it's your opinion, Doctor—?"

"I've given you my opinion. The can of tuna was spoiled. Didn't you ever hear of spoiled canned goods, Mr. Queen?" He opened his medical bag, grabbed a surgical glove, and stretched it over the top of the dish.

"I've examined the empty tin, Dr. Voluta." Ellery had fished it out of the tin can container, thankful that in Los Angeles you had to keep cans separate from garbage. "I see no sign of a bulge, do you?"

"You're just assuming that's the tin it came from," the doctor said disagreeably. "How do you know?"

"The cook told me. It's the only tuna she opened today. She opened it just before she went to bed. And I found the tin at the top of the waste can."

Dr. Voluta threw up his hands. "Excuse me. I want to wash up."

Ellery followed him to the door of the downstairs lavatory. "Have to keep my eye on that vial and dish, Doctor," he said apologetically. "Since you won't turn them over to me."

"You don't mean a thing to me, Mr. Queen. I still think it's all a lot of nonsense. But if this stuff has to be analyzed, I'm turning it over to the police personally. Would you mind stepping back? I'd like to close this door."

"The vial," said Ellery.

"Oh, for God's sake." Dr. Voluta turned his back and opened the tap with a swoosh.

They were waiting for Lieutenant Keats. It was almost six o'clock, and through the windows a pale farina-like world was taking shape. The house was cold. Priam was purged and asleep, his black beard jutting from the blankets on his reclining chair with a moribund majesty, so that all Ellery had been able to think of—before Alfred Wallace shut the door politely in his face—was Sennacherib the Assyrian in his tomb; and that was no help. Wallace had locked Priam's door from the inside. He was spending what was left of the night on the day-bed in Priam's room reserved for his use during emergencies.

Crowe Macgowan had been snappish. "If I hadn't made that promise, Queen, I'd never have had Delia call you. All this stench about a little upchucking. Leave him to Voluta and go home." And he had gone back to his oak, yawning.

Old Mr. Collier, Delia Priam's father, had quietly made himself a cup of tea in the kitchen and trotted back upstairs with it, pausing only long enough to chuckle to Ellery: "A fool and his gluttony are soon parted."

Delia Priam.... He hadn't seen her at all. Ellery had rather built himself up to their middle-of-the-night meeting, although he was prepared to be perfectly correct. Of course, she couldn't know that. By the time he arrived she had returned to her room upstairs. He was glad, in a way, that her sense of propriety was so delicately tuned to his state of mind. It was, in fact, astoundingly perceptive of her. At the same time, he felt a little empty.

Ellery stared gritty-eyed at Dr. Voluta's blue back. It was an immense back, with great fat wrinkles running across it.

He could, of course, get rid of the doctor and go upstairs and knock on her door. There was always a question or two to be asked in a case like this.

He wondered what she would do.

And how she looked at six in the morning.

He played with this thought for some time.

"Ordinarily," said the doctor, turning and reaching for a towel, "I'd have told you to go to hell. But a doctor with a respectable practice has to be cagey in this town, Mr. Queen, and Laurel started something when she began to talk about murder at Leander Hill's death. I know your type. Publicity-happy." He flung the towel at the bowl, picked up the vial and the plastic dish, holding them firmly. "You don't have to watch me, Mr. Queen. I'm not going to switch containers on you. Where the devil is that detective? I haven't had any sleep at all tonight."

"Did anyone ever tell you, Doctor," said Ellery through his teeth, "that you look like Charles Laughton in *The Beachcomber?*"

They glared at each other until a car drew up outside and Keats hurried in.

At four o'clock that afternoon Ellery pulled his rented Kaiser up before the Priam house to find Keats's car already there. The maid with the tic, which was in an active state, showed him into the living-room. Keats was standing before the fieldstone fireplace, tapping his teeth with the edge of a sheet of paper. Laurel Hill, Crowe Macgowan, and Delia Priam were seated before him in a student attitude. Their heads swivelled as Ellery came in, and it seemed to him that Laurel was coldly expectant, young Macgowan uneasy, and Delia frightened.

"Sorry, Lieutenant. I had to stop for gas. Is that the lab report?"

Keats handed him the paper. Their eyes followed. When Ellery handed the paper back, their eyes went with it.

"Maybe you'd better line it up for these folks, Mr. Queen," said the detective. "I'll take it from there."

"When I got here about five this morning," nodded Ellery, "Dr. Voluta was sure it was food poisoning. The facts were these: Against Voluta's medical advice, Mr. Priam invariably has something to eat before going to sleep. This habit of his seems to be a matter of common knowledge. Since he doesn't sleep too well, he tends to go to bed at a late hour. The cook, Mrs. Guittierez, is on the other hand accustomed to retiring early. Consequently, Mr. Priam usually tells Mr. Wallace what he expects to feel like having around midnight, and Mr. Wallace usually transmits this information to the cook before she goes to bed. Mrs. Guittierez then prepares the snack as ordered, puts it into the refrigerator, and retires.

73

"Last night the order came through for tuna fish, to which Mr. Priam is partial. Mrs. Guittierez got a can of tuna from the pantry—one of the leading brands, by the way—opened it, prepared the contents as Mr. Priam likes it—with minced onion, sweet green pepper, celery, lots of mayonnaise, the juice of half a freshly squeezed lemon, freshly ground pepper and a little salt, a dash of Worcestershire sauce, a half-teaspoon of dried mustard, and a pinch of oregano and powdered thyme—and placed the bowl, covered, in the refrigerator. She then cleaned up and went to bed. Mrs. Guittierez left the kitchen at about twenty minutes to ten, leaving a night-light burning.

"At about ten minutes after midnight," continued Ellery, speaking to the oil painting of the Spanish grandee above the fireplace so that he would not be disturbed by a certain pair of eyes, "Alfred Wallace was sent by Roger Priam for the snack. Wallace removed the bowl of tuna salad from the refrigerator, placed it on a tray with some caraway-seed rye bread, sweet butter, and a sealed bottle of milk, and carried the tray to Mr. Priam's study. Priam ate heartily, although he did not finish the contents of the tray. Wallace then prepared him for bed, turned out the lights, and took what remained on the tray back to the kitchen. He left the tray there as it was, and himself went upstairs to his room.

"At about three o'clock this morning Wallace was awakened by the buzzer of the intercom from Mr. Priam's room. It was Priam, in agony. Wallace ran downstairs and found him violently sick. Wallace immediately phoned Dr. Voluta, ran upstairs and awakened Mrs. Priam, and the two of them did what they could until Dr. Voluta's arrival, which was a very few minutes later."

Macgowan said irritably, "Damned if I can see why you tell us—"

Delia Priam put her hand on her son's arm and he stopped.

"Go on, Mr. Queen," she said in a low voice. When she talked, everything in a man tightened up. He wondered if she quite realized the quality and range of her power.

74

"On my arrival I found the tray in the kitchen, where Wallace said he had left it. When I had the facts I phoned Lieutenant Keats. While waiting for him I got together everything that had been used in the preparation of the midnight meal—the spices, the empty tuna tin, even the shell of the lemon, as well as the things on the tray. There was a quantity of the salad, some rye bread, some of the butter, some of the milk. Meanwhile Dr. Voluta preserved what he could of the regurgitated matter. When Lieutenant Keats arrived, we turned everything over to him."

Ellery stopped and lit a cigarette.

Keats said: "I took it all down to the Crime Laboratory and the report just came through." He glanced at the paper. "I won't bother you with the detailed report. Just give you the highlights.

"Chemical analysis of the regurgitated matter from Mr. Priam's stomach brought out the presence of arsenic.

"Everything is given a clean bill—spices, tuna tin, lemon, bread, butter, milk—everything, that is, but the tuna salad itself.

"Arsenic of the same type was found in the remains of the tuna salad.

"Dr. Voluta was wrong," said Keats. "This is not a case of ptomaine poisoning caused by spoiled fish. It's a case of arsenical poisoning caused by the introduction of arsenic into the salad. The cook put the salad in the refrigerator about 9.40 last night. Mr. Wallace came and took it to Mr. Priam around ten minutes after midnight. During that period the kitchen was empty, with only a dim light burning. During those two and a half hours someone sneaked into the kitchen and poisoned the salad."

"There can't have been any mistake," added Ellery. "There is a bowl of something for Mr. Priam in the refrigerator every night. It's a special bowl, used only for his snacks. It's even more easily identified than that—it has the name *Roger* in gilt lettering on it, a gift to Roger Priam from Alfred Wallace last Christmas."

"The question is," concluded Keats, "who tried to poison Mr. Priam."

75

He looked at the three in a friendly way.

Delia Priam, rising suddenly, murmured, "It's so incredible," and put a handkerchief to her nose.

Laurel smiled at the older woman's back. "That's the way it's seemed to me, darling," she said, "ever since Daddy's death."

"Oh, for pete's sake, Laur," snapped Delia's son, "don't keep smiling like Lady Macbeth, or Cassandra, or whoever it was. The last thing in the world Mother and I want is a mess."

"Nobody's accusing you, Mac," said Laurel. "My only point is that now maybe you'll believe I wasn't talking through clouds of opium."

"All *right!*"

Delia turned to Keats. Ellery saw Keats look her over uncomfortably, but with that avidity for detail which cannot be disciplined in the case of certain women. She was superb today, all in white, with a large wooden crucifix on a silver chain girding her waist. No slit in this skirt; long sleeves; and the dress came up high to the neck. But her back was bare to the waist. Some Hollywood designer's idea of personalized fashion; didn't she realize how shocking it was? But then women, even the most respectable, have the wickedest innocence in this sort of thing, mused Ellery; it really wasn't fair to a hard-working police officer who wore a gold band on the fourth finger of his left hand. "Lieutenant, do the police have to come into this?" she asked.

"Ordinarily, Mrs. Priam, I could answer a question like that right off the bat." Keats's eyes shifted; he put an unlit cigarette between his lips and rolled it nervously to the corner of his mouth. A note of stubbornness crept into his voice. "But this is something I've never run into before. Your husband refuses to co-operate. He won't even discuss it with me. All he said was that he won't be caught that way again, that he could take care of himself, and that I was to pick up my hat on the way out."

Delia went to a window. Studying her back, Ellery thought that she was relieved and pleased. Keats should have kept her on a hook; he'd have to have a little skull session with Keats on the best way to handle Mrs. Priam. But that back *was* disturbing.

"Tell me, Mrs. Priam, is he nuts?"

"Sometimes, Lieutenant," murmured Delia without turning, "I wonder."

"I'd like to add," said Keats abruptly, "that Joe Dokes and his Ethiopian brother could have dosed that tuna. The kitchen back door wasn't locked. There's gravel back there, and woods beyond. It would have been a cinch for anyone who'd cased the household and found out about the midnight snack routine. There seems to be a tie-up with somebody from Mr. Priam's and Mr. Hill's past—somebody who's had it in for both of them for a long time. I'm not overlooking that. But I'm not overlooking the possibility that that's a lot of soda pop, too. It could be a cover-up. In fact, I think it is. I don't go for this revenge-and-slow-death business. I just wanted everybody to know that. Okay, Mr. Queen, I'm through."

He kept looking at her back.

Brother, thought Ellery with compassion.

And he said, "You may be right, Keats, but I'd like to point out a curious fact that appears in this lab report. The quantity of arsenic apparently used, says the report, was 'not sufficient to cause death.'"

"A mistake," said the detective. "It happens all the time. Either they use 'way too much' or 'way too little.'"

"Not all the time, Lieutenant. And from what's happened so far, I don't see this character—whoever he is—as the impulsive, emotional type of killer. If this is all tied up, it has a pretty careful and cold-blooded brain behind it. The kind of criminal brain that doesn't make simple mistakes like under-dosing. 'Not sufficient to cause death' ... that was deliberate."

"But why?" howled young Macgowan.

"'Slow dying,' Mac!" said Laurel triumphantly. "Remember?"

"Yes, it connects with the note to Hill," said Ellery in a glum tone. "Non-lethal dose. Enough to make Priam very sick, but not fatally. 'Slow and sure.' 'For each pace forward a warning.' The poisoning attack is a warning to Roger Priam to follow up whatever was in the box he received the morning Hill got the dead dog. Priam's warning number one—unknown. Warning number two—poisoned tuna. Lovely problem."

"I don't admire your taste in problems," said Crowe Macgowan. "What's it mean? All this—this stuff?"

"It means, Mac, that I'm forced to accept your assignment," replied Ellery. "And yours, Laurel, and yours, Delia. I shouldn't take the time, but what else can I do?"

Delia Priam came to him and took his hands and looked into his eyes and said, with simplicity, "Thank you, Ellery. It's such a ... relief knowing it's going to be handled ... by you."

She squeezed, ever so little. It was all impersonally friendly on her part; he felt that. It had to be, with her own son present. But he wished he could control his sweat-glands.

Keats lipped his unlit cigarette.

Macgowan looked down at them, interested.

Laurel said, "Then we're all nicely set," in a perfectly flat voice, and she walked out.

6

The night was chilly, and Laurel walked briskly along the path, the beam of her flashlight bobbing before her. Her legs were bare under the long suède coat and they felt goose-pimply.

When she came to the great oak she stabbed at the green ceiling with her light.

"Mac. You awake?"

Macgowan's big face appeared in her beam.

"Laurel?" he said incredulously.

"It's not Esther Williams."

"Are you crazy, walking alone in these woods at night?" The rope ladder hurtled to her feet. "What do you want to be? A sex murder in tomorrow's paper?"

"You'd be the natural suspect." Laurel began to climb, her light streaking about the clearing.

"Wait, will you! I'll put on the flood." Macgowan disappeared. A moment later the glade was bright as a studio set. "That's why I'm nervous," he grinned, reappearing. His long arm yanked her to the platform. "Boy, is this cosy. Come on in."

"Turn off the flood, Mac. I'd like some privacy."

"Sure!" He was back in a moment, lifting her off her feet. She let him carry her into his tree house and deposit her on the roll-away bed, which was made up for the night. "Wait till I turn the radio off." When he straightened up his head barely missed the ceiling. "*And* the light."

"Leave the light."

"Okay, okay. Aren't you cold, baby?"

"That's the only thing you haven't provided for, Mac. The California nights."

"Didn't you know I carry my own central heating? Shove over."

"Sit down, Mac."

"Huh?"

"On the floor. I want to talk to you."

"Didn't you ever hear of the language of the eyes and so forth?"

"Tonight it has to come out here." Laurel leaned back on her arms, smiling at him. He was beginning to glower. But then he folded up at her feet and put his head on her knees. Laurel moved him, drew her coat over her legs, and replaced his head.

"All right, then, let it out!"

"Mac," said Laurel, "why did *you* hire Ellery Queen?"

He sat still for a moment. Then he reached over to a shelf, got a cigarette, lit it, and leaned back.

"That's a hell of a question to ask a red-blooded man in a tree house at twelve o'clock at night."

"Just the same, answer it."

"What difference does it make? You hired him, Delia hired him, everybody was doing it, so I did it, too. Let's talk about something else. If we've got to talk."

"Sorry. That's my subject for tonight."

He encircled his mammoth legs, scowling through the smoke at his bare feet. "Laurel, how long have we known each other?"

"Since we were kids." She was surprised.

"Grew up together, didn't we?"

"We certainly did."

80

"Have I ever done anything out of line?"

"No," Laurel laughed softly, "but it's not because you haven't tried."

"Why, you little squirt, I could break you in two and stuff both halves in my pants pocket. Don't you know I've been in love with you ever since I found out where babies come from?"

"Why, Mac," murmured Laurel. "You've never said that to me before. Used that word, I mean."

"Well, I've used it," he growled. "Now let me hear your side of it."

"Say it again, Mac?"

"Love! I love you!"

"In that tone of voice?"

She found herself off the bed and on the floor, in his arms. "Damn you," he whispered, "I love you."

She stared up at him. "Mac—"

"I love you...."

"Mac, let go of me!" She wriggled out of his arms and jumped to her feet. "I suppose," she cried, "that's the reason you hired him! Because you love me, or—or something like that. Mac, what's the *reason*? I've got to know!"

"Is that all you have to say to a guy who tells you he loves you?"

"The reason, Mac."

Young Macgowan rolled over on his back and belched smoke. Out of the reek his voice mumbled something ineffectual. Then it stopped. When the smoke cleared, he was lying there with his eyes shut.

"You won't tell me."

"Laur, I can't. It's got ... nothing to do with anything. Just some cock-eyed thing of my own."

Laurel seated herself on the bed again. He was very long, and broad, and brown and muscular and healthy-looking. She took a Dunhill from her coat pocket and lit it with shaky fingers. But when she spoke, she sounded calm. "There are too many mys-

81

teries around here, Chesty. I know there's one about you, and where you're concerned...."

His eyes opened.

"No, Mac, stay there. I'm not entirely a fool. There's something behind this tree house and all this learned bratwurst about the end of civilization, and it's not the hydrogen bomb. Are you just lazy? Or is it a new thrill for some of your studio girls?—the ones who want life with a little extra something they can't get in a motel?" He flushed, but his mouth continued sullen. "All right, we'll let that go. Now about this love business."

She put her hand in his curly hair, gripping. He looked up at her, thoroughly startled. She leaned forward and kissed him on the lips.

"That's for thanks. You're such a beautiful man, Mac ... you see, a girl has her secrets, too—No! Mac, no. If we ever get together, it's got to be in a clean house. On the ground. Anyway, I have no time for love now."

"No time!"

"Darling, something's happening, and it's ugly. There's never been any ugliness in my life before ... that I can remember, that is. And he was so wonderful to me. The only way I can pay him back is by finding whoever murdered him and seeing him die. How stupid does that sound? And maybe I'm kind of bloodthirsty myself. But it's all in the world I'm interested in right now. If the law gets him, fine. But if ..."

"For God's sake!" Crowe scrambled to his feet, his face bilious. A short-nosed little automatic had materialized in Laurel's hand and it was pointing absently at his navel.

"If they don't, I'll find him myself. And when I do, Mac, I'll shoot him as dead as that dog. If they send me to the gaschamber for it."

"Laurel, put that blamed thing back in your pocket!"

"No matter who it is." Her green, brown-flecked eyes were bright. The gun did not move. "Even if it turned out to be you, Mac. Even if we were married—had a baby. If I found out it was you, Mac, I'd kill you, too."

"And I thought Roger was tough." Macgowan stared at her. "Well, if you find out it was me, it'll serve me right. But until you do—"

Laurel cried out. The gun was in his hand. He turned it over curiously.

"Nasty little bean-shooter. Until you do, Red, don't let anybody take this away from you," and he dropped it politely into her pocket, picked her up, and sat down on the bed with her.

A little later Laurel was saying faintly, "Mac, I didn't come here for this."

"Surprise."

"Mac, what do you think of Ellery Queen?"

"I think he's got a case on Ma," said the giant. "Do we have to talk?"

"How acute of you. I think he has, too. But that's not what I meant. I meant professionally."

"Oh, he's a nice enough guy...."

"Mac!"

"Okay, okay." He got up sullenly, dumping her. "If he's half as good as his rep—"

"That's just it. Is he?"

"Is he what? What are we talking about?" He poured himself a drink.

"Is he even *half* as good?"

"How should I know? You want one?"

"No. I've dropped in on him twice and phoned him I don't know how many times in the past couple of days, and he's always there. Sitting in his crow's nest, smoking and scanning the horizon."

"Land ho. It's a way of life, Laurel." Macgowan tossed his drink off and made a face. "That's the way these big-shot dicks work sometimes. It's all up here."

"Well, I'd like to see a little activity on the other end." Laurel jumped up suddenly. "Mac, I can't stand this doing nothing. How about you and me taking a crack at it? On our own?"

"Taking a crack at what?"

83

"At what he ought to be doing."

"Detecting?" The big fellow was incredulous.

"I don't care what you call it. Hunting for facts, if that sounds less movie-ish. Anything that will get somewhere."

"Red Hill, Lady Dick and Her Muscle Man," said young Macgowan, touching the ceiling with both hands. "You know? It appeals to me."

Laurel looked up at him coldly. "I'm not gagging, Mac."

"Who's gagging? Your brain, my sinews—"

"Never mind. Good night."

"Hey!" His big hand caught her in the doorway. "Don't be so half-cocky. I'm really going birdy up here, Laurel. It's tough squatting in this tree waiting for the big boom. How would you go about it?"

She looked at him for a long time. "Mac, don't try to pull anything cute on me."

"My gosh, what would I pull on *you!*"

"This isn't a game, like your ape-man stunt. We're not going to have any code words in Turkish or wear disguises or meet in mysterious bistros. It's going to be a lot of footwork and maybe nothing but blisters to show for it. If you understand that and still want to come in, all right. Anything else, I go it solo."

"I hope you'll put a shirt on, or at least long pants," the giant said morosely. "Where do we start?"

"We should have started on that dead dog. Long ago. Where it came from, who owned it, how it died, and all that. But now that's as cold as I am.... I'd say, Mac," said Laurel, leaning against the jamb with her hands in her pockets, "the arsenic. That's fresh, and it's something to go on. Somebody got into the kitchen over there and mixed arsenic in with Roger's tuna. Arsenic can't be too easy to get hold of. It must leave a trail of some sort."

"I never thought of that. How the dickens would you go about tracing it?"

"I've got some ideas. But there's one thing we ought to do

84

before that. The tuna was poisoned in the house. So that's the place to start looking."

"Let's go." Macgowan reached for a dark blue sweater.

"*Now?*" Laurel sounded slightly dismayed.

"Know a better time?"

Mrs. Williams came in and stumbled over a chair. "Mr. Queen? You in here?"

"Present."

"Then why don't you put on a light?" She found the switch. Ellery was bunched in a corner of the sofa, feet on the picture window, looking at Hollywood. It looked like a fireworks display, popping lights in all colours. "Your dinner's cold."

"Leave it on the kitchen table, Mrs. Williams. You go on home."

She sniffed. "It's that Miss Hill and the naked man, only he's got clothes on this evening."

"Why didn't you say so!" Ellery sprang from the sofa. "Laurel, Mac! Come in."

They were smiling, but Ellery thought they both looked a little peaked. Crowe Macgowan was in a respectable suit; he even wore a tie.

"Well, well, still communing with mysterious thoughts, eh, Queen? We're not interrupting anything momentous?"

"As far as I can see," said Laurel, "he hasn't moved from one spot in sixty hours. Ellery," she said abruptly, "we have some news for you."

"News? For me?"

"We've found out something."

"I wondered why Mac was dressed," said Ellery. "Here, sit down and tell me all about it. You two been on the trail?"

"There's nothing to this detective racket," said the giant, stretching his legs. "You twerps have been getting away with mayhem. Tell him, Red."

"We decided to do a little detecting on our own—"

85

"That sounds to me," murmured Ellery, "like the remark of a dissatisfied client."

"That's what it is." Laurel strode around smoking a cigarette. "We'd better have an understanding, Ellery. I hired you to find a killer. I didn't expect you to produce him in twenty-four hours necessarily, but I did expect *something—some* sign of interest, maybe even a twitch or two of activity. But what have you done? You've sat here and smoked!"

"Not a bad system, Laurel," said Ellery, reaching for a pipe. "I've worked that way for years."

"Well, I don't care for it!"

"Am I fired?"

"I didn't say that—"

"I think all the lady wants to do," said young Macgowan, "is give you a jab, Queen. She doesn't think thinking is a substitute for footwork."

"Each has its place," Ellery said amiably "—sit down, Laurel, won't you? Each has its place, and thinking's place can be very important. I'm not altogether ignorant of what's been going on, seated though I've remained. Let's see if I can't—er—think this out for you...." He closed his eyes. "I would say," he said after a moment, "that you two have been tracking down the arsenic with which Priam's tuna was poisoned." He opened his eyes. "Is that right so far?"

"That's right," cried Macgowan.

Laurel glared. "How did you know?"

Ellery tapped his forehead. "Never sell cerebration short. Now! What exactly have you accomplished? I look into my mental ball and I see ... you and Mac ... discovering a ... can of ... a can of rat poison in the Priam cellar." They were open-mouthed. "Yes. Rat poison. And you found that this particular rat poison contains arsenic ... arsenic, the poison which was also found in Priam's salad. How'm I doin'?"

Laurel said feebly, "But I can't imagine how you ..."

Ellery had gone to the blonde-wood desk near the window

86

and pulled a drawer open. Now he took out a card and glanced over it. "Yes. You traced the purchase of that poison, which bears the brand name of D-e-t-h hyphen o-n hyphen R-a-t-z. You discovered that this revoltingly named substance was purchased on May the thirteenth of this year at ... let me see ... at Kepler's Pharmacy at 1723 North Highland."

Laurel looked at Macgowan. He was grinning. She glared at him and then back at Ellery.

"You questioned either Mr. Kepler himself," Ellery went on, "or his clerk, Mr. Candy—unfortunately my crystal ball went blank at this point. But one of them told you that the can of Deth-on-Ratz was bought by a tall, handsome man whom he identified—probably from a set of snapshots you had with you—as Alfred Wallace. Correct, Laurel?"

Laurel said tightly, "How did you find out?"

"Why, Red, I leave these matters to those who can attend to them far more quickly and efficiently than I—or you, Red. Or the Atomic Age Tree Boy over here. Lieutenant Keats had all that information within a few hours and he passed it along to me. Why should I sauté myself in the California sun when I can sit here in comfort and think?"

Laurel's lip wiggled and Ellery burst into laughter. He shook up her hair and tilted her chin. "Just the same, that was enterprising of you, Laurel. That was all right."

"Not so all right." Laurel sank into a chair, tragic. "I'm sorry, Ellery. You must think I'm an imbecile."

"Not a bit of it. It's just that you're impatient. This business is a matter of legs, brains, and bottoms, and you've got to learn to wait on the last-named with philosophy while the other two are pumping away. What else did you find out?"

"Nothing," said Laurel miserably.

"I thought it was quite a piece," said Crowe Macgowan. "Finding out that Alfred bought the poison that knocked Roger for a loop ... that ought to mean something, Queen."

"If you jumped to that kind of conclusion," said Ellery dryly,

"I'm afraid you're in for a bad time. Keats found out something else."

"What's that?"

"It was your mother, Mac, who thought she heard mice in the cellar. It was your mother who told Wallace to buy the rat poison."

The boy gaped, and Laurel looked down at her hands suddenly.

"Don't be upset, Mac. No action is going to be taken. Even though the mice seem to have been imaginary—we could find no turds or holes.... The fact is, we have nothing positive. There's no direct evidence that the arsenic in Priam's tuna salad came from the can of rat poison in the cellar. There's no direct evidence that either your mother or Wallace did anything but try to get rid of mice who happen not to have been there."

"Well, of course not." Macgowan had recovered; he was even looking pugnacious. "Stupid idea to begin with. Just like this detective hunch of yours, Laurel. Everything's under control. Let's leave it that way."

"All right," said Laurel. She was still studying her hands.

But Ellery said, "No. I don't see it that way. It's not a bad notion at all for you two to root around. You're on the scene—"

"If you think I'm going to rat on my mother," began Crowe angrily.

"We seem to be in a rodent cycle," Ellery complained. "Are you worried that your mother may have tried to poison your stepfather, Mac?"

"No! I mean—you know what I mean! What kind of rat—skunk do you think I am?"

"I got you into this, Mac," Laurel said. "I'm sorry. You can back out."

"I'm *not* backing out! Seems to me you two are trying to twist every word I say!"

"Would you have any scruples," asked Ellery with a smile, "where Wallace is concerned?"

88

"Hell, no. Wallace doesn't mean anything to me. Delia does." Her son added, with a sulky shrewdness, "I thought she did to you, too."

"Well, she does." The truth was, Keats's information about Delia Priam and the rat poison had given him a bad time. "But let's stick to Wallace for the moment. Mac, what do you know about him?"

"Not a thing."

"How long has he been working for your stepfather?"

"About a year. They come and go. Roger's had a dozen stooges in the last fifteen years. Wallace is just the latest."

"Well, you keep your eye on him. And Laurel—"

"On Delia," said Macgowan sarcastically.

"Laurel on everything. Keep giving me reports. Anything out of the ordinary. This case may prove to be a series of excavations, with the truth at the bottom level. Dig in."

"I could go back to the beginning," mumbled Laurel, "and try to trace the dead dog...."

"Oh, you don't know about that, do you?" Ellery turned to the writing-desk again.

"About the *dog*?"

He turned around with another card. "The dog belonged to somebody named Henderson who lives on Clybourn Avenue in the Toluca Lake district. He's a dwarf who gets occasional work in films. The dog's name was Frank. Frank disappeared on Decoration Day. Henderson reported his disappearance to the Pound Department, but his description was vague and unfortunately Frank had no licence—Henderson, it seems, is against bureaucracy and regimentation. When the dog's body was picked up at your house, Laurel, in view of its lack of identification it was disposed of in the usual way. It was only afterwards that Henderson identified the collar, which was returned to him.

"Keats has seen the collar, although Henderson refuses to part with it for sentimental reasons. Keats doubts, though, that anything can be learned from it. There's no trace of the little silver box which was attached to the collar. The receipt Henderson signed at the Pound Department mentions it, but Henderson says he threw it away as not belonging to him.

"As for what the dog died of, an attendant at the Pound remembered the animal and he expressed the opinion that Frank had died of poisoning. Asked if it could have been arsenic poisoning, the man said, yes, it could have been arsenic poisoning. In the absence of an analysis of the remains, the opinion is worthless. All we can do is speculate that the dog was fed something with arsenic in it, which is interesting as speculation but meaningless as evidence. And that's the story of the dead dog, Laurel. You can forget it."

"I'll help wherever I can," said Laurel in a subdued voice. "And again, Ellery—I'm sorry."

"No need to be. My fault for not having kept you up to date." Ellery put his arm around her, and she smiled faintly. "Oh, Mac," he said. "There's something personal I want to say to Laurel. Would you mind giving me a couple of minutes with her alone?"

"Seems to me," grumbled the giant, rising, "as a bloodhound you've got a hell of a wolf strain in you, Queen." His jaw protruded. "Lay off my mother, hear me? Or I'll crack your clavicles for soup!"

"Oh, stop gibbering, Mac," said Laurel quickly.

"Laur, do you want to be alone with this character?"

"Wait for me in the car."

Mac almost tore the front door off its hinges.

"Mac is something like a Great Dane himself," Laurel murmured, her back to the door. "Huge, honest, and a little dumb. What is it, Ellery?"

"Dumb about what, Laurel?" Ellery eyed her. "About me? That wasn't dumb. I admit I've found Delia Priam very attractive."

"I didn't mean dumb about you." Laurel shook her head. "Never mind, Ellery. What did you want?"

"Dumb about Delia? Laurel, you know something about Mac's mother—"

"If it's Delia you want to question me about, I—I can't answer. May I go now, please?"

"Right away." Ellery put his hand on the door-knob, looking down at her cinnamon hair. "You know, Laurel, Lieutenant Keats has done some work at your house, too."

Her eyes flew to his. "What do you mean?"

"Questioning your housekeeper, the chauffeur, the house-man."

"They didn't say anything about me!"

"You're dealing with a professional, Laurel, and a very good one. They didn't realize they were being pumped." His eyes were grave. "A few weeks ago you lost or mislaid a small silver box, Laurel. A sort of pill-box."

She had gone pale, but her voice was steady. "That's right."

"From the description Mrs. Monk, Simeon, and Ichiro gave— you'd asked them to look for it—the box must have been about the same size and shape as the one you told me contained the warning note to your father. Keats wanted to quiz you about it immediately, but I told him I'd handle it myself. Laurel, was it your silver box that was attached to the collar of Henderson's defunct dog?"

"I don't know."

"Why didn't you mention to me the fact that a box of the same description belonging to you had disappeared shortly before June second?"

"Because I was sure it couldn't have been the same one. The very idea was ridiculous. How could it have been my box? I got it at The May Company, and I think The Broadway and other department stores have been carrying it, too. It's advertised for carrying vitamin tablets and things like that. There must have been thousands of them sold all over Los Angeles. I really bought it to give to daddy. He had to take certain pills and he could have carried this around in his watch-pocket. But I mislaid it—"

"Could it have been your pill-box?"

"I suppose it could, but—"

"And you never found the one you lost?"

She looked at him, worried. "Do you suppose it was?"

"I'm not supposing much of anything yet, Laurel. Just trying to get things orderly. Or just trying to get things." Ellery opened the door and looked out cautiously. "Be sure to tell your muscular admirer that I'm returning you to him *virgo intacto*. I'm sort of sentimental about my clavicles." He smiled and squeezed her fingers.

He watched until they were out of sight around the lower curve of the hill, not smiling at all.

Ellery went down to his cold supper and chewed away. The cottage was cheerlessly silent. His jaws made sounds.

Then there was a different sound.

A tap on the kitchen door?

Ellery stared. "Come in?"

And there she was.

"Delia." He got out of his chair, still holding the knife and fork.

She was in a long loose coat of some dark blue material. It had a turned-up collar which framed her head. She stood with her back against the door, looking about the room.

"I've been waiting in the back garden in the dark. I saw Laurel's car. And after Laurel and ... Crowe drove away I thought I'd better wait a little longer. I wasn't sure that your housekeeper was gone."

"She's gone."

"That's good." She laughed.

"Where is your car, Delia?"

"I left it in a side lane at the bottom of the hill. Walked up. Ellery, this is a darling kitchen—"

"Discreet," said Ellery. He had not stirred.

"Aren't you going to ask me in?"

He said slowly, "I don't think I'm going to."

Her smile withered. But then it burgeoned again. "Oh, don't sound so serious. I was passing by and I thought I'd drop in and see how you were getting on—"

"With the case."

"Of course." She had dimples. Funny, he had never noticed them before.

"This isn't a good idea, Delia."

"*What* isn't?"

"This is a small town, Delia, and it's all eyes and ears. It doesn't take much in Hollywood to destroy a woman's reputation."

"Oh, that." She was silent. Then she showed her teeth. "Of course, you're right. It was stupid of me. It's just that sometimes ..." She stopped, and she shivered suddenly.

"Sometimes what, Delia?"

"Nothing. I'm going—Is there anything new?"

"Just that business about the rat poison."

She shrugged. "I really thought there were mice."

"Of course."

"Good night, Ellery."

"Good night, Delia."

He did not offer to walk her down the hill and she did not seem to expect it.

He stared at the kitchen door for a long time.

Then he went upstairs and poured himself a stiff drink.

At three in the morning Ellery gave up trying to sleep and crawled out of bed. He turned on the lights in the living-room, loaded and fired his briar, turned the lights out, and sat down to watch Hollywood glimmer scantily below. Light always disturbed him when he was groping in the dark.

And he was groping, and this was darkness.

Of course, it was a puzzling case. But puzzle was merely the absence of answer. Answer it, and the puzzle vanished. Nor was he bothered by the nimbus of fantasy which surrounded the case like a Los Angeles daybreak fog. All crimes were fantastic insofar as they expressed what most people merely dreamed about. The dream of the unknown enemy had been twenty years or more in the making....

He clucked to himself in the darkness. Back to the writer of the note.

The wonder was not that he made gifts of poisoned dogs and wrote odd notes relishing slow death and promising mysterious warnings with special meanings. The wonder was that he had been able to keep his hatred alive for almost a generation; and that was not fantasy, but sober pathology.

Fantasy was variance from normal experience, a matter of degree. Hollywood had always attracted its disproportionate quota of variants from the norm. In Vandalia, Illinois, Roger Priam would have been encysted in the community like a foreign substance, but in the Southern California canyons he was peculiarly soluble. There might be Delia Priams in Seattle, but in the houri paradise of Hollywood she belonged, the female archetype from whom all desire sprang. And Tree Boy, who in New York would have been dragged off to the observation ward of Bellevue Hospital, was here just another object of civic admiration, rating columns of good-natured newspaper space.

No, it wasn't the fantasy.

It was the hellish scarcity of facts.

Here was an enemy out of the past. What past? No data. The enemy was preparing a series of warnings. What were they? A dead dog had been the first. Then the unknown contents of a small cardboard box. Then a deliberately non-lethal dose of arsenic. The further warnings, the warnings that were promised, had not yet come forth. How many would there be? They were warnings of "special meaning." A series, then. A pattern. But what connection could exist between a dead dog and an arsenic-salted tuna-fish salad? It would help, help greatly, to know what had been in that box Roger Priam had received at the same moment that Leander Hill was stooping over the body of the dog and reading the thin, multi-creased note. Yes, greatly. But ... no data. It was probable that, whatever it was, Priam had destroyed it. But Priam knew. How could the man be made to talk? He must be made to talk.

The darkness was darker than even that. Ellery mused, worrying his pipe. There was a pattern, all right, but how could he be sure it was the only pattern? Suppose the dead hound had been the first warning of special meaning in a proposed series to Hill, the other warnings of which were forever lost in the limbo of an unknown mind because of Hill's premature death? And suppose whatever was in Priam's box was the first warning of a *second* series, of which the second warning was the poisoning—a series having no significant relation to the one aborted by Hill's heart attack? It was possible. It was quite possible that there was no connection in *meaning* between Hill's and Priam's warnings.

The safest course for the time being was to ignore the dead dog received by Hill and to concentrate on the living Priam, proceeding on the assumption that the unknown contents of Priam's box and the poisoning of his salad constituted a separate series altogether....

Ellery went back to bed. His last thought was that he must find out at any cost what had been in that box, and that he could only wait for the third warning to Priam.

But he dreamed of Delia Priam in a jungle thicket, showing her teeth.

7

As Ellery was able to put it together when he arrived at Delia Priam's summons that fabulous Sunday morning—from the stories of Delia, Alfred Wallace, and old Mr. Collier—Delia had risen early to go to church. Beyond remarking that her church attendance was "spotty," she was reticent about this; Ellery gathered that she could not go as regularly as she would like because of the peculiar conditions of her life, and that only occasionally was she able to slip away and into one of the old churches where, to "the blessed mutter of the Mass," she returned to her childhood and her blood. This had been such a morning, five days after the poisoning attack on her husband, two after her strange visit to Ellery's cottage.

While Delia had been up and about at an early hour, Alfred Wallace had risen late. He was normally an early riser, because Priam was a demanding charge and Wallace had learned that if he was to enjoy the luxury of breakfast he must get it over with before Priam awakened. On Sundays, however, Priam preferred to lie in bed until midmorning, undisturbed, and this permitted Wallace to sleep until nine o'clock.

Delia's father was invariably up with the birds. On this morning he had breakfasted with his daughter, and when she drove off to Los Angeles, Mr. Collier went out for his early-morning tramp through the woods. On his way back he had stopped before the big oak and tried to rouse his grandson, but as there was no answer from the tree house beyond Crowe's Brobdingnagian snores the old man had returned to the Priam house and gone into the library. The library was downstairs off the main hall, directly opposite the door to Roger Priam's quarters, with the staircase between. This was shortly after eight, Mr. Collier told Ellery; his son-in-law's door was shut and there was no light visible under the door; all seemed as it always was at that hour of a Sunday morning; and the old man had got his postage-stamp albums out of a drawer of the library desk, his stamp hinges, his tongs, and his Scott's catalogue, and he had set to work mounting his latest mail purchases of stamps. "I've done a lot of knocking about the world," he told Ellery, "and it's corking fun to collect stamps from places I've actually been in. Want to see my collection?" Ellery had declined; he was rather busy at the time.

At a few minutes past nine Alfred Wallace came downstairs. He exchanged greetings with Delia's father—the library door stood open—and went in to his breakfast without approaching Priam's door.

Mrs. Guittierez served him, and Wallace read the Sunday papers, which were always delivered to the door, as he ate. It was the maid's and chauffeur's Sunday off and the house was unusually quiet. In the kitchen the cook was getting things ready for Roger Priam's breakfast.

Shortly before ten o'clock Alfred Wallace painstakingly restored the Sunday papers to their original state, pushed back his chair, and went out into the hall carrying the papers. Priam liked to have the newspapers within arm's reach when he awakened Sunday mornings, and he flew into a rage if they were crumpled or disarranged.

Seeing a line of light beneath Priam's door, Wallace quickened his step.

The first *he* knew anything out of the ordinary had occurred, said Mr. Collier, he heard Wallace's cry from Roger Priam's room: "Mr. Collier! Mr. Collier! Come here!" The old man jumped up from his stamp albums and ran across the hall. Wallace was rattling the telephone, trying to get the operator. Just as he was shouting to Collier, "See about Mr. Priam! See if he's all right!" the operator responded, and Wallace—who seemed in a panic—babbled something about the police and Lieutenant Keats. Collier picked his way across the room to his son-in-law's wheel-chair, which was still made up as a bed. Priam, in his night clothes, was up on one elbow, glaring about with a sort of vitreous horror. His mouth was open and his beard was in motion, but no sound passed them. As far as the old man could see, there was nothing wrong with Priam but stupefying fright. Collier eased the paralyzed man backward until he was supine, trying to soothe him; but Priam lay rigid, as if in a coma, his eyes tightly shut to keep out what he had seen, and the old man could get no response from him.

At this moment, Delia Priam returned from church.

Wallace turned from the phone and Collier from Priam at a choked sound from the doorway. Delia was staring into the room with eyes sick with disbelief. She was paler than her husband and she seemed about to faint.

"All this ... all these ..."

She began to titter.

Wallace said roughly, "Get her out of here."

"He's dead. He's dead!"

Collier hurried to her. "No, no, daughter. Just scared. Now you go upstairs. We'll take care of Roger."

"He's not dead? Then why—? How do these—?"

"Delia." The old man stroked her hand.

"Don't touch anything. Anything!"

"No, no, daughter—"

"Nothing must be touched. It's got to be left exactly as you found it. *Exactly.*" And Delia stumbled up the hall to the household telephone and called Ellery.

When Ellery pulled up before the Priam house a radio patrol car was already parked in the driveway. A young officer was in the car, making a report to headquarters by radio, his mouth going like a faucet. His mate was apparently in the house.

"Here, you." He jumped out of the car. "Where you going?" His face was red.

"I'm a friend of the family, Officer. Mrs. Priam just telephoned me." Ellery looked rather wild himself. Delia had been hysterical over the phone, and the only word he had been able to make out, "fogs," had conveyed nothing reasonable. "What's happened?"

"I wouldn't repeat it," said the patrol-man excitedly. "I wouldn't lower myself. They think I'm drunk. What do they think I am? Sunday morning! I've seen a lot of cross-eyed things in this town, but—"

"Here, get hold of yourself, Officer. Has Lieutenant Keats been notified, do you know?"

"They caught him at home. He's on his way here now."

Ellery bounded up the steps. As he ran into the hall he saw Delia. She was dressed for town, in black and modest dress, hat, and gloves, and she was leaning against a wall bloodlessly. Alfred Wallace, dishevelled and unnerved, was holding one of her gloved hands in both of his, whispering to her. The tableau dissolved in an instant; Delia spied Ellery, said something quickly to Wallace, withdrawing her hand, and she ran forward. Wallace turned, rather startled. He followed her with a hasty shuffle, almost as if he were afraid of being left alone.

"Ellery."

"Is Mr. Priam all right?"

"He's had a bad shock."

"Can't say I blame him," Wallace mumbled. The handsome man passed a trembling handkerchief over his cheeks. "The doctor's on his way over. We can't seem to snap Mr. Priam out of it."

"What's this about 'fogs,' Delia?" Ellery hurried up the hall, Delia clinging to his arm. Wallace remained where he was, still wiping his face.

"Fogs? I didn't say fogs. I said—"

Ellery stopped in the doorway.

The other radio-car patrol-man was straddling a chair, cap pushed back on his head, looking about helplessly.

Roger Priam lay stiffly on his bed staring at the ceiling.

And all over Priam's body, on his blanket, on his sheet, in the shelves and compartments of his wheel-chair, on his typewriter, strewn about the floor, the furniture, Wallace's emergency bed, the window sills, the cornices, the fireplace, the mantelpiece—everywhere—were frogs.

Frogs and toads.

Hundreds of frogs and toads.

Tiny tree toads.

Yellow-legged frogs.

Bullfrogs.

Each little head was twisted.

The room was littered with their corpses.

Ellery had to confess to himself that he was thrown. There was a nonsense quality to the frogs that crossed over the line of laughter into the darker regions of the mind. Beyond the black bull calf of the Nile with the figure of an eagle on his back and the beetle upon his tongue stood Apis, a god; beyond absurdity loomed fear. Fear was the timeless tyrant. At mid-twentieth century it took the shape of a gigantic mushroom. Why not frogs? With frogs the terrible Wrath of the Hebrews had plagued the Egyptian, with frogs and blood and wild beasts and darkness and the slaying of the first-born.... He could hardly blame Roger Priam for lying frozen. Priam knew something of the way of gods; he was by way of being a minor one himself.

While Keats and the patrol-men tramped about the house, Ellery drifted around the Priam living-room trying to get a bearing. The whole thing irritated and enchanted him. It made no sense. It related to nothing. There lay its power over the uninitiated; that was its appearance for the mob. But Priam was of the inner temple. He knew something the others did not. He knew the sense this nonsense made. He knew the nature of the mystery to which it related. He knew the nature of this primitive god and he grasped the meaning of the god's symbolism. Knowledge is not always power; certainty does not always bring peace. This knowledge was paralyzing and this certainty brought terror.

Keats found him nibbling his thumb under the Spanish grandee.

"Well, the doctor's gone and the frogs are all collected and maybe you and I had better have a conference about this."

"Sure."

"This is what you'd call Priam's third warning, isn't it?"

"Yes, Keats."

"Me," said the detective, seating himself heavily on a heavy chair, "I'd call it broccoli."

"Don't make that mistake."

Keats looked at him in a resentful way. "I don't go for this stuff, Mr. Queen. I don't believe it even when I see it. Why does he go to all this trouble?" His tone said he would have appreciated a nice, uncomplicated bullet.

"How is Priam?"

"He'll live. The problem was this doctor, Voluta. It seems we took him away from a party—a blonde party—at Malibu. He took the frogs as a personal insult. Treated Priam for shock, put him to sleep, and dove for his car."

"Have you talked to Priam?"

"I talked to Priam, yes. But he didn't talk to me."

"Nothing?"

"He just said he woke up, reached for that push-button-on-a-cord arrangement he's got for turning on the lights, saw the little beasties, and knew no more."

"No attempt at explanation?"

"You don't think he knows the answer to *this* one!"

"The strong-man type represented by our friend Priam, Lieutenant," said Ellery, "doesn't pass out at the sight of a few hundred frogs, even when they're strewn all over his bed. His reaction was *too* violent. Of course he knows the answer. And it scares the wadding out of him."

Keats shook his head. "What do we do now?"

"What did you find out?"

"Not a thing."

"No sign of a point of entry?"

"No. But what sign would there be? You come from the suspicious East, Mr. Queen. This is the great West, where men are men and nobody locks his door but Easterners." Keats rolled a tattered cigarette to the other side of his mouth. "Not even," he said bitterly, "taxpayers who are on somebody's knock-off list." He jumped up with a frustrated energy. "The trouble is, this Priam won't face the facts. Poison him, and he looks thoughtful. Toss a couple hundred dead frogs around his bedroom, and he shakes his head doubtfully. You know what I think? I think everybody in this house, present company excepted, is squirrel food."

But Ellery was walking a tight circle, squinting towards some hidden horizon. "All right, he got in without any trouble—simply by walking in. Presumably in the middle of the night. Priam's door isn't locked at night so that Wallace or the others can get at him in an emergency, consequently he enters Priam's room with equal facility. So there he is, with a bag or a suitcase full of murdered frogs. Priam is asleep—not dead, mind you, just asleep. But he might just as well have been dead, because his visitor distributed two or three hundred frogs about the premises—in the dark, mind you—without disturbing Priam in the least. Any answers, Lieutenant?"

"Yes," said Keats wearily. "Priam polished off a bottle last night. He *was* dead—dead to the world."

Ellery shrugged and resumed his pacing. "Which takes us back to the frogs. A cardboard box containing ... we don't know what; that's warning number one. Food poisoning ... that's warning number two. Warning number three ... a zoo colony of dead frogs. One, unknown; two, poisoned food; three, strangled frogs. It certainly would help to know number one."

"Suppose it was a fried coconut," suggested Keats. "Would it help?"

"There's a connection, Lieutenant. A pattern."

"I'm listening."

"You don't just pick frogs out of your hat. Frogs *mean* something."

"Yeah," said Keats, "warts." But his laugh was unconvincing. "Okay, so they mean something. So this *all* means something. I don't give a damn what it means. I said, what kind of maniac is this Priam? Does he *want* to shove off? Without putting up a battle?"

"He's putting up a battle, Lieutenant," frowned Ellery. "In his peculiar way, a brave one. To ask for help, even to accept help without asking for it, would be defeat for Priam. Don't you understand that? He has to be top man. He has to control his own destiny. He *has* to, or his life has no meaning. Remember, Keats, he's a man who's living his life away in a chair. You say he's asleep now?"

"With Wallace guarding him. I offered a cop, and I nearly got beaned with the *Examiner*. It was all I could do to make Priam promise he'd keep his doors locked from now on. At that, he didn't promise."

"How about that background stuff? On the partners?"

The detective crushed the stained butt in his fist and flipped it in the fireplace. "It's like pulling teeth," he said slowly. "I don't get it. I put two more men on it yesterday." He snapped a fresh cigarette into his mouth. "The way I see it, Mr. Queen, we're doing this like a couple of country constables. We've got to go right to the horse's mouth. Priam's got to talk. He knows the whole story, every answer. Who his enemy is. Why the guy's nursed a grudge for so many years. Why the fancy stuff—"

"And what was in the box," murmured Ellery.

103

"Correct. I promised Dr. Voluta I'd lay off Priam today." Keats clapped his hat on his head. "But tomorrow I think I'm going to get tough."

When the detective had left, Ellery wandered out into the hall. The house was moody with silence. Crowe Macgowan had gone loping over to the Hill house to tell Laurel all about the amphibian invasion. The door to Priam's quarters was shut.

There was no sign or sound of Delia. She was going to her room to lock herself in, she had said, and lie down. She had seemed to have no further interest in her husband's condition. She had looked quite ill.

Ellery turned disconsolately to go, but then—or perhaps he was looking for an excuse to linger—he remembered the library, and he went back up the hall to the doorway opposite Priam's.

Delia's father sat at the library desk intently examining a postage stamp for its water-mark.

"Oh, Mr. Collier."

The old man looked up. Immediately he rose, smiling. "Come in, come in, Mr. Queen. Everything all right now?"

"Well," said Ellery, "the frogs are no longer with us."

Collier shook his head. "Man's inhumanity to everything. You'd think we'd restrict our murderous impulses to our own kind. But no, somebody had to take his misery out on some harmless little specimens of *Hyla regilla*, not to mention—"

"Of what?" asked Ellery.

"*Hyla regilla*. Tree toads, Mr. Queen, or tree frogs. That's what most of those little fellows were." He brightened. "Well, let's not talk about that any more. Although why a grown man like Roger Priam should be afraid of them—with their necks wrung, too!—I simply don't understand."

"Mr. Collier," said Ellery quietly, "have you any idea what this is all about?"

"Oh, yes," said the old man. "I'll tell you what this is all about, Mr. Queen." He waved his stamp-tongs earnestly. "It's about corruption and wickedness. It's about greed and selfishness and guilt and violence and hatred and lack of self-control. It's about black secrets and black hearts, cruelty, confusion, fear. It's about not making the best of things, not being satisfied with what you have, and always wanting what you haven't. It's about envy and suspicion and malice and lust and nosiness and drunkenness and unholy excitement and a thirst for hot running blood. It's about man, Mr. Queen."

"Thank you," said Ellery humbly, and he went home.

And the next morning Lieutenant Keats of the Hollywood Division put on his tough suit and went at Roger Priam as if the fate of the city of Los Angeles hung on Priam's answers. And nothing happened except that Keats lost his temper and used some expressions not recommended in the police manual and had to retreat under a counter-attack of even harder words, not to mention objects, which flew at him and Ellery like mortar fire. Priam quite stripped his wheel-chair of its accessories in his furious search for ammunition.

Overnight the bearded man had bounced back. Perhaps not all the way: his eyes looked shaft-sunken and he had a case of the trembles. But the old fires were in the depths and the shaking affected only his aim, not his strength—he made a bloodless shambles of his quarters.

Keats had tried everything in ascending order—reason, cajolery, jokes, appeals to personal pride and social responsibility, derision, sarcasm, threats, curses, and finally sheer volume of sound. Nothing moved Priam but the threats and curses, and then he responded in kind. Even the detective, who was left livid with fury, had to admit that he had been out-threatened, out-cursed, and out-shouted.

Through it all Alfred Wallace stood impeccably by his employer's wheel-chair, a slight smile on his lips. Mr. Wallace, too, had ricocheted. It occurred to Ellery that in Wallace's make-up there was a great deal of old Collier's *Hyla regilla*—a chameleon quality, changing colour to suit his immediate background. Yesterday Priam had been unnerved, Wallace had been unnerved. Today Priam was strong, Wallace was strong. It was a minor puzzle, but it annoyed him.

Then Ellery saw that he might be wrong and that the phenomenon might have a different explanation altogether. As he crossed the threshold to the echo of Priam's last blast, with Wallace already shutting the door, Ellery glimpsed for one second a grotesquely different Priam. No belligerent now. No man of wrath. His beard had fallen to his chest. He was holding on to the arms of his wheel-chair as if for the reassurance of contact with reality. And his eyes were tightly closed. Ellery saw his lips moving; and if the thought had not been blasphemous, Ellery would have said Priam was praying. Then Wallace slammed the door.

"That was all right, Keats." Ellery was staring at the door. "That got somewhere."

"Where?" snarled the detective. "You heard him. He wouldn't say what was in the cardboard box, he wouldn't say who's after him, he wouldn't say why—he wouldn't say anything but that he'll handle this thing himself and let the blanking so-and-so come get him if he's man enough. So where did we get, Mr. Queen?"

"Closer to the crack-up."

"What crack-up?"

"Priam's. Keats, all that was the bellowing of a frightened steer in the dark. He's even more demoralized than I thought. He played a big scene just now for our benefit—a very good one, considering the turmoil he's in.

"Maybe one more, Keats," murmured Ellery. "One more."

8

Laurel said the frogs were very important. The enemy had slipped. So many hundreds of the warty beasts must have left a trail. All they had to do was pick it up.

"What trail? Pick it up where?" demanded Macgowan.

"Mac, where would you go if you wanted some frogs?"

"I wouldn't want some frogs."

"To a pet shop, of course!"

The giant looked genuinely admiring. "Why can't I think of things like that?" he complained. "To a pet shop let us go."

But as the day wore on young Macgowan lost his air of levity. He began to look stubborn. And when even Laurel was ready to give up, Macgowan jeered, "Chicken!" and drove on to the next shop on their list. As there are a great many pet emporia in Greater Los Angeles, and as Greater Los Angeles includes one hundred towns and thirty-six incorporated cities, from Burbank north to Long Beach south and Santa Monica west to Monrovia east, it became apparent by the end of an endless day that the detective team of Hill and Macgowan had assigned themselves an investigation worthy of their high purpose, if not their talents.

"At this rate we'll be at it till Christmas," said Laurel in despair as they munched De Luxe Steerburgers at a drive-in in Beverly Hills.

"You can give up," growled Crowe, reaching for his Double-Dip Giant Malted. "Me, I'm not letting a couple of hundred frogs throw me. I'll go it alone tomorrow."

"I'm not giving up," snapped Laurel. "I was only going to say that we've gone at this like the couple of amateurs we are. Let's divide the list and split up tomorrow. That way we'll cover twice the territory in the same time."

"Functional idea," grunted the giant. "Now how about getting something to eat? I know a good steak joint not far from here where the wine is on the house."

Early next morning they parcelled the remaining territory and set out in separate cars, having arranged to meet at 6.30 in the parking lot next to Grauman's *Chinese*. At 6.30 they met and compared notes while Hollywood honked its homeward way in every direction.

Macgowan's notes were dismal. "Not a damn lead, and I've still got a list as long as your face. How about you?"

"One bite," said Laurel gloomily. "I played a hunch and went over to a place in Encino. They even carry zoo animals. A man in Tarzana had ordered frogs. I tore over there and it turned out to be some movie star who'd bought two dozen—he called them 'jug-o-rums'—for his rock pool. All I got out of it was an autograph, which I didn't ask for, and a date, which I turned down."

"What's his name?" snarled Crowe.

"Oh, come off it and let's go over to Ellery's. As long as we're in the neighbourhood."

"What for?"

"Maybe he'll have a suggestion."

He leaned on his horn all the way to the foot of the hill.

When Laurel got out of her Austin, Crowe was already bashing Ellery's door.

"Open up, Queen! What do you lock yourself in for?"

"Mac?" came Ellery's voice.

"And Laurel," sang out Laurel.

"Just a minute."

When he unlocked the front door Ellery looked rumpled and heavy-eyed. "Been taking a nap, and Mrs. Williams must have gone. Come in. You two look like the shank end of a hard day."

"Brother," scowled Macgowan. "Is there a tall, cool drink in this oasis?"

"May I use your bathroom, Ellery?" Laurel started for the bedroom door, which was closed.

"I'm afraid it's in something of a mess, Laurel. Use the downstairs lavatory.... Right over there, Mac. Help yourself."

When Laurel came back upstairs her helper was showing Ellery their lists. "We can't seem to get anywhere," Crowe was grumbling. "Two days and nothing to show for them."

"You've certainly covered a lot of territory," applauded Ellery. "There are the fixings, Laurel—"

"Oh, yes."

"You'd think it would be easy," the giant went on, waving his glass. "How many people buy frogs? Practically nobody. Hardly one of the pet shops even handles 'em. Canaries, yes. Finches, definitely. Parakeets, by the carload. Parakeets, macaws, dogs, cats, tropical fish, monkeys, turkeys, turtles, even snakes. And I know now where you can buy an elephant, cheap. But no frogs to speak of. And toads—they just look at you as if you were balmy."

"Where did we go wrong?" asked Laurel, perching on the arm of Crowe's chair.

"In not analyzing the problem before you dashed off. You're not dealing with an idiot. Yes, you could get frogs through the ordinary channels, but they'd be special orders, and special orders leave a trail. Our friend is not leaving any trails for your convenience. Did either of you think to call the State Fish and Game Commission?"

They stared.

"If you had," said Ellery with a smile, "you'd have learned that most of the little fellows we found in Priam's room are a small tree frog or tree toad—*Hyla regilla* is the scientific name—commonly called spring peepers, which are found in great numbers in this part of the country in streams and trees, especially in the foothills. You can even find bullfrogs here, though they're not native to this part of the country—they've all been introduced from the East. So if you wanted a lot of frogs and toads, and you didn't want to leave a trail, you'd go out hunting for them."

"Two whole days," groaned Macgowan. He gulped what was left in his glass.

"It's my fault, Mac," said Laurel miserably. But then she perked up. "Well, it's all experience. Next time we'll know better."

"Next time he won't use frogs!"

"Mac." Ellery was tapping his teeth with the bit of his pipe. "I've been thinking about your grandfather."

"Is that good?" Mac immediately looked bellicose.

"Interesting man."

"You said it. And a swell egg. Keeps pretty much to himself, but that's because he doesn't want to get in anybody's way."

"How long has he been living with you people?"

"A few years. He knocked around all his life, and when he got too old for it he came back to live with Delia. Why this interest in my grandfather?"

"Is he very much attached to your mother?"

"Well, I'll put it this way," said Crowe, squinting through his empty glass. "If Delia was God, Gramp would go to church. He's gone on her and she's the only reason he stays in Roger's vicinity. And I'm not gone on these questions," said Crowe, looking at Ellery, "so let's talk about somebody else, shall we?"

"Don't you like your grandfather, Mac?"

"I love him! Will you change the subject?"

"He collects stamps," Ellery went on reflectively. "And he's just taken to hunting and mounting butterflies. A man of Mr. Collier's age, who has no business or profession and takes up hobbies, Mac, usually doesn't stop at one or two. What other interests has he?"

Crowe set his glass down with a smack. "Damned if I'm going to say another word about him. Laurel, you coming?"

"Why the heat, Mac?" asked Ellery mildly.

"Why the questions about Gramp!"

"Because all I do is sit here and think, and my thoughts have been covering a lot of territory. Mac, I'm feeling around."

"Feel in some other direction!"

"No," said Ellery, "you feel in all directions. That's the first lesson you learn in this business. Your grandfather knew the scientific name of those spring peepers. It suggests that he may have gone into the subject. So I'd like to know: In those long tramps he takes in the foot-hill woods, has he been collecting tree frogs?"

Macgowan had gone rather pale and his handsome face looked pained and baffled. "I don't know."

"He has a rabbit-hutch somewhere near the house, Mac," said Laurel in a low voice. "We could look."

"We could, but we're not going to! I'm not going to! What do you think I am?" His fists were whistling over their heads. "Anyway, suppose he did? It's a free country, and you said yourself there's lots of these peepers around!"

"True, true," Ellery soothed him. "Have another drink. I've fallen in love with the old gent myself. Oh, by the way, Laurel."

"Do I brace myself?" murmured Laurel.

"Well," grinned Ellery, "I'll admit my thoughts have sauntered in your direction, too, Laurel. The first day you came to me you said you were Leander Hill's daughter by adoption."

"Yes."

"And you said something about not remembering your mother. Don't you know anything at all about your real parents, where you came from?"

111

"No."

"I'm sorry if this distresses you—"

"You know what you are?" yelled Macgowan from the sideboard. "You're equally divided between a bottom and a nose!"

"It doesn't distress me, Ellery," said Laurel with a rather unsuccessful smile. "I don't know a thing about where I came from. I was one of those story-book babies—really left on a doorstep. Of course, daddy had no right to keep me—a bachelor and all. But he hired a reliable woman and kept me for about a year before he even reported me. Then he had a lot of trouble. They took me away from him and there was a long court squabble. But in the end they couldn't find out a thing about me, nobody claimed me, and he won out in court and was allowed to make it a legal adoption. I don't remember any of that, of course. He tried for years afterwards to trace my parents, because he was always afraid somebody would pop up and want me back, and he wanted to settle the matter once and for all. But," Laurel made a face, "he never got anywhere and nobody ever did pop up."

Ellery nodded. "The reason I asked, Laurel, was that it occurred to me that this whole business ... the circumstances surrounding your foster-father's death, the threats to Roger Priam ... may somehow tie in with your past."

Laurel stared.

"Now there," said Macgowan, "there is a triumph of the detectival science. How would that be, Chief? Elucidate."

"I toss it into the pot for what it's worth," shrugged Ellery, "admitting as I toss that it's worth little or nothing. But Laurel," he said, "whether that's a cock-eyed theory or not, your past may enter this problem. In another way. I've been a little bothered by *you* in this thing. Your drive to get to the bottom of this, your wanting revenge—"

"What's wrong with that?" Laurel sounded sharp.

"What's wrong with it is that it doesn't seem altogether normal. No, wait, Laurel. The drive is over-intense, the wish for revenge almost neurotic. I don't get the feeling that it's like you—like the you I think you are."

"I never lost my father before."

"Of course, but—"

"You don't know me." Laurel laughed.

"No, I don't." Ellery tamped his pipe absently. "But one possible explanation is that the underlying motivation of your drive is not revenge on a murderer at all, but the desire to find yourself. It could be that you're nursing a subconscious hope that finding this killer will somehow clear up the mystery of your own background."

"I never thought of that." Laurel cupped her chin and was silent for some time. Then she shook her head. "No, I don't think so. I'd like to find out who I am, where I came from, what kind of people and all that, but it wouldn't mean very much to me. They'd be strangers and the background would be ... not home. No, I loved him as if he were my father. He *was* my father. And I want to see the one who drove him into that fatal heart attack get paid back for it."

When they had gone, Ellery opened his bedroom door and said, "All right, Delia."

"I thought they'd never go."

"I'm afraid it was my fault. I kept them."

"You wanted to punish me for hiding."

"Maybe." He waited.

"I like it here," she said slowly, looking around at the pedestrian blonde furniture.

She was seated on his bed, hands gripping the spread. She had not taken her hat off, or her gloves.

She must have sat that way all during the time they were in the other room, Ellery thought. Hanging in mid-air. Like her probable excuse for leaving the Priam house. A visit somewhere in town. Among the people who wore hats and gloves.

"Why do you feel you have to hide, Delia?"

113

"It's not so messy that way. No explanations to give. No lies to make up. No scenes. I hate scenes." She seemed much more interested in the house than in him. "A man who lives alone. I can hardly imagine it."

"Why did you come again?"

"I don't know. I just wanted to." She laughed. "You don't sound any more hospitable this time than you did the last. I'm not very quick, but I'm beginning to think you don't like me."

He said brutally, "When did you get the idea that I did?"

"Oh, the first couple of times we met."

"That was barnyard stuff, Delia. You make every man feel like a rooster."

"And what's your attitude now?" she laughed again. "That you don't feel like a rooster any more?"

"I'll be glad to answer that question, Delia, in the living-room."

Her head came up sharply.

"You don't have to answer any questions," she said. She got up and strolled past him. "In your living-room or anywhere else." As he shut the bedroom door and turned to her, she said, "You really don't like me?" almost wistfully.

"I like you very much, Delia. That's why you mustn't come here."

"But you just said in there—"

"That was in there."

She nodded, but not as if she really understood. She went to his desk, ignoring the mirror above it, and picked up one of his pipes. She stroked it with her forefinger. He concentrated on her hands, the skin glowing under the sheer nylon gloves.

He made an effort. "Delia—"

"Aren't you ever lonely?" she murmured. "I think I die a little every day, just from loneliness. Nobody who talks to you really *talks*. It's just words. People listening to themselves. Women hate me, and men.... At least when they talk to me!" She wheeled, crying, "Am I that stupid? You won't talk to me, either! Am I?"

114

He had to make the effort over again. It was even harder this time. But he said through his teeth, "Delia, I want you to go home."

"Why!"

"Just because you're lonely, and have a husband who's half-dead—in the wrong half—and because I'm not a skunk, Delia, and you're not a tramp. Those are the reasons, Delia; and if you stay here much longer I'm afraid I'll forget all four of them."

She hit him with the heel of her hand. The top of his head flew off and he felt his shoulder-blades smack against the wall.

Through a momentary mist he saw her in the doorway.

"I'm sorry," she said in an agonized way. "You're a fool, but I'm sorry. I mean about coming here. I won't do it again."

Ellery watched her go down the hill. There was fog, and she disappeared in it.

That night he finished most of a bottle of Scotch, sitting at the picture window in the dark and fingering his jaw. The fog had come higher and there was nothing to see but a chaos. Nothing made sense.

But he felt purged, and safe, and wryly noble.

9

June twenty-ninth was a Los Angeles special. The weather man reported a reading of ninety-one and the newspapers bragged that the city was having its warmest June twenty-ninth in forty-three years.

But Ellery, trudging down Hollywood Boulevard in a wool jacket, was hardly aware of the roasting desert heat. He was a man in a dream these days, a dream entirely filled with the pieces of the Hill-Priam problem. So far it was a meaningless dream in which he mentally chased cubist things about a crazy landscape. In that dimension temperature did not exist except on the thermometer of frustration.

Keats had phoned to say that he was ready with the results of his investigation into the past of Hill and Priam. Well, it was about time.

Ellery turned south into Wilcox, passing the post office.

You could drift about in your head for just so long recognizing nothing. There came a point at which you had to find a compass and a legible map or go mad.

This ought to be it.

* * *

He found Keats tormenting a cigarette, the knot of his tie on his sternum and his sandy hair bristling.

"I thought you'd never get here."

"I walked down." Ellery took a chair, settling himself. "Well, let's have it."

"Where do you want it?" asked the detective. "Between the eyes?"

"What do you mean?" Ellery straightened.

"I mean," said Keats, plucking shreds of tobacco from his lips "—damn it, they pack cigarettes looser all the time!—I mean we haven't got a crumb."

"A crumb of what?"

"Of information."

"You haven't found out *anything?*" Ellery was incredulous.

"Nothing before 1927, which is the year Hill and Priam went into business in Los Angeles. There's nothing that indicates they lived here before that year; in fact, there's reason to believe they didn't, that they came here that year from somewhere else. But from where? No data. We've tried everything from tax records to the Central Bureau fingerprint files. I'm pretty well convinced they had no criminal record, but that's only a guess. They certainly had no record in the State of California.

"They came here in '27," said Keats bitterly, "started a wholesale jewellery business as partners, and made a fortune before the crash of '29. They weren't committed to the market and they rode out the depression by smart manipulation and original merchandising methods. Today the firm of Hill & Priam is rated one of the big outfits in its line. They're said to own one of the largest stocks of precious stones in the United States. And that's a lot of help, isn't it?"

"But you don't come into the wholesale jewellery business from outer space," protested Ellery. "Isn't there a record somewhere of previous connections in the industry? At least of one of them?"

"The N.J.A. records don't show anything before 1927."

"Well, have you tried this? Certainly Hill, at least, had to go abroad once in a while in connection with the firm's foreign offices—Laurel told me they have branches in Amsterdam and South Africa. That means a passport, a birth certificate—"

"That was my ace in the hole." Keats snapped a fresh cigarette to his lips. "But it turns out that Hill & Priam don't own those branches, although they do own the one in New York. They're simply working arrangements with established firms abroad. They have large investments in those firms, but all their business dealings have been, and still are, negotiated by and through agents. There's no evidence that either Hill or Priam stepped off American soil in twenty-three years, or at least during the twenty-three years we have a record of them." He shrugged. "They opened the New York branch early in 1929, and for a few years Priam took care of it personally. But it was only to get it going and train a staff. He left it in charge of a man who's still running it there, and came back here. Then Priam met and married Delia Collier Macgowan, and the next thing that happened to him was the paralysis. Hill did the transcontinental hopping for the firm after that."

"Priam's never had occasion to produce a birth certificate?"

"No, and in his condition there's no likelihood he ever will. He's never voted, for instance, and while he might be challenged to prove his American citizenship—to force him to loosen up about his place of birth and so on—I'm afraid that would take a long, long time. Too long for this merry-go-round."

"The war—"

"Both Priam and Hill were over the military age limit when World War II conscription began. They never had to register. Search of the records on World War I failed to turn up their names."

"You're beginning to irritate me, Lieutenant. Didn't Leander Hill carry any insurance?"

"None that antedated 1927, and in the photostats connected with what insurance he did take out after that date his place of birth appears as Chicago. I've had the Illinois records checked, and there's none of a Leander Hill; it was a phony. Priam carries no insurance at all. The industrial insurance carried by the firm, of course, is no help.

"In other words, Mr. Queen," said Lieutenant Keats, "there's every indication that both men deliberately avoided leaving, or camouflaged, the trail to their lives preceding their appearance in L.A. It all adds up to one thing—"

"That there was no Leander Hill or Roger Priam in existence before 1927," muttered Ellery. "Hill and Priam weren't their real names."

"That's it."

Ellery got up and went to the window. Through the glass, darkly, he saw the old landscape again.

"Lieutenant." He turned suddenly. "Did you check Roger Priam's paralysis?"

Keats smiled. "Got quite a file on that if you want to read a lot of medical mumbo-jumbo. The sources are some of the biggest specialists in the United States. But if you want it in plain American shorthand, his condition is on the level and it's hopeless. By the way, they were never able to get anything out of Priam about his previous medical history, if that's what you had in mind."

"You're disgustingly thorough, Keats. I wish I could find the heart to congratulate you. Now tell me you couldn't find anything on Alfred Wallace and I'll crown you."

Keats picked up an inkstand and offered it to Ellery. "Start crowning."

"Nothing on Wallace *either*?"

"That's right." Keats spat little dry sprigs of tobacco. "All I could dig up about Mr. Alfred W. dates from the day Priam hired him, just over a year ago."

"Why, that can't be!" exploded Ellery. "Not three in the same case."

"He's not an Angeleno, I'm pretty well convinced of that. But I can't tell you what he *is*. I'm still working on it."

"But ... it's such a short time ago, Keats!"

119

"I know," said Keats, showing his teeth without dropping the cigarette, "you wish you were back in New York among the boys in the big league. Just the same, there's something screwy about Wallace, too. And I thought, Mr. Queen, having so little to cheer you up with today, I'd cut out the fancy stuff and try a smash through the centre of the line. I haven't talked to Wallace. How about doing it now?"

"You've got him here?" exclaimed Ellery.

"Waiting in the next room. Just a polite invitation to come down to the station here and have a chat. He didn't seem to mind—said it was his day off anyway. I've got one of the boys keeping him from getting bored."

Ellery pulled a chair into a shadowed corner of the office and snapped, "Produce."

Alfred Wallace came in with a smile, the immaculate man unaffected by the Fahrenheit woes of lesser mortals. His white hair had a foaming wave to it; he carried a debonair slouch hat; there was a small purple aster in his lapel.

"Mr. Queen," said Wallace pleasantly. "So you're the reason Lieutenant Keats has kept me waiting over an hour."

"I'm afraid so." Ellery did not rise.

But Keats was polite. "Sorry about that, Mr. Wallace. Here, have this chair.... But you can't always time yourself in a murder investigation."

"You mean what *may* be a murder investigation, Lieutenant," said Wallace, seating himself, crossing his legs, and setting his hat precisely on his knee. "Or has something new come up?"

"Something new could come up, Mr. Wallace, if you'll answer a few questions."

"Me?" Wallace raised his handsome brows. "Is that why you've placed this chair where the sun hits my face?" He seemed amused.

Keats silently pulled the cord of the venetian blind.

"Thanks, Lieutenant. I'll be glad to answer any questions you ask. If, of course, I can."

"I don't think you'll have any trouble answering this one, Mr. Wallace: Where do you come from?"

"Ah," Wallace looked thoughtful. "Now that's just the kind of question, Lieutenant, I can't answer."

"You mean you won't answer."

"I mean I can't answer."

"You don't know where you come from, I suppose."

"Exactly."

"If that's going to be Mr. Wallace's attitude," said Ellery from his corner, "I think we can terminate the interview."

"You misunderstand me, Mr. Queen. I'm not being obstructive." Wallace sounded earnest. "I can't tell you gentlemen where I come from because I don't know myself. I'm one of those interesting cases you read about in the papers. An amnesia victim."

Keats glanced at Ellery. Then he rose. "Okay, Wallace. That's all."

"But that's not all, Lieutenant. This isn't something I can't prove. In fact, now that you've brought it up, I insist on proving it. You're making a recording of this, of course? I would like this to go into the record."

Keats waved his hand. His eyes were intent and a little admiring.

"One day about a year and a half ago—the exact date was January the sixteenth of last year—I found myself in Las Vegas, Nevada, on a street corner," said Alfred Wallace calmly. "I had no idea what my name was, where I came from, how I had got there. I was dressed in filthy clothing which didn't fit me and I was rather banged up. I looked through my pockets and found nothing—no wallet, no letters, no identification of any kind. There was no money, not even coins. I went up to a policeman and told him of the fix I was in, and he took me to a police station. They asked me questions and had a doctor in to examine me. The doctor's name was Dr. James V. Cutbill, and his address was 515 North Fifth Street, Las Vegas. Have you got that, Lieutenant?

"Dr. Cutbill said I was obviously a man of education and good background, about fifty years old or possibly older. He said it looked like amnesia to him. I was in perfect physical condition, and from my speech a North American. Unfortunately, Dr. Cutbill said, there were no identifying marks of any kind on my body and no operation scars, though he did say I'd had my tonsils and adenoids out probably as a child. This, of course, was no clue. There were some fillings in my teeth, of good quality, he thought, but I'd had no major dental work done. The police photographed me and sent my picture and a description to all Missing Persons Bureaus in the United States. There must be one on file in Los Angeles, Lieutenant Keats."

Keats grew fiery red. "I'll check that," he growled. "And lots more."

"I'm sure you will, Lieutenant," said Wallace with a smile. "The Las Vegas police fixed me up with some clean clothes and found me a job as a handyman in a motel, where I got my board and a place to sleep, and a few dollars a week. The name of the motel is *The 711*, on Route 91 just north of town. I worked there for about a month, saving my pay. The Las Vegas police told me no one of my description was listed as missing anywhere in the country. So I gave up the job and hitch-hiked into California.

"In April of last year I found myself in Los Angeles. I stayed at the Y, the Downtown Branch on South Hope Street; I'm surprised you didn't run across my name on their register, Lieutenant, or haven't you tried to trace me?—and I got busy looking for employment. I'd found out I could operate a typewriter and knew shorthand, that I was good at figures—apparently I'd had business training of some sort as well as a rather extensive education—and when I saw an ad for a secretarial companion-nurse job to an incapacitated business man, I answered it. I told Mr. Priam the whole story, just as I've told it to you. It seems he'd been having trouble keeping people in recent years and, after checking back on my story, he took me on for a month's trial.

And here," said Wallace with the same smile, "here I am, still on the job."

"Priam took you on without references?" said Keats, doodling. "How desperate was he?"

"As desperate as he could be, Lieutenant. And then Mr. Priam prides himself on being a judge of character. I was really glad of that, because to this day I'm not entirely sure what my character is."

Ellery lit a cigarette. Wallace watched the flame of the match critically. When Ellery blew the flame out, Wallace smiled again. But immediately Ellery said, "How did you come to take the name Alfred Wallace if you remembered nothing about your past? Or did you remember that?"

"No, it's just a name I plucked out of the ether, Mr. Queen. 'Alfred,' 'Wallace'—they're very ordinary names and more satisfying than John Doe. Lieutenant Keats, aren't you going to check my story?"

"It's going to be checked," Keats assured him. "And I'm sure we'll find it happened exactly as you've told it, Wallace—dates, names, and places. The only thing is, it's all a dodge. That's something I feel in my bones. As one old bone-feeler to another, Mr. Queen, how about it?"

"Did this doctor in Las Vegas put you under hypnosis?" Ellery asked the smiling man.

"Hypnosis? No, Mr. Queen. He was just a general practitioner."

"Have you seen any other doctor since? A psychiatrist, for example?"

"No, I haven't."

"Would you object to being examined by a psychiatrist of—let's say—Lieutenant Keats's choosing?"

"I'm afraid I would, Mr. Queen," murmured Wallace. "You see, I'm not sure I want to find out who I really am. I might discover, for example, that I'm an escaped thief, or that I have a bow-legged wife and five idiot children somewhere. I'm perfect-ly happy where I am. Of course, Roger Priam isn't the easiest employer in the world, but the job has its compensations. I'm living in royal quarters. The salary Priam pays me is very large—he's a generous employer, one of his few virtues. Old, fat Mrs. Guittierez is an excellent cook, and even though Muggs, the maid, is a straitlaced virgin with halitosis who's taken an unreasonable dislike to me, she does keep my room clean and polishes my shoes regularly. And the position even solves the problem of my sex life—oh, I shouldn't have mentioned that, should I?" Wallace looked distressed; he waved his muscular hand gently. "A slip of the tongue, gentlemen. I do hope you'll forget I said it."

Keats was on his feet. Ellery heard himself saying, "Wallace. Just what did you mean by that?"

"A gentleman, Mr. Queen, couldn't possibly have the bad taste to pursue such a question."

"A gentleman couldn't have made the statement in the first place. I ask you again, Wallace: How does your job with Priam take care of your sex life?"

Wallace looked pained. He glanced up at Keats. "Lieutenant, must I answer that question?"

Keats said slowly, "You don't have to answer anything. You brought this up, Wallace. Personally, I don't give a damn about your sex life unless it has something to do with this case. If it has, you'd better answer it."

"It hasn't, Lieutenant. How could it have?"

"I wouldn't know."

"Answer the question," said Ellery in a pleasant voice.

"Mr. Queen seems more interested than you, Lieutenant."

"Answer the question," said Ellery in a still pleasanter voice.

Wallace shrugged. "All right. But you'll bear witness, Lieu-tenant Keats, that I've tried my best to shield the lady in the case." He raised his eyes suddenly to Ellery, and Ellery saw the smile in them, a wintry shimmer. "Mr. Queen, I have the great good luck to share my employer's wife's bed. As the spirit moves. And the flesh being weak, and Mrs. Priam being the most attractive piece I've yet seen in this glorious state, I must admit that the spirit moves several times a week and has been doing so for about a year. Does that answer your question?"

"Just a minute, Wallace," Ellery heard Keats say.

And Keats was standing before him, between him and Wallace. Keats was saying in a rapid whisper, "Queen, look, let me take it from here on in. Why don't you get out of here?"

"Why should I?" Ellery said clearly.

Keats did not move. But then he straightened up and stepped aside.

"You're lying, of course," Ellery said to Wallace. "You're counting on the fact that no decent man could ask a decent woman a question like that, and so your lie won't be exposed. I don't know what slimy purpose your lie serves, but I'm going to step on it right now. Keats, hand me that phone."

And all the time he was speaking Ellery knew it was true. He had known it was true the instant the words left Wallace's mouth. The story of the amnesia was true only so far as the superficial facts went; Wallace had prepared a blind alley for himself, using the Las Vegas police and a mediocre doctor to seal up the dead end. But this was all true. He knew it was all true, and he could have throttled the man who sat half-way across the room smiling that iced smile.

"I don't see that that would accomplish anything," Keats was saying. "She'd only deny it. It wouldn't prove a thing."

"He's lying, Keats."

Wallace said with delicate mockery, "I'm happy to hear you take that attitude, Mr. Queen. Of course. I'm lying. May I go, Lieutenant?"

"No, Wallace." Keats stuck his jaw out. "I'm not letting it get this far without knowing the whole story. You say you've been cuckolding Priam for almost a year now. Is Delia Priam in love with you?"

125

"I don't think so," said Wallace. "I think it's the same thing with Delia that it is with me. A matter of convenience."

"But it stopped some time ago, didn't it?" Keats had a wink in his voice; man-to-man stuff. "It's not still going on."

"Certainly it's still going on. Why should it have stopped?"

Keats's shoulders bunched. "You must feel plenty proud of yourself, Wallace. Eating a man's food, guzzling his liquor, taking his dough, and sleeping with his wife while he's helpless in a wheel-chair on the floor below. A cripple who couldn't give you what you rate even if he knew what was going on."

"Oh, didn't I make that clear, Lieutenant?" said Alfred Wallace, smiling. "Priam does know what's going on. In fact, looking back, I can see that he engineered the whole thing."

"What are you giving me!"

"You gentlemen apparently don't begin to understand the kind of man Priam is. And I think you ought to know the facts of life about Priam, since it's his life you're knocking yourselves out to save."

Wallace ran his thumb tenderly around the brim of his hat. "I don't deny that I didn't figure Priam right myself in the beginning, when Delia and I first got together. I sneaked it, naturally. But Delia laughed and told me not to be a fool, that Priam knew, that he wanted it that way. Although he'd never admit it or let on—to me, or to her.

"Well," said Wallace modestly. "Of course I thought she was kidding me. But then I began to notice things. Looks in his eye. The way he kept pushing us together. That sort of thing. So I did a little investigating on the quiet.

"I found out that in picking secretaries Priam had always hired particularly virile-looking men.

"And I remembered the questions he asked me when I applied for the job—how he kept looking me over, like a horse." Wallace took a cigar from his pocket and lit it. Puffing with enjoyment, he leaned back. "Frankly, I've been too embarrassed to put the question to Delia directly. But unless I'm mistaken, and I don't think I am, Priam's secretaries have always done double duty. Well, for the last ten years, anyway. It also explains the rapid turnover. Not every man is as virile as he looks," Wallace said with a laugh, "and then there are always some mushy-kneed lads who'd find a situation like that uncomfortable.... But the fact remains. Priam's hired men to serve not only the master of the house, you might say, but the mistress, too."

"Get him out of here," Ellery said to Keats. But to his surprise no words came out.

"Roger Priam," continued Alfred Wallace, waving his cigar, "is an exaggerated case of crudity, raw power, and frustration. The clue to his character—and, gentlemen, I've had ample opportunity to judge it—is his compulsive need to dominate everything and everyone around him. He tried to dominate old Leander Hill through the farce of pretending he, Roger Priam, was running a million-dollar business from a wheel-chair at home. He tried to dominate Crowe Macgowan before Crowe got too big for him, according to Delia. And he's always dominated Delia, who doesn't care enough about anything to put up a scrap—dominated her physically, until he became paralyzed, Delia's told me, with the most incredible vulgarities and brutalities.

"Now imagine," murmured Wallace, "what paralysis from the waist down did to Priam's need to dominate his woman. Physically he was no longer a man. And his wife was beautiful; to this day every male who meets her begins strutting like a bull. Priam knew, knowing Delia, that it was only a question of time before one of them made the grade. And then where would he be? He might not even know about it. It would be entirely out of his control. Unthinkable! So Priam worked out the solution in his warped way—to dominate Delia by proxy.

"By God, imagine that! He deliberately picks a virile man—the substitute for himself physically and psychologically—and flings them at each other's heads, letting nature take its course."

Wallace flicked an ash into the tray on Keats's desk. "I used to

127

think he'd taken a leaf out of Faulkner's *Sanctuary*, or Krafft-Ebing, except that I've come to doubt if he's read a single book in forty-five years. No, Priam couldn't explain all this—to himself least of all. He's an ignorant man; he wouldn't even know the words. Like so many ignorant men, he's a man of pure action. He throws his wife and hand-picked secretary together, thus performing the function of a husband vicariously, and by pretending to be deaf to what goes on with domestic regularity over his head he retains his mastery of the situation. He's the god of the machine, gentlemen, and there is no other god but Roger Priam. That is, to Roger Priam." Wallace blew a fat ring of cigar-smoke and rose. "And now, unless there's something else, Lieutenant, I'd like to salvage what's left of my day off."

Keats said in a loud voice, "Wallace, you're a fork-tongued female of a mucking liar. I don't believe one snicker of this dirty joke. And when I prove you're a liar, Wallace, I'm going to leave my badge home with my wife and kids, and I'm going to haul you into some dark alley, and I'm going to kick the—out of you."

Wallace's smile thinned. His face reassembled itself and looked suddenly old. He reached over Keats's desk and picked up the telephone.

"Here," he said, holding the phone out to the detective. "Or do you want me to get the number for you?"

"Scram."

"But you want proof. Delia will admit it if you ask her in the right way, Lieutenant. Delia's a very civilized woman."

"Get out."

Wallace laughed. He replaced the phone gently, adjusted his fashionable hat on his handsome head, and walked out humming.

Keats insisted on driving Ellery home. The detective drove slowly through the five o'clock traffic.

Neither man said anything.

He had seen them for that moment in the Priam hallway, the day he

128

had come at her summons to investigate the plague of dead frogs. Wallace had been standing close to her, far closer than a man stands to a woman unless he knows he will not be repulsed. And she had not repulsed him. She had stood there accepting his pressure while Wallace squeezed her hand and whispered in her ear.... He remembered one or two of Wallace's glances at her, the glances of a man with a secret knowledge, glances of amused power.... "I always take the line of least resistance...." He remembered the night she had hidden herself in his bedroom at the sound of her son's and Laurel's arrival. She had come to him that night for the purpose to which her life in the Priam house had accustomed her. Probably she had a prurient curiosity about "celebrities" or she was tired of Wallace. (And this was Wallace's revenge?) He would have read the signs of the nymph easily enough if he had not mistaken her flabbiness for reserve—

"We're here, Mr. Queen," Keats was saying.

They were at the cottage.

"Oh. Thanks." Ellery got out automatically. "Good night."

Keats failed to drive away. Instead he said, "Isn't that your phone ringing?"

"Yes. Why doesn't Mrs. Williams answer it?" Ellery said with irritation. Then he laughed. "She isn't answering it because I gave her the afternoon off. I'd better go in."

"Wait." Keats turned his motor off and vaulted to the road. "Maybe it's my office. I told them I might be here."

Ellery unlocked the front door and went in. Keats straddled the threshold.

"Hello?"

Keats saw him stiffen.

"Yes, Delia."

Ellery listened in silence. Keats heard the vibration of the throaty tones, faint and warm and humid.

"Keats is with me now. Hide it till we get there, Delia. We'll be right over."

Ellery hung up.

"What does the lady want?" asked Keats.

129

"She says she's just found another cardboard box. It was in the Priam mail-box on the road, apparently left there a short time ago. Priam's name hand-printed on it. She hasn't told Priam about it, asked what she ought to do. You heard what I told her."

"Another warning!"

Keats ran for his car.

10

Keats stopped his car fifty feet from the Priam mailbox and they got out and walked slowly toward it, examining the road. There were tyre-marks in profusion, illegibly intermingled. Near the box they found several heel-marks of a woman's shoe, but that was all.

The door of the box hung open and the box was empty.

They walked up the driveway to the house. Keats neither rang nor knocked. The maid with the tic came hurrying towards them as he closed the door.

"Mrs. Priam said to come upstairs," she whispered. "To her room." She glanced over her shoulder at the closed door of Roger Priam's den. "And not to make any noise, she said, because *he's* got ears like a dog."

"All right," said Keats.

Muggs fled on tiptoe. The two men stood there until she had disappeared beyond the swinging door at the rear of the hall. Then they went upstairs, hugging the balustrade.

As they reached the landing, a door opposite the head of the stairs swung in. Keats and Ellery went into the room.

Delia Priam shut the door swiftly and sank back against it.

She was in brief tight shorts and a strip of sun halter. Her thighs were long and heavy and swelled to her trunk; her breasts spilled over the halter. The glossy black hair lay carelessly piled; she was barefoot—her high-heeled shoes had been kicked off. The rattan blinds were down and in the gloom her pale eyes glowed sleepily.

Keats looked her over deliberately.

"Hello, Ellery." She sounded relieved.

"Hello, Delia." There was nothing in his voice, nothing at all.

"Don't you think you'd better put something on, Mrs. Priam?" said Keats. "Any other time this would be a privilege and a pleasure, but we're here on business." He grinned with his lips only. "I don't think I could think."

She glanced down at herself, startled. "I'm sorry, Lieutenant. I was up on the sun deck before I walked down to the road. I'm very sorry." She sounded angry and a little puzzled.

"No harm done, Delia," said Ellery. "This sort of thing is all in the eye of the beholder."

She glanced at him quickly. A frown appeared between her heavy brows.

"Is something wrong, Ellery?"

He looked at her.

The colour left her face. Her hands went to her naked shoulders and she hurried past them into a dressing-room, slamming the door.

"Bitch," said Keats pleasantly. He took a cigarette out of his pocket and jammed it between his lips. The end tore and he spat it out, turning away.

Ellery looked around.

The room was overpowering, with dark Spanish furniture and wallpaper and drapes which flaunted masses of great tropical flowers. The rug was a sullen Polynesian red with a two-inch pile. There were cushions and hassocks of unusual shapes and colours. Huge majolicas stood about filled with lilies. On the wall hung heroic Gauguin reproductions and above the bed a large black iron crucifix that looked very old. Niches were crowded with ceramics, wood carvings, metal sculptures of exotic subjects, chiefly modern in style and many of them male nudes. There was an odd book-shelf hanging by an iron chain, and Ellery strolled over to it, his legs brushing the bed. Thomas Aquinas, Kinsey, Bishop Berkeley, Pierre Loti, Havelock Ellis. *Lives of the Saints* and *Fanny Hill* in a Paris edition. The rest were mystery stories; there was one of his, his latest. The bed was a wide and herculean piece set low to the floor, covered with a cloth-of-gold spread appliquéd, in brilliant colours of metallic thread, with a vast tree of life. In the ceiling, directly above the bed and of identical dimensions, glittered a mirror framed in fluorescent tubing.

"For some reason," remarked Lieutenant Keats in the silence, "this reminds me of that movie actor, What's-His-Name, of the old silent days. In the wall next to his john he had a perforated roll of rabbit fur." The dressing-room door opened and Keats said, "Now that's a relief, Mrs. Priam. Thanks a lot. Where's this box?"

She went to a trunk-sized teak chest covered with brasswork chased intricately in the East Indian manner, which stood at the foot of the bed, and she opened it. She had put on a severe brown linen dress and stockings as well as flat-heeled shoes; she had combed her hair back in a knot. She was pale and frigid, and she looked at neither man.

She took out of the chest a white cardboard box about five inches by nine and an inch deep, bound with ordinary white string, and handed it to Keats.

"Have you opened this, Mrs. Priam?"

"No."

"Then you don't know what's in it?"

"No."

"You found it exactly where and how, again?"

"In our mailbox near the road. I'd gone down to pick some flowers for the dinner-table and I noticed it was open. I looked in and saw this. I took it upstairs, locked it in my chest, and phoned."

The box was of cheap quality. It bore no imprint. To the string was attached a plain manila shipping tag. The name "Roger Priam" was lettered on the tag in black crayon, in carefully characterless capitals.

"Dime store stock," said Keats, tapping the box with a fingernail. He examined the tag. "And so is this."

"Delia." At the sound of his voice she turned, but when she saw his expression she looked away. "You saw the box your husband received the morning Hill got the dead dog. Was it like this? In quality, kind of string, tag?"

"Yes. The box was bigger, that's all." There was a torn edge to the furry voice.

"No dealer's imprint?"

"No."

"Does the lettering on this tag look anything like the lettering on the other tag?"

"It looks just like it." She put her hand on his arm suddenly, but she was looking at Keats. "Lieutenant, I'd like to speak to Mr. Queen privately for a minute."

"I don't have any secrets from Keats." Ellery was glancing down at his arm.

"Please?"

Keats walked over to one of the windows with the box. He lifted the blind, squinting along the slick surface of the box.

"Ellery, is it what happened the other night?" Her voice was at its throatiest, very low.

"Nothing happened the other night."

"Maybe that's the trouble." She laughed.

"But a great deal has happened since."

She stopped laughing. "What do you mean?"

He shrugged.

"Ellery. Who's been telling you lies about me?"

Ellery glanced again at her hand. "It's my experience, Delia, that to label something a lie before you've heard it expressed is to admit it's all too true."

He took her hand between his thumb and forefinger as if it were something sticky, and he dropped it.

Then he turned his back on her.

Keats had the box to his ear and he was shaking it with absorption. Something inside rustled slightly. He hefted the box.

"Nothing loose. Sounds like a solid object wrapped in tissue paper. And not much weight." He glanced at the woman. "I don't have any right to open this, Mrs. Priam. But there's nothing in the statutes to stop *you* ... here and now."

"I wouldn't untie that string, Lieutenant Keats," said Delia Priam in a trembling voice, "for all the filth in your mind."

"What did I do?" Keats raised his reddish brows as he handed the box to Ellery. "That puts it up to you, Mr. Queen. What do you want to do?"

"You can both get out of my bedroom!"

Ellery said, "I'll open it, Keats, but not here. And not now. I think this ought to be opened before Roger Priam, with Mrs. Priam there, and Laurel Hill, too."

"You can get along without me," she whispered. "Get out."

"It's important for you to be there," Ellery said to her.

"You can't tell me what to do."

"In that case I'll have to ask the assistance of someone who can."

"No one can."

"Not Wallace?" smiled Ellery. "Or one of his numerous predecessors?"

Delia Priam sank to the chest, staring.

"Come on, Keats. We've wasted enough time in this stud pasture."

Laurel was over in ten minutes, looking intensely curious. Padding after her into the cave-like gloom of the house came the man of the future. Young Macgowan had returned to the Post-Atomic Age.

"What's the matter now?" he inquired plaintively.

No one replied.

By a sort of instinct, he put a long arm about his mother and kissed her. Delia smiled up at him anxiously, and when he straightened she kept her grasp on his big hand. Macgowan seemed puzzled by the atmosphere. He fixed on Keats as the cause, and he glared murderously from the detective to the unopened box.

"Loosen up, boy," said Keats. "Tree life is getting you. Okay, Mr. Queen?"

"Yes."

Young Macgowan didn't know. Laurel knew—Laurel had known for a long time—but Delia's son was wrapped in the lamb's wool of mother-adoration. I'd hate to be the first one, Ellery thought, to tell him.

As for Laurel, she had glanced once at Delia and once at Ellery, and she had become mousy.

Ellery waited on the threshold to the hall as Keats explained about the box.

"It's the same kind of tag, same kind of crayon lettering, as on the dead dog," Laurel said. She eyed the box grimly. "What's inside?"

"We're going to find that out right now." Ellery took the box from Keats and they all followed him up the hall to Priam's door.

"Furl your mains'l," said a voice. It was old Mr. Collier, in the doorway across the hall.

"Mr. Collier. Would you care to join us? There's something new."

"I'll sit up in the rigging," said Delia's father. "Hasn't there been enough trouble?"

"We're trying to prevent trouble," said Keats mildly.

"So you go looking for it. Doesn't make sense to me," said the old man, shaking his head. "Live and let live. Or die and let die.

If it's right one way, it's right the other." He stepped back and shut the library door emphatically.

Ellery tried Priam's door. It was locked. He rapped loudly.

"Who is it?" The bull voice sounded slurry.

Ellery said, "Delia, you answer him."

She nodded mechanically. "Roger, open the door, won't you?" She sounded passive, almost bored.

"Delia? What d'ye want?" They heard the trundling of his chair and some glassy sounds. "Damn this rug! I've told Alfred a dozen times to tack it down—" The door opened and he stared up at them. The shelf before him supported a decanter of whisky, a siphon, and a half-empty glass. His eyes were bloodshot. "What's this?" he snarled at Ellery. "I thought I told you two to clear out of my house and stay out." His fierce eyes lighted on the box in Ellery's hand. They contracted, and he looked up and around. His glance passed over his wife and stepson as if they had not been there. It remained on Laurel's face for a moment with a hatred so concentrated that Crowe Macgowan made an unconscious growling sound. Laurel's lips tightened.

He put out one of his furry paws. "Give me the box."

"No, Mr. Priam."

"That tag's got my name on it. Give it to me!"

"I'm sorry, Mr. Priam."

He raised the purplish ensign of his rage, his eyes flaming. "You can't keep another man's property!"

"I have no intention of keeping it, Mr. Priam. I merely want to see what's inside. Won't you please back into the room so that we can come in and do this like civilized people?"

Ellery kept looking at him impassively. Priam glared in return, but his hands went to the wheels of his chair. Grudgingly, they pushed backwards.

Keats shut the door very neatly. Then he put his back against it. He remained there, watching Priam.

Ellery began to untie the box.

He seemed in no hurry.

Priam's hands were still at the sides of his chair. He was sitting forward, giving his whole attention to the untying process. His beard rose and fell with his chest. The purple flag had come down, leaving a sort of grey emptiness, like a foggy sky.

Laurel was intent.

Young Macgowan kept shifting from foot to naked foot, uneasily.

Delia Priam stood perfectly still.

"Lieutenant," said Ellery suddenly, as he worked over the last knot, "what do you suppose we'll find in here?"

Keats said, "After those dead frogs I wouldn't stick my chin out." He kept looking at Priam.

"Do you have to take out the knots?" cried Crowe, "Open it!"

"Would anyone care to guess?"

"*Please.*" Laurel, begging.

"Mr. Priam?"

Priam never stirred. Only his lips moved, and the beard around them. But nothing came out.

Ellery whipped the lid off.

Roger Priam threw himself back, almost upsetting the chair. Then, conscious of their shock, he fumbled for the glass of whisky. He tilted his head, drinking, not taking his glance from the box.

All that had been exposed was a layer of white tissue.

"From the way you jumped, Mr. Priam," said Ellery conversationally, "anyone would think you expected a hungry rattler to pop out at you, or something equally live and disagreeable. What is it you're afraid of?"

Priam set the glass down with a bang. His knuckles were livid. "I ain't afraid," he spluttered. "Of anything!" His chest spread. "Stop needling me, you—! Or I swear—"

He brought his arm up blindly. It struck the decanter and the decanter toppled from the shelf, smashing on the floor.

Ellery was holding the object high, stripped of its tissue wrappings. He held it by its edges, between his palms.

His own eyes were amazed, and Keats's.

Because there was nothing in what he was displaying to make a man cringe.

It was simply a wallet, a man's wallet of breast-pocket size made of alligator leather, beautifully grained and dyed forest green. There were no hideous stains on it; it had no history; it was plainly brand-new. And high-priced; it was edged in gold. Ellery flipped it open. Its pockets were empty. There had been no note or card in the box.

"Let me see that," said Keats.

Nothing to make a man cower, or a woman grow pale.

"No initials," said Keats. "Nothing but the maker's name." He scratched his cheek, glancing at Priam again.

"What is it, Lieutenant?" asked Laurel.

"What is what, Miss Hill?"

"The maker's name."

"Leatherland, Inc., Hollywood, California."

Priam's beard had sunk to his chest.

Paler than Priam. For Delia Priam's eyes had flashed to their widest at sight of the wallet, all the colour running out of her face. Then the lids had come down as if to shut out a ghost.

Shock. But the shock of what? Fear? Yes, there was fear, but fear followed the shock; it did not precede.

Suddenly Ellery knew what it was.

Recognition.

He mulled over this, baffled. It was a new wallet. She couldn't possibly have seen it before. Unless ... For that matter, neither could Priam. Did it mean the same thing to both of them? Vaguely, he doubted this. Their reactions had thrown off different qualities. Lightning had struck both of them, but it was as if Priam were a meteorologist who understood the nature of the disaster, his wife an ignorant bystander who knew only that she had been stunned. I'm reading too much into this, Ellery thought. You can't judge the truth of anything from a look.... It's useless to attempt to talk to her now.... In an indefinable way he was glad. It was remarkable how easily passion was killed by a dirty fact. He felt nothing when he looked at her now, not even revulsion. The sickness in the pit of his stomach was for himself and his gullibility.

"Delia, where you going?"

She was walking out.

"Mother."

So Crowe had seen it, too. He ran after her, caught her at the door.

"What's the matter?"

She made an effort. "It's all too silly, darling. It's getting to be too much for me. A wallet! And such a handsome one, too. Probably a gift from someone who thinks it's Roger's birthday. Let me go, Crowe. I've got to see Mrs. Guittierez about dinner."

"Oh. Sure." Mac was relieved.

And Laurel....

"The only thing that would throw me," Keats was drawling, "I mean if I was in Mr. Priam's shoes—"

Laurel had been merely puzzled by the wallet.

"—is what the devil I'd be expected to do with it. Like a battleship getting a lawn-mower."

Laurel had been merely puzzled by the wallet, but when she had glimpsed Delia's face her own had reflected shock. The shock of recognition. Again. But this was not recognition of the object *per se*. This was recognition of Delia's recognition. A chain reaction.

"When you stop to think of it, everything we know about these presents so far shows one thing in common—"

"In common?" said Ellery. "What would that be, Keats?"

"Arsenic, dead frogs, a wallet for a man who never leaves his house. They've all been so damned *useless*."

140

Ellery laughed. "There's a theory, Mr. Priam, that's in your power to affirm or deny. Was your first gift useless, too? The one in the first cardboard box?"

Priam did not lift his head.

"Mr. Priam. What was in that box?"

Priam gave no sign that he heard.

"What do these things mean?"

Priam did not reply.

"May we have this wallet for examination?" asked Keats.

Priam simply sat there.

"Seems to me I caught the flicker of one eyelash, Mr. Queen." Keats wrapped the wallet carefully in the tissue paper and tucked it back in the box. "I'll drop you off at your place and then take this down to the Lab."

They left Roger Priam in the same attitude of frozen chaos.

Keats drove slowly, handling the wheel with his forearms and peering ahead as if answers lay there. He was chewing on a cigarette, like a goat.

"Now I'm wrong about Priam," laughed Ellery. "Perfect score."

Keats ignored the addendum. "Wrong about Priam how?"

"I predicted he'd blow his top and spill over at warning number four. Instead of which he's gone underground. Let's hope it's only a temporary recession."

"You're sure this thing is a warning."

Ellery nodded absently.

"Me, I'm not," Keats complained. "I can't seem to get the feel of this case. It's like trying to catch guppies with your bare hands. Now the arsenic, that I could hold on to, even though I couldn't go anywhere with it. But all the rest of it ..."

"You can't deny the existence of all the rest of it, Keats. The dead dog was real enough. The first box Priam got was real, and whatever was in it. There was nothing vapoury about those

141

dead frogs and toads, either. Or about the contents of this box. Or, for that matter," Ellery shrugged, "about the thing that started all this, the note to Hill."

"Oh, yes," growled the detective.

"Oh yes what?"

"The note. What do we know about it? Not a thing. It's not a note, it's a copy of a note. Or is it even that? That might be only what it *seems*. Maybe the whole business was dreamed up by Hill."

"The arsenic, froglets, and wallet weren't dreamed up by Hill," said Ellery dryly, "not in the light of his current condition and location. No, Keats, you're falling for the temptation to be a reasonable man. You're not dealing with a reasonable thing. It's a fantasy, and it calls for faith." He stared ahead. "There's something that links these four 'warnings,' as the composer of the note calls them, links them in a series. They constitute a group."

"How?" Bits of tobacco flew. "Poisoned food, dead frogs, a seventy-five-dollar wallet! And God knows what was in that first box to Priam—judging by what followed, it might have been a size three Hopalong Cassidy suit, or a Bock Beer calendar of the year 1897. Mr. Queen, you *can't* connect those things. They're not connectable." Keats waved his arms, and the car swerved. "The most I can see in this is that each one stands on its own feet. The arsenic? That means: Remember how you tried to poison *me*?—this is a little reminder. The frogs? That means ... Well, you get the idea."

But Ellery shook his head. "If there's one thing in this case I'm sure of, it's that the warnings have related meanings. And the over-all meaning ties up with Priam's past and Hill's past and their enemy's past. What's more, Priam knows its significance, and it's killing him.

"What we've got to do, Lieutenant, is crack Priam, or the riddle, before it's too late."

"I'd like to crack Priam," remarked Keats. "On the nut."

They drove the rest of the way in silence.

142

Keats phoned just before midnight.

"I thought you'd like to know what the Lab found out from examination of the wallet and box."

"What?"

"Nothing. The only prints on the box were Mrs. Priam's. There were no prints on the wallet at all. Now I'm going home and see if I'm still married. How do you like California?"

11

Outside her garage, Laurel looked around. Her look was furtive.
He hadn't been in the walnut tree this morning, thank goodness,
and there was no sign of him now. Laurel slipped into the
garage, blinking as she came out of the sun, and ran to her
Austin.

"Morning, Little Beaver."

"Mac! Damn you."

Crowe Macgowan came around the big Packard, grinning. "I
had a hunch you had a little something under your arm-pit last
night when you told me how late you were going to sleep this
morning. Official business, hm?" He was dressed. Mac looked
very well when he was dressed, almost as well as when he
wasn't. He even wore a hat, a Swiss yodeller sort of thing with a
little feather. "Shove over."

"I don't want you along today."

"Why not?"

"Mac, I just don't."

"You'll have to give me a better reason than that."

"You ... don't take this seriously enough."

"I thought I was plenty serious on the frog safari."

144

"Well … Oh! all right. Get in."

Laurel drove the Austin down to Franklin and turned west, her chin northerly. Macgowan studied her profile in peace.

"La Brea to Third," he said, "and west on Third to Fairfax. Aye, aye, Skipper?"

"Mac! You've looked it up."

"There's only one Leatherland, Inc. of Hollywood, California, and it's in Farmers' Market."

"I wish you'd let me drop you!"

"Nothing doing. Suppose you found yourself in an opium den?"

"There are no opium dens around Fairfax and Third."

"Then maybe a gangster. All the gangsters are coming west, and you know how tourists flock to Farmers' Market."

Laurel said no more, but her heart felt soggy. Between her and the traffic hung a green alligator.

She parked in the area nearest Gilmore Stadium. Early as they were, the paved acres were jammed with cars.

"How are you going to work this?" asked Crowe, shortening his stride as she hurried along.

"There's nothing much to it. Their designs are exclusive, they make everything on the premises, and they have no other outlets. I'll simply ask to see some men's wallets, work my way around to alligator, then to green alligator—"

"And then what?" he asked dryly.

"Why … I'll find out who's bought one recently. They certainly can't sell many green alligator wallets with gold trimming. Mac, what's the idea? Let go!"

They were outside The Button Box. Leatherland, Inc. was nearby, a double-windowed shop with a ranch-house and corral fence décor, bannered with multi-coloured hides and served by a bevy of well-developed cowgirls.

"And how are you going to get one of those babes to open up?" asked Crowe, keeping Laurel's arm twisted behind her back with his forefinger. "In the first place, they don't carry their customers' names around in their heads; they don't have that kind of head. In the second place, they're not going to go through their sales slips—for you, that is. In the third place, what's the matter with me?"

"I might have known."

"All I have to do is flash my genuine Red Ryder sheriff's badge, turn on the charm, and we're in. Laurel, I'm typecasting."

"Take off your clothes," said Laurel bitterly, "and you'll get more parts than you can handle."

"Watch me—fully dressed and lounging-like."

He went into the shop confidently.

Laurel pretended to be interested in a hand-tooled, silver-studded saddle in the window.

Although the shop was crowded, one of the cowgirls spotted Crowe immediately and cantered up to him. Everything bouncing, Laurel observed, hoping one of the falsies would slip down. But it was well-anchored, and she could see him admiring it. So could the cowgirl.

They engaged in a dimpled conversation for fully two minutes. Then they moved over to the rear of the shop. He pushed his hat back on his head the way they did in the movies and leaned one elbow on the showcase. The rodeo Venus began to show him wallets, bending and sunfishing like a bronc. This went on for some time, the sheriff's man leaning farther and farther over the case until he was practically breathing down her sternum. Suddenly he straightened, looked around, put his hand in his pocket, and withdrew it cupped about something. The range-type siren dilated her eyes....

When Crowe strolled out of the shop he passed Laurel with a wink.

She followed him, furious and relieved. The poor goop still didn't catch on, she thought. But then men never noticed anything but women; men like Mac, that is. She turned a corner and ran into his arms.

"Come to popsy," he grinned. "I've got all the dope."

"Are you sure that's all you've got?" Laurel coldly swept past him.

"And I thought you'd give me a gold star!"

"It's no make-up off my skin, but as your spiritual adviser—if you're lining up future mothers of the race for the radioactive new world, pick specimens who look as if they can climb a tree. You'd have to send that one up on a breeches-buoy."

"What do you mean, is that all I've got? You saw me through the window. Could anything have been more antiseptic?"

"I saw you take down her phone number!"

"Shucks, gal. That was professional data. Here." He picked Laurel up, dropped her into the Austin, and got in beside her. "They made up a line of men's wallets in alligator leather last year, dyed three or four different colours. All the other colours sold but the green—they only unloaded three of those. Two of the three greens were bought before Christmas, almost seven months ago, as gifts. One by a Broadway actor to be sent to his agent back in New York, the other by a studio executive for some big-shot French producer—the shop mailed that one to Paris. The third and only other one they've sold is unaccounted for."

"It would be," said Laurel morosely, "seeing that that's the one we're interested in. How unaccounted for, Mac?"

"My cowgirl dug out the duplicate sales slip. It was a cash-and-carry and didn't have the purchaser's name on it."

"What was the date?"

"This year. But what month this year, or what day of what month this year, sales slip showeth not. The carbon slipped or something and the date was smudged."

"Well, didn't she remember what the purchaser looked like? That might tell us something."

"It wasn't my babe's customer, because the initials of the sales-girl on the slip were of someone else."

"Who? Didn't you find out?"

147

"Sure I found out."

"Then why didn't you speak to *her?* Or were you too wrapped up in Miss Falsies?"

"Miss who? Say, I thought those were too good to be true. I couldn't speak to the other gal. The other gal quit last week."

"Didn't you get her name and address?"

"I got her name, Lavis La Grange, but my babe says it wasn't Lavis's real name and she doesn't know what Lavis's real name is. Certainly not Lavis or La Grange. Her address is obsolete, because she decided she'd had enough of the glamorous Hollywood life and went back home. But when I asked my babe where Lavis's home is, she couldn't say. For all she knows it could be Labrador. And anyway, even if we could locate Lavis, my babe says she probably wouldn't remember. My babe says Lavis has the brain of a barley seed."

"So we can't even fix the buyer's sex," said Laurel bitterly. "Some man-hunters we are."

"What do we do now, report to the Master?"

"You report to the Master, Mac. What's there to report? He'll probably know all this before the day's out, anyway. I'm going home. You want me to drop you?"

"You've got more sex appeal. I'll stick with you."

Young MacGowan stuck with Laurel for the remainder of the day; technically, in fact, until the early hours of the next, for it was five minutes past two when she climbed down the rope ladder from the tree house to the floodlit clearing. He leaped after her and encircled her neck with his arm all the way to her front door.

"Sex fiends," he said cheerfully.

"You're doing all right," said Laurel, who felt black and blue; but then she put her mouth up to be kissed, and he kissed it, and that was a mistake because it took her another fifteen minutes to get rid of him.

Laurel waited behind the closed door ten minutes longer to be sure the coast was clear.

Then she slipped out of her house and down to the road.

She had her flashlight and the little automatic was in her coat pocket.

Just before she got to the Priam driveway she turned off into the woods. Here she stopped to put a handkerchief over the lens of her flash. Then, directing the feeble beam to the ground, she made her way toward the Priam house.

Laurel was not feeling adventurous. She was feeling sick. It was the sickness not of fear but of self-appraisal. How did the heroines of fiction do it? The answer was, she decided, that they were heroines of fiction. In real life when a girl had to let a man make love to her in order to steal a key from him she was nothing but a tramp. Less than a tramp, because a tramp got something out of her trampery—money, or an apartment, a few drinks, or even, although less likely, fun. It was a fairly forthright transaction. But she ... she had had to pretend, all the while searching desperately for the key. The worst part of it was trying to dislike it. That damned Macgowan was so purely without guile and he made love so cheerfully—and he was such a darling—that the effort to hate him, it, and herself came off poorly. What a bitchy thing to do, Laurel moaned as her fingers tightened about the key in her pocket.

She stopped behind a French lilac-bush. The house was dark. No light anywhere. She moved along the strip of lawn below the terrace.

Even then it wouldn't have been so nasty if it hadn't concerned his *mother*. How could Mac have lived with Delia all these years and remained blind to what she was? Why did Delia have to be *his* mother?

Laurel tried the front door carefully. It was locked, sure enough. She unlocked it with the key, silently thankful that the Priams kept no dogs. She closed the door just as carefully behind her. Wielding the handkerchief-covered flashlight for a moment, she oriented herself; then she snapped it off.

She crept upstairs close to the banisters.

On the landing she used the flash again. It was almost three o'clock. The four bedroom doors were closed. There was no sound either from this floor or the floor above, where the chauffeur slept. Mrs. Guittierez and Muggs occupied two servants' rooms off the kitchen downstairs.

Laurel tiptoed across the hall and put her ear against a door. Then, quickly and noiselessly, she opened the door and went into Delia Priam's bedroom. How co-operative of Delia to go up to Santa Barbara, where she was visiting "some old Montecito friends" for the week-end. The cloth-of-gold tree of life spread over the bed immaculately. In whose bed was she sleeping tonight?

Laurel hooked the flash to the belt of her coat and began to open dresser drawers. It was the weirdest thing, rummaging through Delia's things in the dead of night by the light of a sort of dark lantern. It didn't matter that you weren't there to take anything. What chiefly made a sneak thief was the technique. If Delia's father, or the unspeakable Alfred, were to surprise her now ... Laurel held on to the thought of the leaden, blue-lipped face of Leander Hill.

It was not in the dresser. She went into Delia's clothes closet.

The scent Delia used was strong, and it mingled disagreeably with the chemical odour of mothproofing and the cedar lining of the walls. Delia's perfume had no name. It had been created exclusively for her by a British Colonial manufacturer, a business associate of Roger Priam's, after a two-week visit to the Priam house years before. Each Christmas thereafter Delia received a quart bottle of it from Bermuda. It was made from the essence of the passion flower. Laurel had once suggested sweetly to Delia that she name it *Prophetic*, but Delia had seemed not to think that very funny.

It was not in the closet. Laurel came out and shut the door, inhaling.

Had she been wrong after all? Maybe it was an illusion, built on the substructure of her loathing for Delia and that single, startling look on Delia's face as Ellery had held up the green wallet.

But suppose it wasn't an illusion. Then the fact that it wasn't where she would ordinarily have kept such a thing might be significant. Because Delia had hurried out of Roger's den immediately. She might have gone directly upstairs to her bedroom, taken it from among the others, and stowed it away where it was unlikely to be found. By Muggs, for instance.

Where might Delia have hidden it? All Laurel wanted was to see it, to verify its existence....

It was not in the brass-bound teak chest at the foot of the bed. Laurel took everything out and then put everything back.

After conquering three temptations to give it up and go home and crawl into bed and pull the bedclothes of oblivion over her head, Laurel found it. It was in the clothes closet after all. But not, Laurel felt, in an honest place. It was wedged in the dolman sleeve of one of Delia's winter coats, a luxurious white duvateen, which in turn was encased in a transparent plastic bag. Innocent and clever. Only a detective, Laurel thought, would have found it. Or another woman.

Laurel felt no triumph, just a shooting pain, like the entry of a hypodermic needle; and then a hardening of everything.

She had been right. She *had* seen Delia carrying one. Weeks before.

It was a woman's envelope bag of forest green alligator leather, with gold initials. The maker's name was Leatherland, Inc. of Hollywood, California.

A sort of Eve to the Adam of the wallet someone had sent to Roger Priam. A mate to the fourth warning.

"I suppose I should have told you yesterday," Laurel said to Ellery in the cottage on the hill, "that Mac and I were down to Farmers' Market on the trail of the green wallet. But we didn't find out anything, and anyway I knew you'd know about it."

"I've had a full report from Keats." Ellery looked at Laurel quizzically. "We had no trouble identifying Tree Boy from the sales-girl's description, and it stood to reason you'd put him up to it."

"Well, there's something else you don't know."

"The lifeblood of this business is information, Laurel. Is it very serious? You look depressed."

"Me?" Laurel laughed. "It's probably a result of confusion. I've found out something about somebody in this case that *could* mean ..."

"Could mean what?" Ellery asked gravely, when she paused.

"That we've found the right one!" Laurel's eyes glittered. "But I can't quite put it into place. It seems to mean so much, only ... Ellery, last night—really in the early hours of this morning—I did something dishonest and—and horrible. Since Roger was poisoned, Alfred Wallace has been locking the doors at night. I stole a key from Mac and in the middle of the night I let myself in, sneaked upstairs—"

"And you went into Delia Priam's bedroom and searched it."

"How did you know!"

"Because I caught the look on your face day before yesterday when *you* saw the look on *Delia's* face. That man's alligator wallet meant something to her. She either recognized it or something about it reminded her directly of something like it. And her start of recognition produced some sort of recognition in you, too, Laurel. Delia left the room at once, and before we went away we made sure of where she'd gone. She'd gone right up to her bedroom.

"She left for Santa Barbara yesterday afternoon, and last night—while you were luring the key out of young Macgowan, probably—I pulled a second-story job and gave the bedroom a going-over. Keats, of course, couldn't risk it; the L.A. Police have had to lean over backwards lately, and if Keats had been caught housebreaking there might have been a mess that would spoil everything. There wasn't enough, of course, to justify a warrant and an open search.

152

"I left Delia's alligator bag in the sleeve of the white coat, where I found it. And where, I take it, you found it a few hours later. I hope you left everything exactly as it was."

"Yes," moaned Laurel. "But all that breast-beating for nothing."

Ellery lit a cigarette. "Now let me tell you something *you* don't know, Laurel." His eyes, which had not laughed at all, became as smoky as his cigarette. "That green alligator pocketbook of Delia's was a gift. She did didn't buy it herself. Luckily, the sales-girl who sold it remembered clearly what the purchaser looked like, even though it was a cash sale. She gave an excellent and recognizable description, and when she was shown the corresponding photograph she identified it as the man she had described. The purchase was made in mid-April of this year, just before Delia's birthday, and the purchaser was Alfred Wallace."

"Alfred—" Laurel was about to go on, but then her teeth closed on her lower lip.

"It's all right, Laurel," said Ellery. "I know all about Delia and Alfred."

"I wasn't sure." Laurel was silent. Then she looked up. "What do you think it means?"

"It could mean nothing at all," Ellery said slowly. "Coincidence, for example, although coincidence and I haven't been on speaking terms for years. More likely whoever it is we're after may have noticed Delia's bag and, consciously or unconsciously, it suggested to him the nature of the fourth warning to Priam. Delia's suspicious actions can be plausibly explained, in this interpretation, as the fear of an innocent person facing a disagreeable involvement. Innocent people frequently act guiltier than guilty ones.

"It could mean that," said Ellery, "or ..." He shrugged. "I'll have to think about it."

153

12

But Ellery's thoughts were forced to take an unforeseen turn. In this he was not unique. Suddenly something called the 38th Parallel, half a planet away, had become the chief interest in the lives of a hundred and fifty million Americans.

Los Angeles particularly suffered a bad attack of jitters.

A few days before, Koreans from the north had invaded South Korea with Soviet tanks and great numbers of Soviet 7.63-millimetre submachine guns. The explosive meaning of this act took some time to erupt the American calm. But when United States occupation troops were rushed to South Korea from Japan and were overwhelmed, and the newspapers began printing reports of American wounded murdered by the invaders, conviction burst. The President made unpleasantly reminiscent announcements, reserves were being called, the United Nations were in an uproar, beef and coffee prices soared, there were immediate rumours about sugar and soap scarcities, hoarding began, and everyone in Los Angeles was saying that World War III had commenced and that Los Angeles would be the first city on the North American continent to feel the incinerating breath of the atom bomb—and how do we know it won't be tonight? San

Diego, San Francisco, and Seattle were not sleeping soundly, either, but that was no consolation to Los Angeles.

It was impossible to remain unaffected by the general nervousness. And, absurd as the thought was, there was always the possibility that it was only too well grounded.

The novel, which had been sputtering along, coughed and went into a nose dive. Ellery hounded the radio, trying to shut out the prophecies of doom which streaked up from his kitchen like flak in wailing Louisiana accents from eight to five daily. His thoughts kept coming back to Tree Boy. Crowe Macgowan no longer seemed funny.

He had not heard from Lieutenant Keats for days.

There was no word from the Priam establishment. He knew that Delia had returned from Montecito, but he had not seen or heard from her.

Laurel phoned once to seek, not give, information. She was worried about Macgowan.

"He just sits and broods, Ellery. You'd think with what's happening in Korea he'd be going around saying I told you so. Instead of which I can't get him to open his big mouth."

"The world of fantasy is catching up with Crowe, and it's probably a painful experience. There's nothing new at the Priams'?"

"It's quiet. Ellery, what do you suppose this lull means?"

"I don't know."

"I'm so confused these days!" Laurel's was something of a wail, too. "Sometimes I think what's going on in the world makes all this silly and unimportant. And I suppose in one way it is. But then I think, no, it's not silly and it is important. Aggressive war is murder, too, and you don't take *that* lying down. You have to fight it on every front, starting with the picayune personal ones. Or else you go down."

"Yes," said Ellery with a sigh, "that makes sense. I only wish this particular front weren't so ... fluid, Laurel. You might say we've got a pretty good general staff, and a bang-up army behind us, but our Intelligence is weak. We have no idea where and when the next attack is coming, in what form and strength—or the meaning of the enemy's strategy. All we can do is sit tight and keep on the alert."

Laurel said quickly, "Bless you," and she hung up quickly, too.

The enemy's next attack came during the night of July 6–7. It was, surprisingly, Crowe Macgowan who notified Ellery. His call came at a little after one in the morning, as Ellery was about to go to bed.

"Queen. Something screwy just happened. I thought you'd want to know." Macgowan sounded tired, not like himself at all.

"What, Mac?"

"The library's been broken into. One of the windows. Seems like a case of ordinary housebreaking, but I dunno."

"The *library*? Anything taken?"

"Not as far as I can see."

"Don't touch anything. I'll be over in ten minutes."

Ellery rang up Keats's home, got a sleepy "What, again?" from the detective, and ran.

He found young Macgowan waiting for him in the Priam driveway. There were lights on upstairs and down, but Roger Priam's French windows off the terrace were dark.

"Before you go in, maybe I'd better explain the set-up...."

"Who's in there now?"

"Delia and Alfred."

"Go on. But make it snappy, Mac."

"Last couple of nights I've been sleeping in my old room here at the house—"

"What? No more tree?"

"You wanted it presto, didn't you?" growled the giant. "I hit the sack early tonight, but I couldn't seem to sleep. Long time later I heard sounds from downstairs. Seemed like the library; my room's right over it. I thought maybe it was Gramp and I felt a yen to talk to him. So I got up and went down the hall and at the top of the stairs I called, 'Gramp?' No answer, and it was quiet down there. Something made me go back up the hall and look in the old gent's room. He wasn't there; bed hadn't been slept in. So I went back to the head of the stairs and there was Wallace."

"Wallace?" repeated Ellery.

"In a robe. He said he'd heard a noise and was just going to go downstairs." Macgowan sounded odd; his eyes were hard in the moonlight. "But you know something, Queen? I got a queer feeling as I spotted Wallace at the head of those stairs. I couldn't make up my mind whether he was about to go down ... or had just come up."

He stared at Ellery defiantly.

A car was tearing up the road.

Ellery said, "Life is full of these dangling participles, Mac. Did you find your grandfather?"

"No. Maybe I'd better take a look in the woods." Crowe sounded casual. "Gramp often takes a walk in the middle of the night. You know how it is when you're old."

"Yes." Ellery watched Delia's son stride off, pulling a flashlight from his pocket as he went.

Keats's car slammed to a stop a foot from Ellery's rear.

"Hi."

"What is it this time?" Keats had a leather jacket on over an undershirt, and he sounded sore.

Ellery told him, and they went in.

Delia Priam was going through the library desk, looking baffled. She was in a brown monkish negligée of some chicknapped material, girdled by a heavy brass chain. Her hair hung down her back and there were purplish shadows, almost welts, under her eyes. Alfred Wallace, in a Paisley dressing-gown, was seated comfortably in a club chair, smoking a cigarette.

Delia turned, and Wallace rose, as the two men came into the library, but neither said anything.

157

Keats went directly to the only open window. He examined the sash about the catch without touching it.

"Jimmied. Have any of you touched this window?"

"I'm afraid," said Wallace, "we all did."

Keats mumbled something impolite and went out. A few moments later Ellery heard him outside, below the open window, and saw the beam of his flash.

Ellery looked around. It was the kind of library he liked; this was one room in which the prevailing Priam gloom was mellow. Leather shone, and the black oak panelling was a friendly background for the books. Books from floor to ceiling on all four walls, and a fieldstone fireplace with a used look. It was a spacious room, and the lamps were good.

"Nothing missing, Delia?"

She shook her head. "I can't understand it." She turned away, pulling her robe closer about her.

"Crowe and I probably scared him off." Alfred Wallace sat down again, exhaling smoke.

"Your father's stamp albums?" Ellery suggested to Delia's back. He had no idea why he thought of old Collier's treasures, except that they might be valuable.

"As far as I know, they haven't been touched."

Ellery wandered about the room.

"By the way, Crowe tells me Mr. Collier hasn't been to bed. Have you any idea where he is, Delia?"

"No." She wheeled on him, eyes flashing. "My father and I don't check up on each other. And I can't recall, Mr. Queen, that I ever gave you permission to call me by my first name. Suppose you stop it."

Ellery looked at her with a smile. After a moment she turned away again. Wallace continued to smoke.

Ellery resumed his ambling.

When Keats returned he said shortly, "There's nothing out there. Have you got anything?"

"I think so," said Ellery. He was squatting before the fireplace. "Look here."

Delia Priam turned at that, and Wallace.

The fireplace grate held the remains of a wood fire. It had burned away to a fine ash. On the ashes lay a heat-crimped and badly charred object of no recognizable shape.

"Feel the ashes to the side, Keats."

"Stony cold."

"Now the ashes under that charred thing."

The detective snatched his hand away. "Still hot!"

Ellery said to Delia, "Was there a wood fire in this grate tonight ... Mrs. Priam?"

"No. There was one in the morning, but it burned out by noon."

"This object was just burned here, Keats. On top of the cold ashes."

The lieutenant wrapped a handkerchief around his hand and cautiously removed the charred thing. He laid it on the hearth.

"What was it?"

"A book, Keats."

"Book?" Keats glanced around at the walls. "I wonder if—"

"Can't tell any more. Pages all burned away and what's left of the binding shows nothing."

"It must have been a special binding." Most of the volumes on the shelves were leather-bound. "Don't they stamp the titles into these fancy jobs?" Keats prodded the remains of the book, turning it over. "Ought to be some indication left."

"There would have been, except that whoever burned this indulged in a little vandalism before he set fire to it. Look at these slashes on the spine—and here. The book was mutilated with a sharp instrument before it was tossed into the grate."

Keats looked up at Delia and Wallace, who were stooping over them. "Any idea what this book was?"

"Damn you! Are you two here again?"

159

Roger Priam's wheel-chair blocked the doorway. His hair and beard were threatening. His pyjama coat gaped, exposing his simian chest; a button was missing, as if he had torn at himself in a temper. His chair was made up as a bed and the blankets trailed on the floor.

"Ain't nobody going to open his mouth? Man can't get any shut-eye in his own house! Alfred, where the hell have you been? Not in your room, because I couldn't get you on the intercom!" He did not glance at his wife.

"Something's happened down here, Mr. Priam," said Wallace soothingly.

"Happened! What now?"

Ellery and Keats were watching Priam closely. The library desk and a big chair stood between the wheel-chair and the fireplace; Priam had not seen the burned book.

"Somebody broke into your library here tonight, Mr. Priam," rasped Keats, "and don't think I'm happy about it, because I'm as sick of you as you are of me. And if you're thinking of blasting me out again, forget it. Breaking and entering is against the law, and I'm the cop on the case. Now you're going to answer questions about this or, by God, I'll pull you in on a charge of obstructing a police investigation. Why was this book cut up and burned?"

Keats stalked across the room carrying the charred remains. He thrust the thing under Priam's nose.

"Book ... burned?"

All his rage had fled, exposing the putty colour beneath. Priam glared down at the twisted cinder in Keats's hand, pulling away a little.

"Do you recognize this?"

Priam's head shook.

"Can't you tell us what it is?"

"No." The word came out cracked. He seemed fascinated by the binding.

Keats turned in disgust. "I guess he doesn't know at that. Well—"

"Just a moment, Lieutenant." Ellery was at the shelves, riffling through books. They were beautiful books, the products of private presses chiefly—hand-made paper, lots of gold leaf, coloured inks, elaborate endpaper designs, esoteric illustrations, specially designed type fonts; each was hand-bound and expensively hand-tooled. And the titles were impeccable, all the proper classics. The only thing was, after riffling through two dozen books, Ellery had still to find one in which the pages had been cut.

The books had never been read. It was likely, from their stiff pristine condition, that they had not been opened since leaving the hands of the bookbinder.

"How long have you had these books, Mr. Priam?"

"How long?" Priam licked his lips. "How long is it, Delia?"

"Since shortly after we were married."

"Library means books," Priam muttered, nodding. "Called in a fancy dealer and had him measure the running feet of shelf space and told him to go out and get enough books to fill the space. Highbrow stuff, I told him; only the best." He seemed to gain confidence through talking; a trace of arrogance livened his heavy voice. "When he lugged them around, I threw 'em back in his face. 'I said the best!' I told him. 'Take this junk back and have it bound up in the most expensive leather and stuff you can find. It's got to look the money or you don't get a plugged nickel.'"

Keats had dropped his impatience. He edged back.

"And a very good job he did, too," murmured Ellery. "I see they're in the original condition, Mr. Priam. Don't seem to have been opened, any of them."

"Opened! And crack those bindings? This collection is worth a fortune, Mister. I've had it appraised. Won't let *nobody* read 'em."

161

"But books are made to be read, Mr. Priam. Haven't you ever been curious about what's in these pages?"

"Ain't read a book since I played hooky from public school," retorted Priam. "Books are for women and long-hairs. Newspapers, that's different. And picture magazines." His head jerked up with a belligerent reflex. "What are you getting at?"

"I'd like to spend about an hour here, Mr. Priam, looking over your collection. I give you my word, I'll handle your books with the greatest care. Would you have any objection to that?"

Cunning pin-pointed Priam's eyes. "You're a book-writer yourself, ain't you?"

"Yes."

"Ever write articles like in the Sunday magazine sections?"

"Occasionally."

"Maybe you got some idea about writing up an article on the Priam Book Collection. Hey?"

"You're a shrewd man, Mr. Priam," said Ellery with a smile.

"I don't mind," the bearded man said with geniality. There was colour in his cheekbones again. "That book-dealer said no millionaire's library ought to be without its own special catalogue. 'It's too good a collection, Mr. Priam,' he says to me. 'There ought to be a record of it for the use of bib- bib-'"

"Bibliophiles?"

"That's it. Hell, it was little enough, and besides I figured it might come in handy for personal publicity in my jewellery business. So I told him to go ahead. You'll find a copy of the catalogue right there on that stand. Cost me a lot of money—specially designed, y'know, four-colour job on special paper. And there's a lot of technical stuff in it, in the descriptions of the books. Words I can't even pronounce," Priam chuckled, "but, God Almighty, you don't have to be able to pronounce it if you can pay for it." He waved a hairy hand. "Don't mind at all, Mister—what was the name again?"

"Queen."

"You go right ahead, Queen."

"Very kind of you, Mr. Priam. By the way, have you added any books since your catalogue was made up?"

"Added any?" Priam stared. "I got all the good ones. What would I want with more? When d'ye want to do it?"

"No time like the present, I always say, Mr. Priam. The night is killed, anyway."

"Maybe tomorrow I'll change my mind, hey?" Priam showed his teeth again in what he meant to be a friendly grin. "That's all right, Queen. Shows you're no dope, even if you do write books. Go to it!" The grin faded as he turned his animal eyes on Wallace. "You push me back, Alfred. And better bunk downstairs for the rest of the night."

"Yes, Mr. Priam," said Alfred Wallace.

"Delia, what are you standing around for? Go back to bed."

"Yes, Roger."

The last they saw of Priam he was waving amiably as Wallace wheeled him across the hall. From his gesture it was apparent that he had talked himself out of his fears, if indeed he had not entirely forgotten their cause.

When the door across the hall had closed, Ellery said: "I hope you don't mind, Mrs. Priam. We've got to know which book this was."

"You think Roger's a fool, don't you?"

"Why don't you go to bed?"

"Don't ever make that mistake. Crowe!" Her voice softened. "Where've you been, darling? I was beginning to worry. Did you find your grandfather?"

Young Macgowan filled the doorway; he was grinning. "You'll never guess where." He yanked, and old Collier appeared. There was a smudge of chemical stain along his nose and he was smiling happily. "Down in the cellar."

"Cellar?"

"Gramp's fixed himself up a dark room, Mother. Gone into photography."

"I've been using your Contax all day, daughter. I hope you

163

don't mind. I've got a great deal to learn," said Collier, shaking his head. "My pictures didn't come out very well. Hello there! Crowe tells me there's been more trouble."

"Have you been in the cellar all this time, Mr. Collier?" asked Lieutenant Keats.

"Since after supper."

"Didn't you hear anything? Somebody jimmied that window."

"That's what my grandson told me. No, I didn't hear anything, and if I had I'd probably have locked the cellar door and waited till it was all over! Daughter, you look all in. Don't let this get you down."

"I'll survive, Father."

"You come on up to bed. Good night, gentlemen." The old man went away.

"Crowe." Delia's face set. "Mr. Queen and Lieutenant Keats are going to be working in the library for a while. I think perhaps you'd better stay ... too."

"Sure, sure," said Mac. He stooped and kissed her. She went out without a glance at either of the older men. Macgowan shut the door after her. "What's the matter?" he asked Ellery in a plaintive tone. "Don't you two get along any more? What's happened?"

"If you must keep an eye on us, Mac," snapped Ellery, "do it from that chair in the corner, where you'll be out of the way. Keats, let's get going."

The "Priam Collection" was a bibliographic montrosity, but Ellery was in a scientific, not an aesthetic, mood and his methodology had nothing to do with art or even morals; he simply had the Hollywood detective read off the titles on Priam's shelves and he checked them against the gold-crusted catalogue.

It took them the better part of two hours, during which Crowe Macgowan fell asleep in the leather chair.

When at last Keats stopped, Ellery said: "Hold it," and he began to thumb back along the pages of the catalogue.

"Well?" said Keats.

"You failed to read just one title." Ellery set the catalogue down and picked up the charred corpse of the book. "This used to be an octavo volume bound in laminated oak, with hand-blocked silk endpapers, of *The Birds*, by Aristophanes."

"The what, by whom?"

"*The Birds*. A play by Aristophanes, the great satirical dramatist of the fifth century before Christ."

"I don't see the joke."

Ellery was silent.

"You mean to tell me," demanded the detective, "that the burning of this book by a playwright dead a couple of dozen centuries is another of these warnings?"

"It must be."

"How can it be?"

"Mutilated and burned, Keats. At least two of the four previous warnings also involved violence in some form: the food poisoning, the murder of the frogs ..." Ellery sat up.

"What's the matter?"

"Frogs. Another play by Aristophanes has that exact title. *The Frogs*."

Keats looked pained.

"But that's almost certainly a coincidence. The other items wouldn't begin to fit.... *The Birds*. An unknown what's-it, food poisoning, dead toads and frogs, an expensive wallet, and now a plushy edition of a Greek social satire first performed—unless I've forgotten my Classics II—in 414 B.C."

"And I'm out of cigarettes," grunted Keats. Ellery tossed a pack over. "Thanks. You say there's a connection?"

"'And for each pace forward a warning ... a warning of special meaning for you—and for him,'" Ellery quoted. "That's what the note said. 'Meanings for pondering and puzzling.'"

"How right he was. I still say, Queen, if this stuff means anything at all, each one stands on its own tootsies."

"'For each pace forward,' Keats. It's *going* somewhere. No, they're tied. The whole thing's a progression." Ellery shook his head. "I'm not even sure any more that Priam knows what they mean. This one tonight really balls things up. Priam is virtually an illiterate. How could he possibly know what's meant by the destruction of an old Greek play?"

"What's it about?"

"The play? Well ... to the best of my recollection, two Athenians talk the Birds into building an aerial city, in order to separate the Gods from Man."

"That helps."

"What did Aristophanes call his city in the air? Cloud ... Cloud-land ... Cloud-Cuckoo-Land."

"That's the first thing I've heard in this case that rings the bell." Keats got up in disgust and went to the window.

A long time passed. Keats stared out at the night, which was beginning to boil and show a froth. But the room was chilly, and he hunched his shoulders under the leather jacket. Young Macgowan snored innocently in the club chair. Ellery said nothing.

Ellery's silence lasted for so long that after a time Keats, whose brain was empty and wretched, became conscious of its duration. He turned around tiredly and there was a gaunt, unshaven, wild-eyed refugee from a saner world staring back at him with uninvited joy, grudgingly delirious, like a girl contemplating her first kiss.

"What in the hell," said the Hollywood detective in alarm, "is the matter with you?"

"Keats, they have something in common!"

"Sure. You've said that a dozen times."

"Not one thing, but two."

Keats came over and took another of Ellery's cigarettes. "What do you say we break this up? Go home, take a shower, and hit the hay." Then he said, *"What?"*

"Two things in common, Keats!" Ellery swallowed. His mouth was parched and there was a tuneful fatigue in his head, but he knew he had it, he had it at last.

166

"You've *got* it?'

"I know what it means, Keats. I know."

"What? What?"

But Ellery was not listening. He fumbled for a cigarette without looking.

Keats struck a match for him and then, absently, held it to his own cigarette; he went to the window again, inhaling, filling his lungs. The froth on the night had bubbled down, leaving a starchy mass, glimmering like soggy rice. Keats suddenly became aware of what he was doing. He looked startled, then desperate, then defiant. He smoked hungrily, waiting.

"Keats."

Keats whirled. "Yes?"

Ellery was on his feet. "The man who owned the dog. What were his name and address again?"

"Who?" Keats blinked.

"The owner of the dead dog, the one you have reason to believe was poisoned before it was left on Hill's door-step. What was the owner's name? I've forgotten it."

"Henderson. Clybourn Avenue, in Toluca Lake."

"I'll have to see him as soon as I can. You going home?"

"But why—"

"You go on and get a couple of hours' sleep. Are you going to be at the station later this morning?"

"Yeah. But what—?"

But Ellery was walking out of Roger Priam's library with stiff short steps, a man in a dream.

Keats stared after him.

When he heard Ellery's Kaiser drive away, he put Ellery's pack of cigarettes in his pocket and picked up the remains of the burned book.

Crowe Macgowan awoke with a snort.

"You still here? Where's Queen?" Macgowan yawned. "Did you find out anything?"

Keats held his smouldering butt to a fresh cigarette, puffing recklessly. "I'll send you a telegram," he said bitterly, and he went away.

Sleep was impossible. He tossed for a while, not even hopefully.

At a little after six Ellery was downstairs in his kitchen, brewing coffee.

He drank three cups, staring into the mists over Hollywood. A dirty grey world with the sun struggling through. In a short time the mist would be gone and the sun would shine clear.

The thing was sharply brilliant. All he had to do was get rid of the mist.

What he would see in that white glare Ellery hardly dared anticipate. It was something monstrous, and in its monstrous way beautiful; that, he could make out dimly.

But first there was the problem of the mist.

He went back upstairs, shaved, took a shower, changed into fresh clothing, and then he left the cottage and got into his car.

13

It was almost eight o'clock when Ellery pulled up before a small stucco house tinted cobalt blue on Clybourn Avenue off Riverside Drive.

A hand-coloured wooden cut-out resembling Dopey, the Walt Disney dwarf, was stuck into the lawn on a stake, and on it a flowery artist had lettered the name Henderson.

The uniformly closed venetian blinds did not look promising.

As Ellery went up the walk a woman's voice said, "If you're lookin' for Henderson, he's not home."

A stout woman in an orange wrapper was leaning far over the railing of her red cement stoop next door, groping with ringed fingers for something hidden in a violet patch.

"Do you know where I can reach him?"

Something swooshed, and six sprinklers sent up watery bouquets over the woman's lawn. She straightened, red-faced and triumphant.

"You can't," she said, panting. "Henderson's a picture actor. He's being a pirate mascot on location around Catalina or somewhere. He expected a few weeks' work. You a press agent?"

"Heaven forbid," muttered Ellery. "Did you know Mr. Henderson's dog?"

"His dog? Sure I knew him. Frank, his name was. Always tearin' up my lawn and chasin' moths through my pansy-beds—though don't go thinkin'," the fat woman added hastily, "that I had anything to do with poisonin' Frank, because I just can't abide people who do things like that to animals, even the destroyin' kind. Henderson was all broke up about it."

"What kind of dog was Frank?" Ellery asked.

"Kind?"

"Breed."

"Well ... he wasn't very big. Nor so little, neither, when you stop to think of it—"

"You don't know his breed?"

"I think some kind of a hunting dog. Are you from the Humane Society or the Anti-Vivisection League? I'm against experimentin' with animals myself, like the *Examiner*'s always sayin'. If the good Lord—"

"You can't tell me, Madam, what kind of hunting dog Frank was?"

"Well ..."

"English setter? Irish? Gordon? Llewellyn? Chesapeake? Weimaraner?"

"I just guess," said the woman cheerfully, "I don't know."

"What colour was he?"

"Well, now, sort of brown and white. No, black. Come to think of it, not really white, neither. More creamy, like."

"More creamy, like. Thank you," said Ellery. And he got into his car and moved fifty feet, just far enough to be out of his informant's range.

After thinking for a few minutes, he drove off again.

He cut through Pass and Olive, past the Warner Brothers' studio, into Barham Boulevard to the Freeway. Emerging through the North Highland exit into Hollywood, he found a parking space on McCadden Place and hurried around the corner to the Plover Bookshop.

It was still closed.

He could not help feeling that this was inconsiderate of the Plover Bookshop. Wandering up Hollywood Boulevard disconsolately, he found himself opposite Coffee Dan's. This reminded him vaguely of his stomach, and he crossed over and went in for breakfast. Someone had left a newspaper on the counter, and as he ate he read it conscientiously. When he paid his check, the cashier said, "What's the news from Korea this morning?" and he had to answer stupidly, "Just about the same," because he could not remember a word he had read.

Plover was open!

He ran in and seized the arm of a clerk. "Quick," he said fiercely. "A book on dogs."

"Book on dogs," said the clerk. "Any particular kind of book on dogs, Mr. Queen?"

"Hunting dogs! With illustrations! In colour!"

Plover did not fail him. He emerged carrying a fat book and a charge slip for seven and a half dollars, plus tax.

He drove up into the hills rashly and caught Laurel Hill a moment after she stepped into her stall shower.

"Go away," Laurel said, her voice sounding muffled. "I'm naked."

"Turn that water off and come out here!"

"Why, Ellery."

"Oh ...! I'm not the least bit interested in your nakedness—"

"Thanks. Did you ever say that to Delia Priam?"

"Cover your precious hide with this! I'll be in the bedroom." Ellery tossed a bath-towel over the shower door and hurried out. Laurel kept him waiting five minutes. When she came out of the bathroom she was swaddled in a red, white, and blue robe of terry cloth.

"I didn't know you cared. But next time would you mind at least knocking? Gads, look at my hair—"

"Yes, yes," said Ellery. "Now, Laurel, I want you to project yourself back to the morning when you and your father stood

171

outside your front door and looked at the body of the dead dog. Do you remember that morning?"

"I think so," said Laurel steadily.

"Can you see that dog right now?"

"Every hair of him."

"Hold on to him!" Ellery yanked her by the arm and she squealed, grabbing at the front of her robe. She found herself staring down at her bed. Upon it, open to an illustration in colour of a springer spaniel, lay a large book. "Was he a dog like this?"

"N-no ..."

"Go through the book page by page. When you come to Henderson's pooch, or a reasonable facsimile thereof, indicate same in an unmistakable manner."

Laurel looked at him suspiciously. It was too early in the morning for him to have killed a bottle, and he was shaved and pressed, so it wasn't the tag end of a large night. Unless ...

"Ellery!" she screamed. "You've found out something!"

"Start looking," hissed Ellery viciously; at least it sounded vicious to his ears, but Laurel only looked overjoyed and began to turn pages like mad.

"Easy," he cried. "You may skip it."

"I'll find your old hound." Pages flew like locust petals in a May wind. "Here he is—"

"Ah."

Ellery took the book.

The illustration showed a small, almost dumpy, dog with short legs, pendulous ears, and a wiry upcurving tail. The coat was smooth. Hindlegs and forequarters were an off-white, as was the muzzle; the little dog had a black saddle and black ears with secondary pigmentation of yellowish brown extending into his tail.

The caption under the illustration said: *BEAGLE.*

"Beagle." Ellery glared. "Beagle.... Of course. Of *course.* No other possibility. None whatever. If I'd had the brain of a woodlouse.... Beagle, Laurel, beagle!" And he swept her off her feet and planted five kisses on the top of her wet head. Then he tossed her on her unmade bed and before her horrified eyes went into a fast tap—an accomplishment which was one of his most sacred secrets, unknown even to his father. And Ellery chanted, "*Merci*, my pretty one, my she-detective. You have follow ze clue of ze ar-sen-ique, of ze little frog, of ze wallette, of ze everysing, but ze sing you know all ze time—zat is to say, ze beagle. Oh, ze beagle!" And he changed to a soft-shoe.

"But what's the breed of dog got to do with anything, Ellery?" moaned Laurel. "The only connection I can see with the word beagle is its slang meaning. Isn't a 'beagle' a detective?"

"Ironic, isn't it?" chortled Ellery; and he exited doing a Shuffle-Off-to-Buffalo, blowing farewell kisses and almost breaking the prominent nose of Mrs. Monk, Laurel's housekeeper, who had it pressed in absolute terror to the bedroom door.

Twenty minutes later Ellery was closeted with Lieutenant Keats at the Hollywood Division. Those who passed the closed door heard the murmur of the Queen voice, punctuated by a weird series of sounds bearing no resemblance to Keats's usual tones.

The conference lasted well over an hour.

When the door opened, a suffering man appeared. Keats looked as if he had just picked himself up from the floor after a kick in the groin. He kept shaking his head and muttering to himself. Ellery followed him briskly. They vanished in the office of Keats's chief.

An hour and a half later they emerged. Keats now looked convalescent, even robust.

"I still don't believe it," he said, "but what the hell, we're living in a funny world."

"How long do you think it will take, Keats?"

"Now that we know what to look for, not more than a few days. What are you going to do in the meantime?"

"Sleep and wait for the next one."

"By that time," grinned the detective, "maybe we'll have a pretty good line on this inmate."

They shook hands solemnly and parted, Ellery to go home to bed and Keats to set the machinery of the Los Angeles police department going on a twenty-four-hour-a-day inquiry into a situation over twenty years old ... this time with every prospect of success.

In three days not all the mouldy threads were gathered in, but those they had been able to pick up by teletype and long-distance phone tied snugly around what they already knew. Ellery and Keats were sitting about at the Hollywood Division trying to guess the lengths and textures of the missing ends when Keats's phone rang. He answered it to hear a tense voice.

"Lieutenant Keats, is Ellery Queen there?"

"It's Laurel Hill for you."

Ellery took the phone. "I've been neglecting you, Laurel. What's up?"

Laurel said with a rather hysterical giggle, "I've committed a crime."

"Serious?"

"What's the rap for lifting what doesn't belong to you?"

Ellery said sharply, "Something for Priam again?"

He heard a scuffle, then Crowe Macgowan's voice saying hastily, "Queen, she didn't swipe it. I did."

"He did not!" yelled Laurel. "I don't care, Mac! I'm sick and tired of hanging around not knowing—"

"Is it for Roger Priam?"

"It is," said Macgowan. "A pretty big package this time. It was left on top of the mail-box. Queen, I'm not giving Roger a hold over Laurel. I took it and that's that."

"Have you opened it, Mac?"

"No."

"Where are you?"

"Your house."

"Wait there and keep your hands off it." Ellery hung up. "Number six, Keats!"

They found Laurel and Macgowan in Ellery's living-room, hovering hostilely over a package the size of a men's suit-box, wrapped in strong manila paper and bound with heavy string. The now-familiar shipping tag with Priam's name lettered on it in black crayon—the now-familiar lettering—was attached to the string. The package bore no stamps, or markings of any kind.

"Delivered in person again," said Keats. "Miss Hill, how did you come to get hold of this?"

"I've been watching for days. Nobody tells me anything, and I've got to do *something*. And, darn it, after hours and hours of hiding behind bushes I missed her after all."

"Her?" said Crowe Macgowan blankly.

"Well, her, or him, or whoever it is." Laurel turned old rose.

Crowe stared at her.

"Let's get technical," said Keats. "Go ahead and open it, Macgowan. Then we won't have to lie awake nights with a guilty conscience."

"Very humorous," mumbled Delia's son. He snapped the string and ripped off the wrapping in silence.

The box was without an imprint, white, and of poor quality. It bulged with its contents.

Mac removed the lid.

The box was crammed with printed documents in a great variety of sizes, shapes, and coloured inks. Many were engraved on banknote paper.

"What the devil." Keats picked one out at random. "This is a stock certificate."

"So is this," said Ellery. "And this …" After a moment they stared at each other. "They all seem to be stock certificates."

"I don't get it." Keats worried his thumbnail. "This doesn't fit in with what you figured out, Queen. It couldn't."

Ellery frowned. "Laurel, Mac. Do these mean anything to you?"

175

Laurel shook her head, staring at a name on the certificate she had picked up. Now she put it down, slowly, and turned away.

"Why, this must represent a fortune," exclaimed Crowe. "Some warning!"

Ellery was looking at Laurel. "We'd better have a breakdown on the contents of this box, Keats, and then we can decide how to handle it.—Laurel, what's the matter?"

"Where you going?" demanded Macgowan.

Laurel turned at the door. "I'm sick of this. I'm sick of the whole thing, the waiting and looking and finding and doing absolutely nothing. If you and the lieutenant have anything, Ellery, what is it?"

"We're not through making a certain investigation, Laurel."

"Will you ever be?" She said it drearily. Then she went out, and a moment later they heard the Austin scramble away.

About seven o'clock that evening Ellery and Keats drove up to the Priam house in Keats's car, Ellery carrying the box of stock certificates. Crowe Macgowan was waiting for them at the front door.

"Where's Laurel, Mac? Didn't you get my phone message?" said Ellery.

"She's home." Crowe hesitated. "I don't know what's the matter with her. She's tossed off about eight Martinis and I couldn't do a thing with her. I've never seen Laurel act like that. She doesn't take a drink a week. I don't like it."

"Well, a girl's entitled to a bender once in a while," jeered Keats. "Your mother in?"

"Yes. I've told her. What did you find out?"

"Not much. The wrappings and box were a wash-out. Our friend likes gloves. Did you tell Priam?"

"I told him you two were coming over on something important. That's all."

Keats nodded, and they went to Roger Priam's quarters.

Priam was having his dinner. He was wielding a sharp blade

176

and a fork on a thick rare steak. Alfred Wallace was broiling another on a portable barbecue. The steak was smothered with onions and mushrooms and barbecue sauce from several chafing dishes, and a bottle of red wine showed three-quarters empty on the tray. Priam ate in character: brutally, teeth tearing, powerful jaws crunching, eyes bulging with appetite, flecks of sauce on his agitated beard.

His wife, in a chair beside him, watched him silently, as one might watch a zoo animal at feeding time.

The entrance of the three men caught the meat-laden fork in mid-air. It hung there for a moment, then it completed its journey, but slowly, and Priam's jaws ground away mechanically. His eyes fixed and remained on the box in Ellery's hands.

"Sorry to interrupt your dinner, Mr. Priam," said Keats, "but we may as well have this one out now."

"The other steak, Alfred." Priam extended his plate. Wallace refilled it in silence. "What's this, now?"

"Warning number six, Mr. Priam," said Ellery.

Priam attacked his second steak.

"I see it's no use," he said in almost a friendly tone, "trying to get you two to keep your noses out of my business."

"I took it," said Crowe Macgowan abruptly. "It was left on the mail-box and I lifted it."

"Oh, you did." Priam inspected his stepson.

"I live here, too, you know. I'm getting pretty fed up with this, and I want to see it cleaned out."

Priam hurled his plate at Crowe Macgowan's head. It hit the giant a glancing blow above the ear. He staggered, crashed back into the door. His face went yellow.

"*Crowe!*"

He brushed his mother aside. "Roger, if you ever do that again," he said in a low voice, "I'll kill you."

"Get out!" Priam's voice was a bellow.

"Not while Delia's here. If not for that I'd be in a uniform right now. God knows why she stays, but as long as she does, I

177

do, too. I don't owe you a thing, Roger. I pay my way in this dump. And I have a right to know what's going on.... It's all right, Mother." Delia was dabbing at his bleeding ear with her handkerchief; her face was pinched and old-looking. "Just remember what I said, Roger. Don't do that again."

Wallace got down on his hands and knees and began to clean up the mess.

Priam's cheekbones were a violent purple. He had gathered himself in, bunched and knotted. His glare at young Macgowan was palpable.

"Mr. Priam," said Ellery pleasantly, "have you ever seen these stock certificates before?"

Ellery laid the box on the tray of the wheel-chair. Priam looked at the mass of certificates for a long time without touching them—almost, Ellery would have said, without seeing them. But gradually awareness crept over his face, and as it advanced it touched the purple like a chemical, leaving pallor behind.

Now he seized a stock certificate, another, another. His great hands began to scramble through the box, scattering its contents. Suddenly his hands fell and he looked at his wife.

"I remember these." And Priam added, with the most curious emphasis, "Don't you, Delia?"

The barb penetrated her armour. "I?"

"Look at 'em, Delia." His bass was vibrant with malice. "If you haven't seen them lately, here's your chance."

She approached his wheel-chair reluctantly, aware of something unpleasant that was giving him a feeling of pleasure. If he felt fear at the nature of the sixth warning, he showed no further trace of it.

"Go ahead, Delia." He held out an engraved certificate. "It won't bite you."

"What are you up to now?" growled Crowe. He strode forward.

"You saw them earlier today, Macgowan," said Keats. Crowe stopped, uneasy. The detective was watching them all with a brightness of eye he had not displayed for some time ... watching them all except Wallace, whom he seemed not to be noticing, and who was fussing with the barbecue as if he were alone in the room.

Delia Priam read stiffly, "Harvey Macgowan."

"Sure is," boomed her husband. "That's the name on the stock, Delia. Harvey Macgowan. Your old man, Crowe." He chuckled.

Macgowan looked foolish. "Mother, I didn't notice the name at all."

Delia Priam made an odd gesture. As if to silence him. "Are they all—?"

"Every one of them, Mrs. Priam," said Keats. "Do they mean anything to you?"

"They belonged to my first husband. I haven't seen these for ... I don't know how many years."

"You inherited these stocks as part of Harvey Macgowan's estate?"

"Yes. If they're the same ones."

"They're the same ones, Mrs. Priam," Keats said dryly. "We've done a bit of checking with the old probate records. They were turned over to you at the settlement of your first husband's estate. Where have you kept them all these years?"

"They were in a box. Not this box.... It's so long ago, I don't remember."

"But they were part of your effects? When you married Mr. Priam, you brought them along with you? Into this house?"

"I suppose so. I brought everything." She was having difficulty enunciating clearly. Roger Priam kept watching her lips, his own parted in a grin.

"Can't you remember exactly where you've kept these, Mrs. Priam? It's important."

"Probably in the storeroom in the attic. Or maybe among some trunks and boxes in the cellar."

"That's not very helpful."

"Stop badgering her, Keats," said young Macgowan. Because he was bewildered, his jaw stuck out. "Do you remember where you put your elementary school diploma?"

"Not quite the same thing," said the detective. "The face value of these stocks amounts to a little over a million dollars."

"That's nonsense," said Delia Priam with a flare of asperity. "These shares are worthless."

"Right, Mrs. Priam. I wasn't sure everybody knew. They're worth far less than the paper they're printed on. Every company that issued these shares is defunct."

"What's known on the stock market," said Roger Priam with every evidence of enjoyment, "as cats and dogs."

"My first husband sank almost everything he had in these pieces of paper," said Delia in a monotone. "He had a genius for investing in what he called 'good things' that always turned out the reverse. I didn't know about it until after Harvey died. I don't know why I've hung on to them."

"Why, to show 'em to your loving second husband, Delia," said Roger Priam, "right after we were married; remember? And remember I advised you to wallpaper little Crowe's little room with them as a reminder of his father? I gave them back to you and I haven't seen them again till just now."

"They've been somewhere in the house, I tell you! Where anyone could have found them!"

"And where someone did," said Ellery. "What do you make of it, Mr. Priam? It's another of these queer warnings you've been getting—in many ways the queerest. How do you explain it?"

"These cats and dogs?" Priam laughed. "I'll leave it to you, my friends, to figure it out."

There was contempt in his voice. He had either convinced himself that the whole fantastic series of events was meaningless, the work of a lunatic, or he had so mastered his fears of what he knew to be a reality that he was able to dissemble like a veteran actor. Priam had the actor's zest; and, shut up in a room for so many years, he may well have turned it into a stage, with himself the star performer.

"Okay," said Lieutenant Keats without rancour. "That seems to be that."

"Do you think so?"

The voice came from another part of the room.

Everyone turned.

Laurel Hill stood inside the screen door to Priam's terrace.

Her face was white, nostrils pinched. Her murky eyes were fixed on Delia Priam.

Laurel wore a suède jacket. Both hands were in the pockets.

"That's the end of that, is it?"

Laurel shoved away from the screen door. She teetered for an instant, regained her balance, then picked her way very carefully half the distance to Delia Priam, her hands still in her pockets.

"Laurel," began Crowe.

"Don't come near me, Mac. Delia, I have something to say to you."

"Yes?" said Delia Priam.

"When that green alligator wallet came, it reminded me of something. Something that belonged to you. I searched your bedroom while you were in Montecito and I found it. One of your bags—alligator, dyed green, and made by the same shop as the wallet. So I was sure you were behind all this, Delia."

"You'd better get her out of here," said Alfred Wallace suddenly. "She's tight."

"Shut up, Alfred." Roger Priam's voice was a soft rumble.

"Miss Hill," said Keats.

"No!" Laurel laughed, not taking her eyes from Delia. "I was sure you were behind it, Delia. But Ellery Queen didn't seem to think so. Of course, he's a great man, so I thought I must be wrong. But these stock certificates belong to you, Delia. You put them away. You knew where they were. You're the only one who could have sent them."

"Laurel," began Ellery, "that's not the least bit logical—"

"*Don't come near me!*" Her right hand came out of her pocket with an automatic.

Laurel pointed its snub nose at Delia Priam's heart.

Young Macgowan was gaping.

"But if you sent this 'warning'—whatever in your poisoned mind it's supposed to mean—you sent the others, too, Delia. And *they* won't do anything about it. It's washed up, they say. Well, I've given them their chance, Delia. You'd have got away with it if only men were involved; your kind always does. But *I'm* not letting you get away with killing my father! You're going to pay for that right now, Delia!—right n ..."

Ellery struck her arm as the gun went off and Keats caught it neatly as it flew through the air. Crowe made a choking sound, taking a step towards his mother. But Delia Priam had not moved. Roger Priam was looking down at his tray. The bullet had shattered the bottle of wine two inches from his hand.

"By God," snarled Priam, "she almost got me. Me!"

"That was a dumb-bunny stunt, Miss Hill," said Keats. "I'm going to have to take you in for attempted homicide."

Laurel was looking in a glazed way from the gun in the detective's hand to the immobile Delia. Ellery felt the girl shrinking in his grip, in spasms, as if she were trying to compress herself into the smallest possible space.

"I'm sorry, Mrs. Priam," Keats was saying. "I couldn't know she was carrying a gun. She never seemed the type. I'll have to ask you to come along and swear out a complaint."

"Don't be silly, Lieutenant."

"Huh?"

"I'm not making any charge against this girl."

"But Mrs. Priam, she shot to kill—"

"Me!" yelled Roger Priam.

"No, it's me she shot at." Delia Priam's voice was listless. "She's wrong, but I understand how you can bring yourself to do a thing like this when you've lost somebody you've loved. I wish I had Laurel's spunk. Crowe, stop looking like a dead carp. I hope you're not going to be stuffy about this and let Laurel down. It's probably taken her weeks to work herself up to this, and at that she had to get drunk to do it. She's a good girl, Crowe. She needs you. And I know you're in love with her."

Laurel's bones all seemed to melt at once. She sighed, and then she was silent.

"I think," murmured Ellery, "that the good girl has passed out."

Macgowan came to life. He snatched Laurel's limp figure from Ellery's arms, looked around wildly, and then ran with her. The door opened before him; Wallace stood there, smiling.

"She'll be all right." Delia Priam walked out of the room. "I'll take care of her."

They watched her go up the stairs behind her son, back straight, head high, hips swinging.

14

By the night of July thirteenth all the reports were in.

"If I'm a detective," Keats said unhappily to Ellery, "then you've got second sight. I'm still not sure how you doped this without inside information."

Ellery laughed. "What time did you tell Priam and the others?"

"Eight o'clock."

"We've just got time for a congratulatory drink."

They were in Priam's house on the stroke of eight. Delia Priam was there, and her father, and Crowe Macgowan, and a silent and drained-looking Laurel. Roger Priam had evidently extended himself for the occasion; he had on a green velvet lounging jacket and a shirt with starched cuffs, and his beard and hair had been brushed. It was as if he suspected something out of the ordinary and was determined to meet it full-dress, in the baronial manner. Alfred Wallace hovered in the background, self-effacing and ineffaceable, with his constant mocking, slightly irritating smile.

"This is going to take a little time," said Lieutenant Keats, "but I don't think anybody's going to be bored.... I'm just along for atmosphere. It's Queen's show."

He stepped back to the terrace-ward wall, in a position to watch their faces.

"Show? What kind of show?" There was fight in the Priam tones, his old hair-trigger belligerence.

"Showdown would be more like it, Mr. Priam," said Ellery.

Priam laughed. "When are you going to get it through your heads that you're wasting your time, not to mention mine? I didn't ask for your help, I don't want your help, I won't take your help—and I ain't giving any information."

"We're here, Mr. Priam, to give you information."

Priam stared. Of all of them, he was the only one who seemed under no strain except the strain of his own untempered arrogance. But there was curiosity in his small eyes.

"Is that so?"

"Mr. Priam, we know the whole story."

"What whole story?"

"We know your real name. We know Leander Hill's real name. We know where you and Hill came from before you went into business in Los Angeles in 1927, and what your activities were before you both settled in California. We know all that, Mr. Priam, and a great deal more. For instance, we know the name of the person whose life was mixed up with yours and Hill's before 1927—the one who's trying to kill you today."

The bearded man held on to the arms of his wheel-chair. But he gave no other sign; his face was iron. Keats, watching from the sidelines, saw Delia Priam sit forward, as at an interesting play; saw the flicker of uneasiness in old Collier's eyes; the absorption of Macgowan; the unchanging smile on Wallace's lips. And he saw the colour of life creep back in Laurel Hill's cheeks.

"I can even tell you," continued Ellery, "exactly what was in the box you received the morning Leander Hill got the gift of the dead dog."

Priam exclaimed, "That's bull! I burned that box and what was in it the same day I got it. Right in that fireplace there! Is the rest of your yarn going to be as big a bluff as this?"

"I'm not bluffing, Mr. Priam."

"You know what was in that box?"

"I know what was in that box."

"Out of the zillions of different things it could have been, you know the one thing it was, hey?" Priam grinned. "I like your nerve, Queen. You must be a good poker player. But that's a game I used to be pretty good at myself. So suppose I call you. What was it?"

He raised a glass of whisky to his mouth.

"Something that looked like a dead eel."

Had Ellery said, "Something that looked like a live unicorn," Priam could not have reacted more violently. He jerked against the tray and most of the whisky sprayed out of his beard. He spluttered, swiping at himself.

As far as Keats could see, the others were merely bewildered. Even Wallace dropped his smile, although he quickly picked it up and put it on again.

"I was convinced from practically the outset," Ellery went on, "that these 'warnings'—to use the language of the original note to Hill—were interconnected; separate but integral parts of an all-over pattern. And they are. The pattern is fantastic—for instance, even now I'm sure Lieutenant Keats still suspects what Hollywood calls a weenie. But fantastic or not, it exists; and the job I set myself was to figure out what it was. And now that I've figured it out, it doesn't seem fantastic at all. In fact, it's straightforward, even simple, and it certainly expresses a material enough meaning. The fantasy in this case, as in so many cases, lies in the mind that evolved the pattern, not in the pattern itself.

"As the warnings kept coming in, I kept trying to discover their common denominator, the cement that was holding them together. When you didn't know what to look for—unlike Mr. Priam, who did know what to look for—it was hard, because in some of them the binding agent was concealed.

"It struck me, after I'd gone over the warnings innumerable times," said Ellery, and he paused to light a cigarette, so that nothing in the room was audible but the scratch of the match and Roger Priam's heavy breathing, "it struck me finally that *every warning centrally involved an animal.*"

Laurel said, "What?"

"I'm not counting the dog used to bring the warning note to Hill. Since it conveyed a warning to Hill and not to you, Mr. Priam, we must consider the dead dog entirely apart from the warnings sent to you. Still, it's interesting to note in passing that Hill's series of warnings, which never got beyond the first, began with an animal, too.

"Omitting for the moment the contents of the first box you received, Mr. Priam," Ellery said, "let's see how the concept 'animal' derives from the warnings we had direct knowledge of. Your second warning was a poisoning attack, a non-fatal dose of arsenic. The animal? *Tuna fish*, the medium by which the poison was administered.

"The third warning? *Frogs and toads.*

"The fourth warning was one step removed from the concept—a wallet. But the wallet was leather, and the leather came from an *alligator.*

"There was no mistaking the animal in the fifth warning. The ancient Greek comedy by Aristophanes—*The Birds.*

"And the sixth warning, Mr. Priam—some worthless old stock certificates—would have given me a great deal of trouble if you hadn't suggested the connection yourself. There's a contemptuous phrase applied to such stocks by market traders, you said— '*cats and dogs.*' And you were quite right—that's what they're called.

"So ... fish, frogs, alligator, birds, cats and dogs. The fish, frogs, and alligator suggested literally, the birds and the cats and dogs suggested by allusion. All animals. That was the astonishing fact. What did you say, Mr. Priam?"

But Priam had merely been bumbling in his beard.

"Now the fact that each of the five warnings I'd had personal contact with concealed, like a puzzle, a different animal—aston-

187

ishing as it was—told me nothing," continued Ellery, throwing his cigarette into Priam's fireplace. "I realized after some skull work that the meaning must go far deeper. It had to be dug out.

"But digging out the deeper meaning was another story.

"You either see it or you don't. It's all there. There's nothing up its sleeve. The trick lies in the fact that, like all great mystifications, it wears the cloak of invisibility. I do not use the word 'great' loosely. It's just that—a great conception—and it wouldn't surprise me if it takes its place among the classic inventions of the criminal mind."

"For God's sake," burst out Crowe Macgowan, "talk something that makes sense!"

"Mac," said Ellery, "what are frogs and toads?"

"What are frogs and toads?"

"That's right. What kind of animals are they?" Macgowan looked blank.

"Amphibians," said old Mr. Collier.

"Thank you, Mr. Collier. And what are alligators?"

"Alligators are reptiles."

"The wallet derived from a reptile. And to which family of animals do cats and dogs belong?"

"Mammals," said Delia's father.

"Now let's re-state our data, still ignoring the first warning, of which none of us had first-hand knowledge but Mr. Priam. The second warning was *fish*. The third warning was *amphibians*. The fourth warning was *reptiles*. The fifth warning was *birds*. The sixth warning was *mammals*.

"Immediately we perceive a change in the appearance of the warnings. From being an apparently unrelated, rather silly conglomeration, they've taken on a related, scientific character.

"Is there a science in which fish, amphibians, reptiles, birds, and mammals are related—what's more, *in exactly that order?*

"In fact, is there a science in which fish are regarded as coming—as it were—second, amphibians third, reptiles fourth, birds fifth, and mammals last?—exactly as the warnings came?

"Any high school biology student could answer the question without straining himself.

"*They are progressive stages in the evolution of man.*"

Roger Priam was blinking steadily, as if there were a growing, rather too bright light.

"So you see, Mr. Priam," said Ellery with a smile, "there was no bluff involved whatever. Since the second warning, fish, represents the second stage in the evolution of man, and the third warning, amphibians, represents the third stage in the evolution of man, and so on, then plainly the first warning could only have represented the first stage in the evolution of man. It's the lowest class of what zoologists call, I believe, craniate vertebrates—the lamprey, which resembles an eel but belongs to a different order. So I knew, Mr. Priam, that when you opened that first box you found in it something that looked like an eel. There was no other possibility."

"I thought it was a dead eel," said Priam rigidly.

"And did you know what the thing that looked like a dead eel meant, Mr. Priam?"

"No, I didn't."

"There was no note in that first box giving you the key to the warnings?"

"No ..."

"He couldn't have expected you to catch his meaning from the nature of the individual warnings themselves," said Ellery with a frown. "To see through a thing like this calls for a certain minimum of education which—unfortunately, Mr. Priam—you don't have. And he knows you don't have it; he knows you, I think, very well."

"You mean he sent all these things," cried Laurel, "not caring whether they were understood or not?"

The question was in Lieutenant Keat's eyes, too.

"It begins to appear," said Ellery slowly, "as if he preferred that they *weren't* understood. It was terror he was after—terror for its own sake." He turned slightly away with a worried look.

"I never did know what they meant," muttered Roger Priam. "It was not knowing that made me ..."

"Then it's high time you did, Mr. Priam." Ellery had shrugged his worry off. "The kind of mentality that would concoct such an unusual series of warnings was obviously not an ordinary one. Granted his motive—which was to inspire terror, to punish, to make his victim die mentally over and over—he must still have had a mind which was capable of thinking in these specialized terms and taking this specific direction. Why did he choose the stages of evolution as the basis of his warnings? How did his brain come to take that particular path? Our mental processes are directly influenced by our capacities, training, and experience. To have founded his terror campaign on the evolution theory, to have worked it out in such systematic detail, the enemy of Leander Hill and Roger Priam must have been a man of scientific training—biologist, zoologist, anthropologist ... or a naturalist.

"When you think of the stages of evolution," continued Ellery, "you automatically think of Charles Darwin. Darwin was the father of the evolutionary theory. It was Darwin's researches over a hundred years ago, his lecture before the Linnean Society in 1858 on *The Theory of Evolution,* his publication the following year of the amplification of his *Theory* which he called *On the Origin of Species,* that opened a new continent of scientific knowledge in man's exploration of his own development.

"So when I saw the outline of a naturalist and accordingly thought of Darwin, the greatest naturalist of all, it was a logical step to think back to Darwin's historic voyage—one of the world's great voyages on perhaps science's most famous ship— the voyage of naturalistic exploration on which Darwin formulated his theory of the origin of species and their perpetuation by natural selection. And thinking back to that produced a really wonderful result." Ellery gripped the back of a chair, leaning over it. "Because the ship on which Charles Darwin set sail from Plymouth, England, in 1831 on that epic voyage was named ... *H.M.S. Beagle.*"

"Beagle." Laurel goggled. *"The dead dog!"*

"There were a number of possibilities," Ellery nodded. "In sending Hill a beagle, the sender might have been providing the master key which was to unlock the door of the warnings to come—beagle, Darwin's ship, Darwin, evolution. But that seemed pretty remote. Neither Hill nor Priam was likely to know the name of the ship on which Darwin sailed more than a hundred years ago, if indeed they knew anything at all about the man who had sailed on it. Or the plotter might have been memorializing in a general way the whole basis of his plot. But this was even unlikelier. Our friend the scientifically-minded enemy hasn't wasted his time with purposeless gestures.

"There were other possibilities along the same line, but the more I puzzled over the dead beagle the more convinced I became that it was meant to refer to something specific and significant in the background of Hill, Priam, and their enemy. What could the connection have been? What simple, direct tie-up could have existed among a naturalist and two non-scientific men, and the word or concept 'beagle,' and something that happened about twenty-five years ago?

"Immediately a connection suggested itself, a connection that covered the premises in the simplest, most direct way. Suppose twenty-five years or so ago a naturalist, together with Hill and Priam, planned a scientific expedition. Today they would probably use a plane; twenty-five years ago they would have gone by boat. And suppose the naturalist, conscious of his profession's debt to the great naturalist Darwin, in embarking on this expedition had the problem of naming, or the fancy to rename, the vessel on which he, Hill, and Priam were to be carried on their voyage of naturalistic exploration....

"I suggested to Lieutenant Keats," said Ellery, "that he try to trace a small ship, probably of the coastal type, which was either built, bought, or chartered for purposes of a scientific expedition—a ship named, or re-named, *Beagle* which set sail from probably an American port in 1925 or so.

"And Lieutenant Keats, with the co-operation of various

police agencies of the coastal cities, succeeded in tracing such a vessel. Shall I go on, Mr. Priam?"

Ellery paused to light a fresh cigarette.

Again there was no sound but the hiss of the match and Priam's breathing.

"Let's take the conventional interpretation of Mr. Priam's silence, Lieutenant," said Ellery, blowing out the match, "and nail this thing down."

Keats pulled a slip of paper from his pocket and came forward.

"The name of the man we want," the detective began, "is Charles Lyell Adam. Charles Lyell Adam came from a very wealthy Vermont family. He was an only child and when his parents died he inherited all their money. But Adam wasn't interested in money. Or, as far as we know, in women, liquor, or good times. He was educated abroad, he never married, and he kept pretty much to himself.

"He was a gentleman, a scholar, and an amateur scientist. His field was naturalism. He devoted all his time to it. He was never attached to a museum, or a university, or any scientific organization that we've been able to dig up. His money made it possible for him to do as he liked, and what he liked to do most was tramp about the world studying the flora and fauna of out-of-the-way places.

"His exact age," continued Keats, after referring to his notes, "isn't known. The Town Hall where his birth was recorded went up in smoke around 1910, and there was no baptismal record—at least, we haven't located one. Attempts to fix his age by questioning old residents of the Vermont town where he was born have produced conflicting testimony—we couldn't find any kin. We weren't able to find anything on him in the draft records of the first World War—he can't be located either as a draftee or an enlisted man. Probably he got some sort of deferment, although

192

we haven't been able to turn up anything on this, either. About all we can be sure of is that, in the year 1925, when Adam organized an expedition bound for the Guianas, he was anywhere from twenty-seven to thirty-nine years old.

"For this expedition," said Keats, "Adam had a special boat built, a fifty-footer equipped with an auxiliary engine and scientific apparatus of his own design. Exactly what he was after, or what he was trying to prove scientifically, no one seems to know. But in the summer of '25 Adam's boat, *Beagle*, cleared Boston Harbour and headed down the coast.

"It stopped over in Cuba for repairs. There was a long delay. When the repairs were finished, the *Beagle* got under way again. And that was the last anybody saw or heard of the *Beagle*, or Charles Lyell Adam, or his crew. The delay ran them into hurricane weather and, after a thorough search turned up no trace of the vessel, the *Beagle* was presumed to have gone down with all hands.

"The crew," said Lieutenant Keats, "consisted of two men, each about forty years old at the time, each a deep-water sailor of many years' experience, like Adam himself. We've got their names—their real names—but we may as well keep calling them by the names they took in 1927: Leander Hill and Roger Priam."

Keats shot the name at the bearded man in the wheel-chair as if it were a tennis ball; and, like spectators at the match, they turned their heads in unison to Priam. And Priam clutched the arms of his chair, and he bit his lip until a bright drop appeared. This drop he licked; another appeared and it oozed into his beard. But he met their eyes defiantly.

"All right," he rumbled. "So now you know it. What about it?"

It was as if he were grounded on a reef and gamely mustering his forces of survival against the winds.

"The rest," said Ellery, squarely to Priam, "is up to you."

"You bet it's up to me!"

"I mean whether you tell us the truth or we try to figure it out, Mr. Priam."

"You're doing the figuring, Mister."

"You still won't talk?"

"You're doing the talking," said Priam.

"We don't have much to go on, as you know very well," said Ellery, nodding as if he had expected nothing else, "but perhaps what we have is enough. You're here, twenty-five years later; and up to recently Leander Hill was here, too. And according to the author of the note that was left in the beagle's collar, Charles Lyell Adam was left for dead twenty-five years ago, under circumstances which justified him—in his own judgment, at any rate—in using the word 'murder,' Mr. Priam ... except that he didn't die and *he's* here.

"Did you and Hill scuttle the *Beagle*, Mr. Priam, when you were Adam's crew and the *Beagle* was somewhere in West Indian waters? Attack Adam, leave him for dead, scuttle the *Beagle*, and escape in a dinghy, Mr. Priam? The Haitians sail six hundred miles in cockleshells as a matter of course, and you and Hill were good enough seamen for Adam to have hired in the first place.

"But seamen don't attempt murder and scuttle good ships for no reason, Mr. Priam. What was the reason? If it had been a personal matter, or mutiny, or shipwreck as a result of incompetence or negligence, or any of the usual reasons, you and Hill could always have made your way back to the nearest port and reported what you pleased to explain the disappearance of Adam and his vessel. But you and Hill didn't do that, Mr. Priam. You and Hill chose to vanish along with Adam—to vanish in your sailor personalities, that is, leading the world to believe that Adam's crew had died with him. You went to a great deal of trouble to bury yourselves, Mr. Priam. You spent a couple of years doing it, preparing new names and personalities for your resurrection. Why? Because you had something to conceal—*something you couldn't have concealed had you come back as Adam's crew.*

194

"That's the most elementary logic, Mr. Priam. Now will you tell us what happened?"

Nothing in Priam stirred, not even the hairs of his beard.

"Then I'll have to tell you. In 1927, you and Hill appeared in Los Angeles and set up a wholesale jewellery business. What did you know about the jewellery business? We know all about you and Hill now, Mr. Priam, from the time you were born until you signed on the *Beagle* for its one and only voyage. You both went to sea as boys. There was nothing in either of your backgrounds that remotely touched jewels or jewellery. And, like most sailors, you were poor men. Still, two years later, here you both were, starting a fabulous business in precious stones. *Was that what you couldn't have concealed had you come back as Adam's crew?* Because the authorities would have said, *Where did these two poor seamen get all this money—or all these jewels?* And that's one question, Mr. Priam, you didn't want asked—either you or Hill.

"So it's reasonable to conjecture, Mr. Priam," said Ellery, smiling, "that the *Beagle* didn't go down in a hurricane after all. That the *Beagle* reached its destination, perhaps an uninhabited island, and that in exploring for the fauna and flora that interested him as a naturalist, Adam ran across something far afield from his legitimate interests. Like an old treasure-chest, Mr. Priam, buried by one of the pirate swarms who used to infest those waters. You can find descendants of those pirates, Mr. Priam, living in the Bahamas today.... An old treasure-chest, Mr. Priam, filled with precious stones. And you and Hill, poor sailors, attacked Adam, took the *Beagle* into blue water, sank her, and got away in her dinghy.

"And there you were, with a pirate's fortune in jewels, and how were you to live to enjoy it? The whole thing was fantastic. It was fantastic to find it, it was fantastic to own it, and it was fantastic to think that you couldn't do anything with it. But one of you got a brilliant idea, and about that idea there was nothing fantastic at all. Bury all trace of your old selves, come back as entirely different men—*and go into the jewellery business.*

"And that's what you and Hill did, Mr. Priam. For two years

you studied the jewellers' trade—exactly where, we haven't learned. When you felt you had enough knowledge and experience, you set up shop in Los Angeles ... and your stock was the chest of precious stones Adam had found on his island, for undisputed possession of which you'd murdered him. And now you *could* dispose of them. Openly. Legitimately. And get rich on them."

Priam's beard was askew on his chest. His eyes were shut, as if he were asleep ... or gathering his strength.

"But Adam didn't die," said Ellery gently. "You and Hill bungled. He survived. Only he knows how he nursed himself back to health, what he lived on, how he got back to civilization, and where, and where he's been since. But by his own testimony, in the note, he dedicated the rest of his life to tracking you and Hill down. For over twenty years he kept searching for the two sailors who had left him for dead—for his two murderers, Mr. Priam. Adam didn't want the fortune—he had his own fortune; and, anyway, he was never very interested in money. What he wanted, Mr. Priam, was revenge. As his note says.

"And then he found you."

And now Ellery's voice was no longer gentle.

"Hill was a disappointment to him. The shock of learning that Adam, against all reason, was alive—and all that that implied— was too much for Hill's heart. Hill was rather different from you, I think, Mr. Priam; whatever he'd been in the old days at sea, he had grown into the semblance of a solid citizen. And perhaps he'd never been really vicious. You were always the bully-boy of the team, weren't you? Maybe Hill didn't do anything but acquiesce in your crime, dazzled by the reward you dangled before his eyes. You needed him to get away; I think you needed his superior intelligence. In any event, after that one surrender to you and temptation, Hill built himself up into what a girl like Laurel could learn to love and respect ... and for the sake of whose memory she was even willing to kill.

"Hill was a man of imagination, Mr. Priam, and I think what

killed him at the very first blow was as much his dread of the effect on Laurel of the revelation of his old crime as the knowledge that Adam was alive and hot for revenge.

"But you're made of tougher material, Mr. Priam. You haven't disappointed Adam; on the contrary. It's really a pleasure for Adam to work on you. He's still the scientist—his method is as scientifically pitiless as the dissection of an old cadaver. And he's having himself a whale of a time, Mr. Priam, with you providing the sport. I don't think you understand with what wonderful humour Charles Lyell Adam is chasing you. Or do you?"

But when Priam spoke, he seemed not to have been listening. At least, he did not answer the question. He roused himself and he said, "Who is he? What's he calling himself now? Do you know that?"

"That's what you're interested in, is it?" Ellery smiled. "Why, no, Mr. Priam, we don't. All we know about him today is that he's somewhere between fifty-two and sixty-four years of age. I'm sure you wouldn't recognize him; either his appearance has been radically changed by time or he's had it changed for him by, say, plastic surgery. But even if Adam looked today exactly as he looked twenty-five years ago, it wouldn't do you—or us, Mr. Priam—any good. Because he doesn't have to be on the scene in person, you see. He could be working through someone else." Priam blinked and blinked. "You're not precisely a well-loved man, Mr. Priam, and there are people very close to you who might not be at all repelled by the idea of contributing to your unhappiness. So if you have any idea that as long as you protect yourself against a middle-aged male of certain proportions you're all right, you'd better get rid of it as quickly as possible. Adam's unofficial accomplice, working entirely for love of the job, you might say, could be of either sex, of any age ... and right here, Mr. Priam, in your own household."

Priam sat still. Not wholly in fear—with a reserve of desperate caution, it seemed, even defiance, like a treed cat.

"What a stinking thing to say—!"

"Shut up, Mac." And this was Keats, in a low voice, but there was a note in it that made Delia's son bring his lips together and keep them that way.

"A moment ago," said Ellery, "I mentioned Adam's sense of humour. I wonder if you see the point, Mr. Priam. Where his joke is heading."

"What?" said Priam in a mumble.

"All his warnings to you have had not one, but two, things in common. Not only has each warning involved an animal—*but each animal was dead.*"

Priam's head jerked.

"His first warning was a dead lamprey. His second warning was a dead fish. His third consisted of dead frogs and toads. The next a dead alligator. The next—*The Birds*—a little symbolism here, because he mutilated and destroyed the book ... the only way in which you can physically 'kill' a book! Even his last warning—the 'cats and dogs'—connotes death; there's nothing quite so 'dead' as the stock of a company that has folded up. Really a humorist, this Adam.

"Right up the ladder of evolution—from the lowest order of vertebrates, the lamprey, to one of the highest, cats and dogs. And every one, in fact or by symbol, was delivered dead.

"But, Mr. Priam, Adam isn't finished." Ellery leaned forward. "He hasn't climbed Darwin's ladder to stop at the next-to-the-last rung. The top rung of that ladder is still to be put in evidence. The highest creature in the class of Mammalia.

"So it's perfectly certain that there's an exhibit yet to come, the last exhibit, and by inference from the preceding ones, a dead exhibit. Charles Lyell Adam is going to produce a *dead man,* Mr. Priam, and there wouldn't be much point to his Darwinian joke if that dead man weren't Roger Priam."

Priam remained absolutely motionless.

"We've gone all over this," said Lieutenant Keats sharply, "and we agree there's only one thing to do. You're tagged for murder, Priam, and it's going to come soon—tomorrow, maybe

198

tonight, maybe an hour from now. I've got to have you alive, Priam, and I want Adam alive, too, if possible, because the law likes us to bring 'em back that way. You're going to have to be guarded night and day, starting right now. A man in this room. One on the terrace there. A couple around the grounds—"

Roger Priam filled his chest.

A roar came out that set the crystals in the chandelier jangling.

"Criminal, am I? On what evidence?" He brandished a club-like forefinger at Lieutenant Keats. "I'm not admitting a thing, you can't prove a thing, and I ain't asking for your protection or taking it!—d'ye get me?"

"What are you afraid of?" jeered the detective. "That we *will* lay our hands on Adam?"

"I've always fought my own scraps and, by God, I'll fight this one!"

"From a wheel-chair?"

"From a wheel-chair! Now get out of my house, you—, and stay out!"

15

They stayed out. Anyone from the outside would have said they were finished with Roger Priam and all his works. Daily Lieutenant Keats might have been seen going about his business; daily Ellery might have been seen staring at his—a blank sheet of paper in a still typewriter—or at night dining alone, with an ear cocked, or afterwards hovering above the telephone. He rarely left the cottage during the day; at night, never. His consumption of cigarettes, pipe tobacco, coffee, and alcohol gave Mrs. Williams a second subject for her interminable monologues; she alternated between predictions of sudden death for the world and creeping ulcers for Ellery.

At one time or another Laurel, Crowe Macgowan, Alfred Wallace, Collier—even Delia Priam—phoned or called in person, either unsolicited or by invitation. But each hung up or went away as worried or perplexed or thoughtful as he had been; and if Ellery unburdened himself to any of them, or vice versa, nothing seemed to come of it.

And Ellery lit another cigarette, or tormented another pipe, or gulped more hot coffee, or punished another highball, and Mrs. Williams's wails kept assailing the kitchen ceiling.

* * *

Then, one humid night at the beginning of the fourth week in July, just after midnight, the call came for which Ellery was waiting.

He listened, he said a few words, he broke the connection, and he called the number of Keats's house.

Keats answered on the first ring.

"Queen?"

"Yes. As fast as you can."

Ellery immediately hung up and ran out to his car. He had parked the Kaiser at the front door every night for a week.

He left it on the road near the Priam mail-box. Keats's car was already there. Ellery made his way along the bordering grass to the side of the house. He used no flashlight. In the shadow of the terrace a hand touched his arm.

"Quick." Keats's whisper was an inch from his ear.

The house was dark, but a faint night light was burning in Roger Priam's room off the terrace. The French door was open, and the terrace was in darkness.

They got down on their knees, peered through the screening of the inner door.

Priam's wheel-chair was in its bed position, made up for the night. He lay on his back, motionless, beard jutting obliquely to the ceiling. Mouth open.

Nothing happened for several minutes.

Then there was the slightest metallic sound.

The night light was in an electric outlet in the wainscoting near the door which led into the hall. They saw the doorknob clearly; it was in motion. When it stopped, the door began to open. It creaked. Came to rest.

Priam did not move.

The door opened swiftly.

But the night light was beyond the doorway, and when the door swung back to the farther wall it cut off most of the slight glow. All they could make out from the terrace was a formless blackness deeper than the darkness at the rear of the room. This gap in the void moved steadily from the doorway to Roger Priam's chair-bed. A tentacular something projected before it. The projection swam into the outermost edge of the night light's orbit and they saw that it was a revolver.

Beside Priam's chair the moving blackness halted.

The revolver came up a little.

Keats stirred. It was more a tightening of his muscles than a true movement; still, Ellery's fingers clamped on the detective's arm.

Keats froze.

And then the whole room exploded, motion gone wild.

Priam's arm flashed upward and his great hand closed like the jaws of a reptile on the wrist of the hand that held the revolver. The crippled man heaved his bulk upright, bellowing. There was the blurriest of struggles; they looked like two squids locked in battle at the bottom of the sea.

Then there was a soggy report, a smart thud, and quiet.

When Ellery snapped the wall switch Keats was already on his knees by the figure on the floor. It lay in a curl, almost comfortably, one arm hidden and the other outstretched. At the end of the outstretched arm lay the revolver.

"Chest," Keats muttered.

Roger Priam was glaring at the two men.

"It's Adam," he said hoarsely. "Where did you two come from? He came to kill me. It's Adam. I told you I could handle him!" He laughed with his teeth, but at once he began to shake, and he squinted at the fallen figure and rubbed his eyes with a trembling hand. "Who is he? Let me see him!"

"It's Alfred."

"*Alfred?*" The beard drooped.

Keats rose to go around Priam's chair. He plucked one of Priam's telephones from its hook and dialled a number.

"*Alfred is Adam?*" Priam sounded dazed, stupid. He recoiled quickly, but it was only Ellery removing his top blanket.

Ellery dropped the blanket over the thing on the floor.

"He's ...?" Priam's tongue came out. "Is he dead?"

"Headquarters?" said Keats. "Keats, Hollywood Division, reporting a homicide. The Hill-Priam case. Roger Priam just shot Alfred Wallace, his secretary-nurse-what-have-you, shot him to death.... That's right. Through the heart. I witnessed the shooting myself, from the terrace—"

"To death," said Priam. "To death. He's dead!... But it was self-defence. You witnessed it—if you witnessed it.... He pussy-footed into my room here. I heard him come in. I made believe I was sleeping. Oh, I was ready for him!" His voice cracked. "Didn't you see him point the gun at me? I grabbed it, twisted his hand! It was self-defence—"

"We saw it all, Mr. Priam," said Ellery in a soothing voice.

"Good, you saw it. He's dead. Damn him, he's dead! Wallace.... Try to kill me, would he? By God, it's over. It's over."

"Yes," Keats was saying into the phone. "When? Okay, no hurry." He hung up.

"You heard Mr. Queen," Priam babbled. "He saw it all, Lieutenant—"

"I know." Keats went over to the blanket and lifted one corner. Then he dropped the blanket and took out a cigarette and lit it. "We'll have to wait." He inhaled.

"Sure, yes, Lieutenant." Priam fumbled with something. The upper half of his bed rose, the lower sank, to form the chair. He groped. "A drink," he said. "You join me? Celebration." He guffawed. "Besides, I'm a little wobbly."

Ellery was wandering around, pulling at an ear, rubbing the back of his neck. There was a ridge between his eyes.

Keats kept smoking and watching him.

"I've got to hand it to him," Priam was saying, busy with a bottle and a glass. "Alfred Wallace.... Must have had his nose fixed. I never recognized him. Smooth, smooth operator. Gets right on the inside. Laughing up his sleeve all the time! But who's laughing now? Here's to him." He raised the glass, grinning, but the wild animal was still in his eyes. He tossed the

203

whisky off. When he set the glass down, his hand was no longer shaking. "But there he is, and here I am, and it's all over." His head came down, and he was silent.

"Mr. Priam," said Ellery.

Priam did not reply.

"Mr. Priam?"

"Hey?" Priam looked up.

"There's one point that still bothers me. Now that it's over, would you straighten me out on it?"

Priam looked at him. Then, deliberately, he reached for the bottle and refilled his glass.

"Why, Mr. Queen, it all depends," he said. "If you expect me to admit a lot of guff—with maybe a stenographer taking it all down from my terrace—you can save your wind. All right, this man was after me. No idea why, friends, except that he went crazy. On that voyage. Absolutely nuts.

"On the *Beagle* he went after me and my shipmate with a machete. We were off some dirty island and we jumped overboard, swam to the beach, and hid in the woods. Hurricane blew up that night and swept the *Beagle* out to sea. We never saw the ship or Adam again. Shipmate and me, we then found a treasure on that island and we finally got it off on a raft we made.

"Reason we laid low and changed our names to Hill and Priam was so Adam could never come back and claim one-third of the treasure—he'd been exploring that island. And maybe he'd still try to kill us even if he didn't claim a third. That's my story, friends. Not a crime in a cargo load." He grinned and tossed off the second glassful. "And I'm sticking to it."

Keats was regarding him with admiration. "It's a lousy story, Priam, but if you stick to it we're stuck with it."

"Anything else, Mr. Queen ..." Priam waved genially. "All you got to do is ask. What's the point that's been giving you such a bad time?"

"The letter Adam sent to Leander Hill," said Ellery.

"The letter—?" Priam stared. "Why in hell would you be worrying about *that?*"

Ellery took a folded sheet of paper from his breast pocket.

"This is a copy of the note Hill found in the silver box on the beagle's collar," he said. "It's been some time and perhaps I'd better refresh your memory by reading it aloud."

"Go ahead." Priam still stared.

"*You believed me dead,*" read Ellery. "*Killed, murdered. For over a score of years I have looked for you—for you and for him. And now I have found you. Can you guess my plan? You'll die. Quickly? No, very slowly. And so pay me back for my long years of searching and dreaming of revenge. Slow dying ... unavoidable dying. For you and for him. Slow and sure—dying in mind and in body. And for each pace forward a warning ... a warning of special meaning for you—and for him. Meanings for pondering and puzzling. Here is warning number one.*"

"See?" said Priam. "Crazy as a bug."

"*Killed, murdered,*" said Keats. "By a hurricane, Mr. Priam?" But he was smiling.

"That was his craziness, Lieutenant. I remember when he was steaming after us on deck, waving the machete around his head, how he kept yelling we were trying to murder him. All the time he was trying to murder us. Ask your brain doctors. They'll tell you." Priam swung about. "Is that what's been bothering you, Mr. Queen?"

"What? Oh! No, not that, Mr. Priam." Ellery scowled down at the paper. "It's the phrasing."

"The what?"

"The way the message is worded."

Priam was puzzled. "What's the matter with it?"

"A great deal is the matter with it, Mr. Priam. I'll go so far as to say that this is the most remarkable collection of words I've ever been priviledged to read. How many words are there in this message, Mr. Priam?"

"How the devil should I know?"

"Ninety-nine, Mr. Priam."

Priam glanced at Keats. But Keats was merely smoking with the gusto of a man who has denied himself too long, and there was nothing on Ellery's face but concern. "So it's got ninety-nine words. I don't get it."

"Ninety-nine words, Mr. Priam, comprising three hundred and ninety-seven letters of the English alphabet."

"I still don't get it." A note of truculence crept into Priam's heavy voice. "What are you trying to prove, that you can count?"

"I'm trying to prove—and I can prove, Mr. Priam—that there's something wrong with this message."

"Wrong?" Priam's beard shot up. "What?"

"The tools of my business, Mr. Priam," said Ellery, "are words. I not only write words of my own, but I read extensively—and sometimes with envy—the words of others. So I consider myself qualified to make the following observation: This is the first time I've ever run across a piece of English prose, deathless or otherwise, made up of as many as ninety-nine words, consisting of almost four hundred individual characters, *in which the writer failed to use a single letter T.*"

"Single letter T," repeated Priam. His lips moved after he stopped speaking, so that for a moment it looked as if he were chewing something with a foreign and disagreeable taste.

"It took me a long time to spot that, Mr. Priam," continued Ellery, walking around near the body of Alfred Wallace. "It's the sort of thing you can't see because it's so obvious. When we read, most of us concentrate on the sense of what we're reading, not its physical structure. Who looks at a building and sees the individual bricks? Yet the secret of the building lies precisely there. There are twenty-six basic bricks in the English language, some of them more important than the rest. There's no guesswork about those bricks, Mr. Priam. Their nature, their usability, their interrelationships, the frequency of their occurrence have been determined as scientifically as the composition of stucco.

"Let me tell you about the letter T, Mr. Priam," said Ellery.

"The letter T is the second most frequently used letter in the English language. Only E occurs more frequently. T is the number two brick of the twenty-six.

"T, Mr. Priam, is the most frequently used *initial* letter in the English language.

"English uses a great many combinations of two letters representing a single speech sound. These are known as digraphs. The letter T, Mr. Priam, is part of the most frequently used digraph—TH.

"T is also part of the most frequently used trigraph—three letters spelling a single speech sound—THE, as in the word BATHE.

"TT, Mr. Priam, gives ground only to SS and EE as the most frequently used *double* letter.

"The same letters, S and E, are the only letters which occur more frequently than T as the *last* letters of words.

"But that isn't all, Mr. Priam," said Ellery. "The letter T is part of the most frequently used three-letter word in the English language—the word THE.

"The letter T is part of the most frequently used four-letter word—THAT—and also of the second most frequently used four-letter word—WITH.

"And as if that weren't enough, Mr. Priam," said Ellery, "we find T in the second most frequently used two-letter word— TO—and in the fourth most frequently used two-letter word— IT. Do you wonder now, Mr. Priam," said Ellery, "why I called Charles Adam's note to your partner remarkable?

"It's so remarkable, Mr. Priam, that it's impossible. No conceivable chance or coincidence could produce a communication of almost a hundred English words that was completely lacking in Ts. *The only way you can get a hundred-word message without a single T is by setting out to do so. You have to make a conscious effort to avoid using it.*

207

"Do you want confirmation, Mr. Priam?" asked Ellery, and now something new had come into his voice; it was no longer thoughtful or troubled. "The writer of this note didn't use a single TO or IT or AT or THE or BUT or NOT or THAT or WITH or THIS. You simply can't escape those words unless you're trying to.

"The note refers to you and Leander Hill; that is, to two people. He says: *I have looked for you and for him*. Why didn't he write: *I have looked for the two of you*, or *I have looked for both of you?*—either of which would have been a more natural expression than *for you and for him*? The fact that in the word TWO and in the word BOTH the letter T occurs can hardly escape us. He just happened to express it that way? Perhaps once; even possibly twice; but he wrote *for you and for him* three times in the same message!

"He writes: *Slow dying ... unavoidable dying*. And again: *dying in mind and in body*. He's no novelist or poet looking for a different way of saying things. And this is a note, not an essay for publication. Why didn't he use the common phrases: *Slow death ... inevitable death ... death mentally and physically?* Even though the whole message concerns death, the word itself—in that form—does not occur even once. If he was deliberately avoiding the letter T, the question is answered.

"*You believed me dead....* Had he expressed this in a normal, natural way he would have written: *You thought I was dead*. But *thought* contains two Ts. We find the word *pondering*, for *to think over*, for obviously the same reason.

"And surely *Here is warning number one* is a circumlocution to avoid writing the more natural *This is the first warning?*

"Am I quibbling? Can this still have been a coincidence, dictated by an eccentric style? The odds against this mount astronomically when you consider two other examples from the note.

"*And for each pace forward a warning*, he writes. He's not talking about physical progress, where a *pace* might have a specialized meaning in the context. There is no reason on earth why he shouldn't have written *And for each step forward*, except that *step* contains a T.

"My last example is equally significant. He writes: *For over a score of years*. Why use the fancy word *score*? Why didn't he write: *For over twenty years*, or whatever the actual number of years was? Because the word *twenty*, or any combination including the word *twenty*—from twenty-one through twenty-nine—gets him involved in Ts."

Roger Priam was baffled. He was trying to capture something, or recapture it. All his furrows were deeper with the effort, and his eyes rolled a little. But he said nothing.

And, in the background, Keats smoked; and, in the foreground, Alfred Wallace lay under the blanket.

"The question is, of course," said Ellery, "why the writer of the note avoided using the letter T.

"Let's see if we can't reconstruct something useful here.

"How was the original of Leander Hill's copy written? By hand, or by mechanical means? We have no direct evidence; the note has disappeared. Laurel caught a glimpse of the original when Hill took it from the little silver box, but Hill half-turned away as he read it and Laurel couldn't specify the character of the writing.

"But the simplest analysis shows the form in which it must have appeared. The letter could not have been hand-written. It is just as easy to write the letter T as any other letter of the alphabet. The writer, considering the theme of his message, could hardly have been playing word games; and no other test but ease or difficulty makes sense.

"If the note wasn't handwritten, then it was typewritten. You saw that note, Mr. Priam—Hill showed it to you the morning after his heart attack. Wasn't it typewritten?"

Priam looked up, frowning in a peculiar way. But he did not answer.

"It was typewritten," said Ellery. "But the moment you assume a typewritten note, the answer suggests itself. The writer

209

was composing his message on a typewriter. He used no Ts. Why look for complicated reasons? If he used no Ts, it's simply because Ts were not available to him. He *couldn't* use Ts. The T key on the machine he was using wouldn't function. It was broken."

Surprisingly, Priam lifted his head and said, "You're guessing."

Ellery looked pained. "I'm not trying to prove how clever I am, Mr. Priam, but I must object to your verb. Guessing is as obnoxious to me as swearing is to a bishop. I submit that I worked this out; I've had little enough fun in this case! But let's assume it's a guess. It's a very sound guess, Mr. Priam, and it has the additional virtue of being susceptible to confirmation.

"I theorize a typewriter with a broken key. Do we know of a typewriter—in this case—which wasn't in perfect working order?"

"Strangely enough, Mr. Priam, we do.

"On my way to your house for the first time, in Laurel Hill's car, I asked Laurel some questions about you. She told me how self-sufficient you've made yourself, how as a reaction to your disability you dislike help of the most ordinary kind. As an example, Laurel said that when she was at your house 'the day before' you were in a foul mood over having to dictate business memoranda to Wallace instead of doing them yourself—*your typewriter had just been sent into Hollywood to be repaired."*

Priam twisted. Keats stood by his wheel-chair, lifting the attached typewriter shelf.

Priam choked a splutter, glancing painfully down at the shelf as Keats swung it up and around.

Ellery and Keats bent over the machine, ignoring the man in the chair.

They glanced at each other.

Keats tapped the T key with a finger-nail. "Mr. Priam," he said, "there's only one key on this machine that's new. It's the T. The note to Hill was typed right here." He spread his fingers over the carriage of Priam's typewriter, almost with affection.

A sound, formless and a little beastly, came out of Priam's throat. Keats stood by him, very close.

"And who could have typed a note on your machine, Mr. Priam?" asked Ellery in the friendliest of voices. "There's no guesswork here. If I'd never seen this typewriter shelf I'd have known the machine is screwed on. It would have to be, to keep it from falling off when the shelf is swung aside and dropped. Besides, Laurel Hill told me so.

"So, except for those times when the typewriter needs a major repair, it's a permanent fixture of your wheel-chair. Was the original of the note to Hill typed on your machine after it was removed for repair but before the broken T key was replaced? No, because the note was delivered to Hill two weeks *before* you sent the machine into Hollywood. Did someone type the note on your machine while you were out of your wheel-chair? No, Mr. Priam, because you're never out of your chair; you haven't left it for fifteen years. Was the note typed on your machine while you were—say—asleep? Impossible; when the chair is a bed the shelf obviously can't come up.

"So I'm very much afraid, Mr. Priam, there's only one conclusion we can reach," said Ellery. "*You typed that warning note yourself.*

"It's you who threatened your partner with death.

"The only active enemy out of your past and Hill's, Mr. Priam, is Roger Priam."

"Don't misunderstand me," said Ellery. "Charles Adam is not imaginary. He was an actual person, as our investigation uncovered. Adam disappeared in West Indian waters 'over a score of years ago,' as you wrote in the note, and he hasn't been seen or heard of since. It was only the note that made us believe Adam was still alive. Knowing now that you wrote the note, we can only conclude that Adam didn't survive the *Beagle*'s voyage twenty-five years ago after all, that you and Hill did succeed in killing him, and that his reappearance here in Southern Califor-

211

nia this summer was an illusion you deliberately engineered.

"Priam," said Ellery, "you knew what a shock it would be to your partner Hill to learn that Adam was apparently alive after so many years of thinking he was dead. Not only alive but explicitly out for revenge. You knew that Hill would be particularly susceptible to such news. He had built a new life for himself. He was bound up emotionally with Laurel, his adopted daughter, who worshipped the man he seemed to be.

"So Adam's 'reappearance' threatened not only Hill's life but, what was possibly even more important to him, the whole structure of Laurel's love for him. There was a good chance, you felt, that Hill's bad heart—he had had two attacks before—could not survive such a shock. And you were right—your note killed him.

"If Hill had any doubts about the authenticity of the note, you dispelled them the morning after the heart attack, when for the first time in fifteen years you took the trouble of having yourself carted over to Hill's house. The cause could only have been a telephone agreement with Hill to have a confidential, urgent talk about the note. You had, I imagine, another and equally pressing reason for that unprecedented visit: You wanted to be sure the note was destroyed so that it couldn't be traced back to your typewriter. Either Hill gave it to you and you destroyed it then or later, or he destroyed it before your eyes. What you didn't know, Priam, and what he didn't tell you, was that he had already made a copy of the note in his own handwriting and hidden it in his mattress. Why? Maybe after the first shock, when Hill thought it over, he hadn't been *quite* convinced. Maybe a sixth sense told him before you got to him that something was wrong. Whether you convinced him during that visit or not, the note was probably already copied and in his mattress, and a native caution—despite all your arguments—made him leave it there and say nothing about it. We can't know and won't ever know just what went on in Hill's mind.

"But the damage was done by the sheer impact of the shock, Priam. Murder by fright," said Ellery. "Far colder-blooded and more deliberate than killing by gun or knife, or even poison. A murder calling for great pains of premeditation. One wonders why. Not merely why you wanted to kill Hill, but why you splashed your crime so carefully with that elaborate camouflage of 'the enemy out of the past.'

"Your motive must have been compelling. It couldn't have been gain, because Hill's death brought you no material benefits; his share of the business went to Laurel. It couldn't have been to avoid exposure as the murderer of Adam twenty-five years ago, for Hill was neck-deep in that crime with you and had benefited from it equally—he was hardly in a position to hold it over you. In fact, he was in a poorer position than you were to hold it over *him*, because Hill had the additional reason to want to keep it from Laurel. Nor is it likely that you killed him to avoid exposure for any other crime of which he might have gained knowledge, such as—I take the obvious theory—embezzlement of the firm's funds. Because the truth is you have had very little to do with the running of Hill & Priam; it was Hill who ran it, while you merely put up a show of being an equal partner in work and responsibility. Never leaving your house, you could hardly have been so in control of daily events as to have been able to steal funds, or falsify accounts, or anything like that. Nor was it trouble over your wife. Hill's relationship with Mrs. Priam was friendly and correct; besides," said Ellery rather dryly, "he was getting past the age for that sort of thing.

"There's only one thing you accomplished, Priam, by killing Leander Hill. So, in the absence of a positive indication in any other direction, I'm forced to conclude that that's why you wanted Hill out of the way.

"And it's confirmed by your character, Priam, the whole drive of your personality.

"By killing Hill *you got rid of your business partner.* That is one of the facts that emerge from his death. Is it the key fact? I think it is.

"Priam, you have an obsessive need to dominate, to dominate

your immediate background and everyone in it. The one thing above all others that you can't stand is dependence on others. With you the alternative is not so much independence of others as making others dependent on you. Because physically you're helpless, you want power. You must be master—even if, as in the case of your wife, you have to use another man to do it.

"You hated Hill because he, not you, was master of Hill & Priam. He ran it and he had run it for fifteen years with no more than token help from you. The firm's employees looked up to him and loathed you. He made policy, purchases, sales; to accounts, big and small, Leander Hill was Hill & Priam and Roger Priam was a forgotten and useless invalid stuck away in a house somewhere. The fact that to Hill you owe your material security and the sound condition of Hill & Priam has festered inside of you for fifteen years. Even while you enjoyed the fruits of Hill's efforts, they left a bitter taste in your mouth that eventually poisoned you.

"You planned his death.

"With Hill out of the way, you would be undisputed master of the business. That you might run it into the ground probably never occurred to you. But if it did, I'm sure the danger didn't even make you hesitate. The big thing was to make everyone involved in or with Hill & Priam come crawling to you. The big thing was to be boss."

Roger Priam said nothing. This time he did not even make the beastly sound. But his little eyes roved.

Keats moved even closer.

"Once you saw what you had to do," continued Ellery, "you realized that you were seriously handicapped. You couldn't come and go as you pleased; you had no mobility. An ordinary murder was out of the question. Of course, you could have disposed of Hill right in this room during a business conference by a shot. But Hill's death wasn't the primary objective. He had to die and leave you free to run the business.

"You had to be able to kill him in such a way that you wouldn't be even suspected.

"It occurred to you, as it's occurred to murderers before, that the most effective way of diverting suspicion from yourself was to create the illusion that you were equally in danger of losing your life, and from the same source. In other words, you had to create a fictitious outside threat directed not merely at Hill but at both of you.

"Your and Hill's connection with Charles Lyell Adam twenty-five years ago provided a suitable, if daring and dangerous, means for creating such an illusion. If Adam were 'alive,' he could have a believable motive to seek the death of both of you. Adam's background could be traced by the authorities; the dramatic voyage of the *Beagle* was traceable to the point of its disappearance with all hands; the facts of your and Hill's existence and present situation in life, plus the hints you could let drop in 'Adam's' note, would lead any competent investigator to the conclusions you wanted him to reach.

"You were very clever, Priam. You avoided the psychological error of making things too obvious. You deliberately told not quite enough in 'Adam's' note. You repeatedly refused on demand to give any information that would help the police or make the investigation easier, although an examination of your 'refusals' shows that you actually helped us considerably. But on the surface you made us work for what we got.

"You made us work hard, because you laid a fantastic trail for us to follow.

"But if your theory-of-evolution pattern was on the fancy side, your logic was made curiously more convincing because of it. To nurse a desire for revenge for almost a generation a man has to be a little cracked. Such a mind might easily run to the involved and the fanciful. At the same time, 'Adam' would naturally tend to think in terms of his own background and experience. Adam having been a naturalist, you created a trail such as an eccentric naturalist might leave—a trail you were sure we

215

would sooner or later recognize and follow to its conclusion, which was that Naturalist Charles Adam was 'the enemy out of the past.'

"Your camouflage was brilliantly conceived and stroked on, Priam. You laid it so thickly on this case that, if you had not foolishly used that broken-T typewriter, we should probably have been satisfied to pin the crime on a man who's really been dead for a quarter of a century."

Priam's big head wavered a little, almost a nod. But it might have been a momentary trembling of the muscles of his neck. Otherwise, he gave no sign that he was even listening.

"In an odd sort of way, Priam, you were unlucky. You didn't realize quite how bad Hill's heart was, or you miscalculated the impact of your paper bullet. Because Hill died as a result of your very first warning. You had sent yourself a warning on the same morning, intending to divide the other warnings between you and Hill, probably, alternating them. When Hill died so immediately, it was too late to pull yourself out. You were in the position of the general who has planned a complicated battle against the enemy, finds that his very first sortie has accomplished his entire objective, but is powerless to stop his orders and preparation for the succeeding attacks. Had you stopped after sending yourself only one warning the mere stoppage would have been suspect. The warnings to yourself had to continue in order that the illusion of Adam-frightening-Hill-to-death should be completely credible.

"You sent six warnings, including the masterly one of having your tuna salad poisoned so that you could eat some, fall sick, and so call attention to your 'fish' clue. After six warnings you undoubtedly felt you had thoroughly fooled us as to the real source of the crime. On the other hand, you recognized the danger of stopping even at six with yourself still alive. We might begin to wonder why—in your case—'Adam' had given up. Murderers have been caught on a great deal less.

"You saw that, for perfect safety, you had to give us a convincing end to the whole business.

216

"The ideal, of course, was for us to 'catch' 'Adam.'

"A lesser man, Priam, wouldn't have wasted ten seconds wrestling with the problem of producing a man dead twenty-five years and handing his living body over to the police. But you didn't abandon the problem merely because it seemed impossible to solve. There's a lot of Napoleon in you.

"And you solved it.

"Your solution was tied up with another unhappy necessity of the case. To carry out your elaborate plot against Hill and yourself, you needed help. You have the use of your brain unimpaired, and the use of your hands and eyes and ears in a limited area, but these weren't enough. Your plans demanded the use of legs, too, and yours are useless. You couldn't possibly, by yourself, procure a beagle, poison it, deliver it and the note to Hill's doorstep; get cardboard boxes and string from the dime store, a dead lamprey from God knows where, poison, frogs, and so on. It's true that the little silver box must have been left here, or dropped, by Laurel; that the arsenic undoubtedly came from the can of Deth-on-Ratz in your cellar; that the tree frogs were collected in these very foothills; that the green alligator wallet must have been suggested by your wife's possession of a handbag of the same material and from the same shop; that you found the worthless stock from Mrs. Priam's first husband's estate in some box or trunk stored in this house; that to leave the bird clue you chose a book from your own library. Whenever possible you procured what you needed from as close by as you could manage, probably because in this way you felt you could control them better. But even for the things in and from this house, you needed a substitute for your legs.

"Who found and used these things at your direction?

"Alfred Wallace could. Secretary, nurse, companion, orderly, handyman ... with you all day, on call all night ... you could hardly have used anyone else. If for no other reason than that Wallace couldn't possibly have been kept ignorant of what was going on. Using Wallace turned a liability into an asset.

"Whether Wallace was your accomplice willingly because you

paid him well, or under duress because you had something on him," said Ellery, looking down at the mound under the blanket, "is a question only you can answer now, Priam. I suppose it doesn't really matter any more. However you managed it, you persuaded Alfred to serve as your legs and as extensions of your eyes and hands. You gave Alfred his orders and he carried them out.

"Now you no longer needed Alfred. And perhaps—as other murderers have found out—tools like Alfred have a way of turning two-edged. Wallace was the only one who knew you were the god of the machine, Priam. No matter what you had on him—if anything—Wallace alive was a continuous danger to your safety and peace of mind.

"The more you mulled, the more feasible Wallace's elimination became. His death would remove the only outside knowledge of your guilt; as your wife's lover he ought to die to satisfy your peculiar psychological ambivalence; and, dead, he became a perfect Charles Adam. Wallace was within Adam's age range had Adam lived; Wallace's background was unknown because of his amnesic history; even his personality fitted with what we might have expected Adam to be.

"If you could make us flush Alfred Wallace from the mystery as Charles Adam, you'd be killing three birds with one stone.

"And so you arranged for Wallace's death."

Roger Priam raised his head. Colour had come back into his cheekbones, and his heavy voice was almost animated.

"I'll have to read some of your books," Priam said. "You sure make up a good story."

"As a reward for that compliment, Priam," said Ellery, smiling, "I'll tell you an even better one.

"A few months ago you ordered Alfred Wallace to go out and buy a gun. You gave Wallace the money for it, but you wanted the gun's ownership traceable to him.

"Tonight you buzzed Wallace on the intercom, directly to his

218

bedroom, and you told Wallace you heard someone prowling around outside the house. You told him to take the gun, make sure it was loaded, and come down here to your room, quietly—"

"That's a lie," said Roger Priam.

"That's the truth," said Ellery.

Priam showed his teeth. "You're a bluffer after all. Even if it was true—which it ain't—how could you know it?"

"Because Wallace told me so."

The skin above Priam's beard changed colour again.

"You see," said Ellery, "I took Wallace into my confidence when I saw the danger he was in. I told him just what to expect at your hands and I told him that if he wanted to save his skin he'd be wise to play ball with Lieutenant Keats and me.

"Wallace didn't need much convincing, Priam. I imagine you've found him the sort of fellow who can turn on a dime; or, to change the figure, the sort who always spots the butter side of the bread. He came over to me without a struggle. And he promised to keep me informed; and he promised, when the time came, to follow not your instructions, Priam, but mine.

"When you told him on the intercom tonight to sneak down here with the loaded revolver, Wallace immediately phoned me. I told him to hold up going downstairs for just long enough to allow the lieutenant and me to get here. It didn't take us long, Priam, did it? We'd been waiting nightly for Wallace's phone call for some time now.

"I'm pretty sure you expected someone to be outside on guard, Priam, although of course you didn't know it would be Keats and me in person on Wallace's notification. You've put up a good show about not wanting police guards, in line with your shrewd performance all along, but you've known from the start that we would probably disregard your wishes in a crisis, and that was just what you wanted us to do.

"When Alfred stole into this room armed with a gun, you knew whoever was on guard—you hoped actually watching from the terrace—would fall for the illusion that Wallace was trying to kill you. If no one was watching, but a guard on the grounds heard the shot, within seconds he'd be in the room, and he'd find Wallace dead—in *your* room, with you obviously awakened from sleep, and only your story to listen to. With the previous build-up of someone threatening your life, he'd have no reason to doubt your version of what happened. If there were no guards at all, you would phone for help immediately, and between your version of the events and the fact that the gun was bought by Wallace you had every reason to believe the matter would end there. It was a bold, even a Bonapartist plan, Priam, and it almost worked."

Priam stirred, and with the stir a fluidity came over him, passing like a ripple. Then he said in a perfectly controlled voice, "Whatever Wallace told you was a damn lie. I didn't tell him to buy a gun. I didn't call him down here tonight. And you can't prove I did. You yourself saw him sneak in here a while back with a loaded gun, you saw me fight for my life, you saw him lose, and now he's *dead*." The bearded man put the lightest stress on the last word, as if to underscore Wallace's uselessness as a witness.

"I'm afraid you didn't listen very closely to what I said, Priam," said Ellery. "I said it *almost* worked. You don't think I'd allow Alfred to risk death or serious injury, do you? What he brought downstairs with him tonight, on my instructions, was a gun loaded with blanks. We've put on a show for you, Priam." And Ellery said, "*Get up, Wallace.*"

Before Priam's bulging eyes the blanket on the floor rose like the magic carpet, and there, under it, stood Alfred Wallace, smiling.

Roger Priam screamed.

16

What no one foresaw—including Ellery—was how Roger Priam would react to his arrest, indictment, and trial. Yet from the moment he showed his hand it was impossible to conceive that he might have acted otherwise. Alfred Wallace was a probable sole exception, but Wallace was being understandably discreet.

Priam took the blame for everything. His contempt for Wallace's part in the proceedings touched magnificence. Wallace, Priam said, had been the merest tool, not understanding what he was being directed to do. One would have thought, to hear Priam, that Wallace was an idiot. And Wallace acted properly idiotic. No one was fooled, but the law operates under rules of evidence, and since there were only two witnesses, the accused and his accomplice, each—for different motives—minimizing Wallace and maximizing Priam, Wallace went scot-free.

As Keats said, in a growl, "Priam's got to be boss, by God, even at his own murder trial."

It was reported that Priam's attorney, a prominent West Coast trial lawyer, went out on the night of the verdict and got himself thoroughly fried, missing the very best part of the show. Because that same night Roger Priam managed to kill himself by swallowing poison. The usual precautions against suicide had been taken, and those entrusted with the safety of the condemned man until his execution were chagrined and mystified. Roger Priam merely lay there with his bearded mouth open in a grin, looking as fiercely joyful as a pirate cut down on his own quarterdeck. No one could dictate to *him*, his grin seemed to say, not even the sovereign State of California. If he had to die, he was picking the method and the time.

He had to be dominant even over death.

To everyone's surprise, Alfred Wallace found a new employer immediately after the trial, an Eastern writer by the name of Queen. Wallace and his suitcase moved into the little cottage on the hill, and Mrs. Williams and her two uniforms moved out, the cause leading naturally to the effect.

Ellery could not say that it was a poor exchange, for Wallace turned out a far better cook than Mrs. Williams had ever been, an accomplishment in his new employee Ellery had not bargained for, since he had hired Wallace to be his secretary. The neglected novel was still the reason for his presence in Southern California, and now that the Hill-Priam case was closed Ellery returned to it in earnest.

Keats was flabbergasted. "Aren't you afraid he'll put arsenic in your soup?"

"Why should he?" Ellery asked reasonably. "I'm paying him to take dictation and type my manuscript. And talking about soup, Wallace makes a mean *sopa de almendras, à Mallorquina*. From Valldemosa—perfectly delicious. How about sampling it tomorrow night?"

Keats said thanks a lot, but he didn't go for that gourmet stuff himself, his speed was chicken noodle soup, besides his wife was having some friends in for television, and he hung up hastily.

To the press Mr. Queen was lofty. He had never been one to hound a man for past errors. Wallace needed a job, and he needed a secretary, and that was that.

Wallace merely smiled.

* * *

Delia Priam sold the hillside property and disappeared.

The usual guesses, substantiated by no more than "a friend of the family who asks that her name be withheld" or "Delia Priam is rumoured," had her variously in Las Vegas at the dice tables with a notorious underworld character; in Taos, New Mexico, under an assumed name, where she was said to be writing her memoirs for newspaper and magazine syndication; flying to Rome heavily veiled; one report insisted on placing her on a remote shelf in India as the "guest" of some wild mountain rajah well-known for his peculiar tastes in Occidental women.

That none of these pleasantly exciting stories was true everyone took for granted, but authoritative information was lacking. Delia Priam's father was not available for comment; he had stuffed some things in a duffel bag and gone off to Canada to prospect, he said, for uranium ore. And her son simply refused to talk to reporters.

To Ellery, privately, Crowe Macgowan confided that his mother had entered a retreat near Santa Maria; he spoke as if he never expected to see her again.

Young Macgowan was cleaning up his affairs preparatory to enlisting in the Army. "I've got ten days left," he told Ellery, "and a thousand things to do, one of which is to get married. I said it was a hell of a preliminary to a trip to Korea, but Laurel's stuck her chin out, so what can I do?"

Laurel looked as if she were recuperating from a serious illness. She was pale and thin but at peace. She held on to Macgowan's massive arm with authority. "I won't lose you, Mac."

"What are you afraid of, the Korean women?" jeered Crowe. "I'm told their favourite perfume is garlic."

"I'm joining the WACs," said Laurel, "if they'll ship one overseas. I suppose it's not very patriotic to put a condition to it, but if my husband is in Asia I want to be in the same part of the world."

"You'll probably wind up in West Germany," growled the large young man. "Why don't you just stay home and write me long and loving letters?"

Laurel patted his arm.

"Why don't *you* just stay home," Ellery asked Crowe, and stick to your tree?"

"Oh, that." Crowe reddened. "My tree is sold."

"Find another."

"Listen, Queen," snarled Delia's son, "you tend to your crocheting and I'll tend to mine. I'm no hero, but there's a war on—beg pardon, a United Nations police action. Besides, they'll get me anyway."

"I understand that," said Ellery with gravity, "but your attitude seems so different these days, Mac. What's happened to the Atomic Age Tree Boy? Have you decided, now that you've found a mate, that you're not worth preserving for the Post-Atomic Era? That's hardly complimentary to Laurel."

Mac mumbled, "You let me alone.... Laurel, no!"

"Laurel, yes," said Laurel. "After all, Mac, you owe it to Ellery. Ellery, about that Tree Boy foolishness...."

"Yes," said Ellery hopefully. "I've been rather looking forward to a solution of that mystery."

"I finally worried it out of him," said Laurel. "Mac, you're fidgeting. Mac was trying to break into the movies. He'd heard that a certain producer was planning a series of Jungle Man pictures to compete with the Tarzan series, and he got the brilliant idea of becoming a jungle man in real life, right here in Hollywood. The Atomic Age silliness was bait for the papers. It worked, too. He got so much publicity that the producer approached him, and he was actually negotiating a secret contract when Daddy Hill died and I began to yell murder. The murder talk, and the newspaper stories involving Mac's stepfather—which I suppose Roger planted himself, or had Alfred plant for him—scared the producer and he called off the negotiations. Crowe was awfully sore at me, weren't you, darling?"

"Not as sore as I am right now. For pete's sake, Laur, do you have to expose my moral underwear to the whole world?"

"I'm only a very small part of it, Mac," grinned Ellery. "So that's why you tried to hire me to solve the case. You thought if I could clear it up pronto, you could still save the deal with the movie producer."

"I did, too," said young Macgowan forlornly. "He came back at me only last week, asking questions about my draft status. I offered him the services of my grandfather, who'd have loved to be a jungle man, but the ungrateful guy told me to go to hell. And here I am, en route. Confidentially, Queen, does Korea smell as bad as they say it does?"

Laurel and Crowe were married by a Superior Court judge in Santa Monica, with Ellery and Lieutenant Keats as witnesses, and the wedding supper was ingested and imbibed at a drive-in near Oxnard, the newlyweds thereafter scouting off in Laurel's Austin in the general direction of San Luis Obispo, Paso Robles, Santa Cruz, and San Francisco. Driving back south on the Coast Highway, Ellery and Keats speculated as to their destination.

"I'd say Monterey," said Keats emotionally. "That's where I spent my honeymoon."

"I'd say, knowing Mac," said Ellery, "San Juan Capistrano or La Jolla, seeing that they lie in the opposite direction."

They were both misty-eyed on the New York State champagne which Ellery had traitorously provided for the California nuptials, and they wound up on a deserted beach at Malibu with their arms around each other, harmonizing *Ten Little Fingers and Ten Little Toes* to the silver-teared Pacific.

After dinner one night in late September, just as Alfred Wallace was touching off the fire he had laid in the living-room, Keats dropped in. He apologized for not having phoned before coming, saying that only five minutes before he had had no idea of visiting Ellery; he was passing by on his way home and he had stopped on impulse.

"For heaven's sake, don't apologize for an act of Christian mercy," exclaimed Ellery. "I haven't seen any face but Wallace's now for more than a week. The lieutenant takes water in his Scotch, Wallace."

"Go easy on it," Keats said to Wallace. "I mean the water. May I use your phone to call my wife?"

"Wonderful. You're going to stay." Ellery studied Keats. The detective looked harassed.

"Well, for a while." Keats went to the phone.

When he came back, a glass was waiting for him on the coffee table before the fire, and Ellery and Wallace were stretching their legs in two of the three armchairs around it. Keats dropped between them and took a long sip. Ellery offered him a cigarette and Wallace held a match to it, and for a few moments Keats frowned into the fire.

"Something wrong, Keats?" Ellery asked finally.

"I don't know." Keats picked up his glass. "I'm an old lady, I guess. I've wanted to chin with you for a long time now. I kept resisting the temptation, feeling stupid. Tonight ..." He raised his glass and gulped.

"What's bothering you?"

"Well ... the Priam case. Of course, it's all over—"

"What about the Priam case?"

Keats made a face. Then he set the glass down with a bang. "Queen, I've been over that spiel of yours—to me at the Hollywood Division, to Priam that night in his room—it must be a hundred times. I don't know, I can't explain it ..."

"You mean my solution to the case?"

"It never seems to come out as pat when I go over it as it did when you...." Keats stopped and rather deliberately turned to look at Alfred Wallace. Wallace looked back politely.

"It's not necessary for Wallace to leave, Keats," said Ellery with a grin. "When I said that night at Priam's that I'd taken Wallace into my confidence, I meant just that. I took him into my confidence completely. He knows everything I know, including the answers to the questions that I take it have been giving you a bad time."

The detective shook his head and finished what was left in his glass. When Wallace rose to refill it, Keats said, "No more now," and Wallace sat down again.

"It's not the kind of thing I can put my mitt on," said the detective uncomfortably. "No *mistakes*. I mean mistakes that you can ..." He drew on his cigarette for support, started over. "For instance, Queen, a lot of the hoopla you attributed to Priam just doesn't *fit*."

"Doesn't fit what?" asked Ellery mildly.

"Doesn't fit Priam. I mean, what Priam was. Take that letter he typed on the broken machine and put in the collar of the dead beagle for delivery to Hill ..."

"Something wrong with it?"

"Everything wrong with it! Priam was an uneducated man. If he ever used a fancy word, I wasn't around to hear it. His talk was crude. But when he wrote that letter ... How could a man like Priam have made such a letter up? To avoid using the letter T, to invent roundabout ways of saying things—that takes ... a *feel* for words, doesn't it? A certain amount of practice in—in composition? And punctuation—the note was dotted and dashed and commaed and everything perfectly."

"What's your conclusion?" asked Ellery.

Keats squirmed.

"Or haven't you arrived at one?"

"Well ... I have."

"You don't believe Priam typed that note?"

"He typed it, all right. Nothing wrong with your reasoning on that.... Look." Keats flipped his cigarette into the fire. "Call me a halfwit. But the more I think about it, the less I buy the payoff. Priam typed that letter, but somebody else *dictated* it. Word for word. Comma for comma." Keats jumped out of the chair as if he felt the need of being better prepared for the attack that was sure to come. But when Ellery said nothing, merely looked thoughtful and puffed on his pipe, Keats sat down again. "You're a kind-hearted character. Now tell me what's wrong with *me*."

"No, you keep going, Keats. Is there anything else that's bothered you?"

"Lots more. You talked about Priam's shrewd tactics, his cleverness; you compared him to Napoleon. Shrewd? Clever? A tactician? Priam was about as shrewd as a bull steer in heat and as clever as a punch in the nose. He couldn't have planned a menu. The only weapon Priam knew was a club.

"He figured out a series of related clues, you said, that added up—for our benefit—to a naturalist. Evolution. The steps in the ladder. Scientific stuff. How could a roughneck smallbrain like Priam have done that? A man who bragged he hadn't read a book since he was in knee pants! You'd have to have a certain amount of technical knowledge even to *think* of that evolutionary stuff as the basis of a red herring, let alone get all the stages correct and in the right order. Then picking a fancy-pants old Greek drama to tie in birds! No, sir, I don't purchase it. Not Priam.

"Oh, I don't question his guilt. He murdered his partner, all right. Hell, he confessed. But he wasn't the bird who figured out the method and thought up the details. That was the work of somebody with a lot better equipment than Roger Priam ever hoped to have."

"In other words, if I get your thought, Keats," murmured Ellery, "you believe Priam needed not only someone else's legs but someone else's grey matter, too."

"That's it," snapped the detective. "And I'll go whole hog. I say the same man who supplied the legs supplied the know-how!" He glared at Alfred Wallace, who was slumped in the chair, hands clasped loosely about the glass on his stomach, eyes gleaming Keats's way. "I mean you, Wallace! You got a lucky break, my friend, Priam sloughing you off as a maroon who trotted around doing what you were told—"

"Lucky nothing," said Ellery. "That was in the cards, Keats. Priam *did* believe Wallace was a stupid tool and that the whole brilliant plot was the product of his own genius; being Priam, he couldn't believe anything else—as Wallace, who knew him intimately, accurately foresaw. Wallace made his suggestions so subtly, led Priam about by his large nose so tactfully, that Priam never once suspected that *he* was the tool, being used by a master craftsman."

Keats glanced again at Wallace. But the man lay there comfortably, even looking pleased.

Keats's head ached. "Then—you mean—"

Ellery nodded. "The real murderer in this case, Keats, was not Priam. It's Wallace. Always was."

Wallace extended a lazy arm and snagged one of Ellery's cigarettes. Ellery tossed him a packet of matches, and the man nodded his thanks. He lit up, tossed the packet back, and resumed his hammocky position.

The detective was confused. He glanced at Ellery, at Wallace, at Ellery again. Ellery was puffing peacefully away at his pipe.

"You mean," said Keats in a high voice, "Hill wasn't murdered by Priam after all?"

"It's a matter of emphasis, Keats. Gangster A, a shot big enough to farm out his dirty work, employs Torpedo C to kill Gangster B. Torpedo C does so. Who's guilty of B's murder? A *and* C. The big shot and the little shot. Priam and Alfred were both guilty."

"Priam hired Wallace to do his killing for him," said Keats foolishly.

"No." Ellery picked up a pipe cleaner and inserted it in the stem of his pipe. "No, Keats, that would make Priam the big shot and Wallace the little. It was a whole lot subtler than that. Priam *thought* he was the big shot and that Wallace was a tool, but he was wrong; it was the other way around. Priam *thought* he was using Wallace to murder Hill, when all the time Wallace was using Priam to murder Hill. And when Priam planned the clean-up killing of Wallace—planned it on his own—Wallace turned Priam's plan right around against Priam and used it to make Priam kill himself."

"Take it easy, will you?" groaned Keats. "I've had a hard week. Let's go at this in words of one syllable, the only kind I can understand.

"According to you, this monkey sitting here, this man you call a murderer—who's taking your pay, drinking your liquor, and smoking your cigarettes, all with your permission—this Wallace planned the murders first of Hill, then of Priam, using Priam without Priam's realizing that he was being used—in fact, in such a way that Priam thought *he* was the works. All my pea-brain wants to know is: *Why?* Why should *Wallace* want to kill Hill and Priam? What did *he* have against 'em?"

"You know the answer to that, Lieutenant."

"Me?"

"Who's wanted to murder Hill and Priam from the start?"

"Who?"

"Yes, who's had that double motive throughout the case?"

Keats sat up gripping the arms of his chair. He looked at Alfred Wallace in a sickly way. "You're kidding," he said feebly. "This whole thing is a rib."

"No rib, Keats," said Ellery. "The question answers itself. The only one who had motive to kill both Hill *and* Priam was Charles Adam. Ditto Wallace? Then why look for two? Things equal to the same thing are equal to each other. Wallace is Adam. Refill now?"

Keats swallowed.

Wallace got up and amiably did the honours, Keats watching as if he half-expected to catch the tall man slipping a white powder into the glass. He drank, and afterwards gazed glumly into the brown liquid.

"I'm not being specially obtuse," Keats said finally. "I'm just trying to wriggle out of this logic of yours. Let's forget logic. You say that proves this smoothie is Charles Adam. How about coincidence? Of all the millions of nose-wipers who *could* have been Priam's man Friday, it turns out to be the one man in the universe who wanted to kill him. Too neat, Queen, not to say gaudy."

"Why do you call it coincidence? There was nothing coincidental about Charles Adam's becoming Priam's wet-nurse. *Adam planned it that way.*

"For twenty-five years he looked for Priam and Hill. One day he found them. Result: He became Priam's secretary-nurse-companion ... not as Adam, of course, but as a specially created character whom he christened Alfred Wallace. My guess is that Adam had more than a little to do with the sudden resignations of several of his predecessors in the job, but it remains a guess—Wallace, quite reasonably, is close-mouthed on the subject. My guess is also that he's been around Los Angeles far longer than the amnesic trail to Las Vegas indicated. Maybe it's been years—eh, Wallace?"

Wallace raised his brows quizzically.

"In any event, he managed finally to land the job and to fool Roger Priam absolutely. Priam went to his death completely unaware that Wallace was *actually* Adam rather than the spurious substitute for Adam Priam thought he was palming off on the authorities. Priam never doubted for a moment that Adam's bones were still lying in the coral sand of that deserted West Indian island."

Ellery stared reflectively at Wallace, who was sipping his Scotch like a gentleman in his club. "I wonder what you really look like, Adam. The newspaper photos we dug up weren't much use.... Of course, twenty-five years have made a big difference. But you wouldn't have trusted to that. Plastic work, almost certainly, and of the highest order; there isn't a sign of it. Maybe a little something to your vocal cords. And lots of practice with such things as gait, tricks of speech, 'characteristic' gestures, and so on. It was probably all done years ago, so that you had plenty of time to obliterate all trace of—forgive me—of the old Adam. Priam never had a chance. Or Hill. And you had the virility Priam demanded in a secretary. You'd undoubtedly found out about that in your preliminary reconnaissance. A glimpse of Delia Priam, and you must have been absolutely delighted. Plum pudding to go with your roast beef."

Wallace smiled appreciatively.

"I don't know when—or how—Priam first let on that he wanted to be rid of Leander Hill. Maybe he never said so at all, in so many words. At least in the beginning. You were with him night and day, and you were studying him. You could hardly have remained blind to Priam's hatred. I think, Wallace," said Ellery, setting his feet on the coffee table, "yes, I think you got hold of Priam's proboscis very early with your magnetic grip,

231

and steered it this way and that. It would be a technique that appealed to you, feeling your victim's desires and directing them, unsuspected, according to your own. Sensing that Priam wanted Hill dead, you led him around to becoming actively conscious of it. Then you let him chew on it. It took months, probably. But you had plenty of time, and you'd proved your patience.

"In the end, it became a passion with him.

"Of course, to do anything at all along that line he needed an accomplice. There couldn't be any question as to who the accomplice might be. It wouldn't surprise me if you dropped a few hints that you weren't altogether unfamiliar with violence ... you had vague 'memories,' perhaps, that came and went conveniently through the curtain of your 'amnesia' ... It was all very gradual, but one day you got there. It was out. And you were to do the 'legwork.'"

Wallace surveyed the flames dreamily. Keats, watching him, listening to Ellery, had the most childish sense that all this was happening elsewhere, to other people.

"Priam had plans of his own. They would be Priam-like plans, crude and explosive—a Molotov cocktail sort of thing. And you 'admired' them. But perhaps something a little less direct ...? In discussing the possibilities you may have suggested that there might be something in the common background of Priam and Hill that would give Priam—always Priam—a psychologically sound spring-board for a really clever plan. Eventually you got the story of Adam—of yourself—out of him. Because, of course, that's what you were after all along.

"After that, it was ridiculously easy. All you had to do was put ideas into Priam's head, so that they could come out of his mouth and, in doing so, convince him that they were original with him. In time you had the whole thing explicit. There was the plot that would give Priam the indestructible garment of innocence, Priam was convinced it was all his idea ... and all the time it was the very plot you'd planned to use yourself. That must have been a great day, Wallace."

Ellery turned to Keats.

"From that point it was a mere matter of operations. He'd mastered the technique of cuckolding Priam, psychologically as well as maritally; at every stage he made Priam think Priam was directing events and that he, Wallace, was carrying them out; but at every stage it was Priam who was ordering exactly what Wallace wanted him to order.

"It was Wallace who dictated the note to Hill, with Priam doing the typing—just as you figured out, Keats. Wallace didn't call it dictation—he undoubtedly called it, humbly, 'suggestions.' And Priam typed away on a machine on which the T key was broken. Accident? There are no accidents where Wallace-Adam is concerned. He'd managed, somehow, and without Priam's knowledge, to break that key; and he managed to persuade Priam that there was no danger in using the typewriter that way, since a vital part of the plan was to see to it that Hill destroyed the note after he read it. Of course, what Wallace wanted was a record of that note *for us*, and if Hill hadn't secretly made a copy of it, you may be sure Wallace would have seen to it that a transcription was found—by me or by you or by someone like Laurel who would take it to us at once. In the end, the clue of the missing T would trap Priam through the new T on Priam's machine ... just as Wallace planned."

The man beyond Keats permitted himself a slight smile. He was looking down at his glass, modestly.

"And when he realized what was at the back of Priam's mind," continued Ellery, "the plan to kill *him* ... Wallace made use of that, too. He took advantage of events so that the biter would be bitten. When I told Wallace what I 'knew,' it coincided perfectly with his final move. The only trouble was—eh, Adam?—I knew a little too much."

Wallace raised his glass. Almost it was a salute. But then he put it to his lips and it was hard to say if the gesture had meant anything at all.

Keats stirred, shifting in the comfortable chair as if it were uncomfortable. There was a wagon track between his eyes, leaving his forehead full of ruts.

"I'm not going good tonight, Queen," he mumbled. "So far this all sounds to me like just theory. You say this man is Charles Adam. You put a lot of arguments together and it sounds great. Okay, so he's Charles Adam. But how could you have been sure? It's *possible* that he wasn't Charles Adam. That he was John Jones, or Stanley Brown, or Cyril St. Clair, or Patrick Silverstein. I say it's *possible*. Show me that it isn't."

Ellery laughed. "You're not getting me involved in a defence of what's been, not always admiringly, called the 'Queen method.' Fortunately, Keats, I *can* show you that it's *not* possible for this man to be anyone else *but* Charles Adam. Where did he tell us he got the name Alfred Wallace?"

"He said he picked it out of thin air when he got an amnesia attack and couldn't remember who he was." Keats glowered. "All of which was horse radish."

"All of which was horse radish," nodded Ellery, "except the fact that, whatever his name was, it certainly *wasn't* Alfred Wallace. He did pick that when he wanted an assumed name."

"So what? There's nothing unusual about the name Alfred Wallace."

"Wrong, Keats. There's something not only unusual and remarkable about the name Alfred Wallace, but unique.

"Alfred Wallace—Alfred Russel Wallace—was a contemporary of Charles Darwin's. Alfred Wallace was the naturalist who arrived at a formulation of the evolution theory almost simultaneously with Darwin, although independently. In fact, their respective announcements were first given to the world in the form of a joint essay read before the Linnean Society in 1858, and published in the Society's *Journal* the same year. Darwin had drafted the outline of his *Theory* in manuscript in 1842. Wallace, ill with fever in South America, came to the same conclusions and sent his findings to Darwin, which is how they came to be published simultaneously."

Ellery tapped his pipe against an ashtray. "And here we have a man up to his ears in the Hill-Priam case who carries the admittedly assumed name of Alfred Wallace. A case in which a naturalist named Charles Adam used the theory of evolution—fathered by Darwin and the 19th century Alfred Wallace—as the basis of a series of clues. Coincidence that the secretary of one of Adam's victims should select as his alias one of the two names associated with evolution? Out of the billions of possible name combinations? Just as Charles Adam founded his entire murder plan on his scientific knowledge, so he drew an alias out of his science's past. He would hardly have stooped to calling himself Darwin; the obviousness of that would have offended him. But the name Alfred Wallace is almost unknown to the general public. Perhaps the whole process was unconscious; it would be a delightful irony if this man, who prides himself on being the god of events, should be mortally tripped by his own unconscious mind."

Keats got up so suddenly that even Wallace was startled.

But the detective was paying no attention to Wallace. In the firelight his fair skin was a pebbled red as he scowled down at Ellery, who was regarding him inquiringly.

"So when you hired him as your secretary, Queen, you knew you were hiring Adam—a successful killer?"

"That's right, Keats."

"Why?"

Ellery waved his dead pipe. "Isn't it evident?"

"Not a bit. Why didn't you tell all this to me a long time ago?"

"You haven't thought it out, Lieutenant." Ellery stared into the fire, tapping his lips with the stem. "Not a word of it constitutes legal evidence. None of it is proof as proof is construed in a court of law. Even if the story could have been spread before the Court, on the record, in the absence of legal proof of any of its component parts it would certainly have resulted in a dismissal of a charge against Wallace, and it might even have so garbled things as to get Priam off, too, or sentenced to a punishment that didn't fit his crime.

"I didn't want to chance Priam's squeezing out by reason of sheer complication and confusion, Keats. I preferred to let him get what was coming to him and try to deal with the gentleman in this chair later. And here he's been for a couple of months, Keats, under my eye and thumb, and I still haven't found the answer. Maybe you have a suggestion?"

"He's a damn murderer," grated Keats. "Granted he got a dirty deal twenty-five years ago ... when he took the law into his own hands he became as bad as they were. And if that sounds like a Sunday-school sermon, let it!"

"No, no, it's very true," said Ellery sadly. "There's no doubt about that at all, Lieutenant. He's a bad one. You know it, I know it, and he knows it. But he isn't talking, and what can you and I prove?"

"A rubber hose—"

"I don't believe would do it," said Ellery. "No, Keats, Wallace-Adam is a pretty special problem. Can we prove that he broke the T key on Priam's typewriter? Can we prove that he suggested the plan behind Priam's murder of Hill? Can we prove that he worked out the series of death threats against Priam ... threats Priam boasted in court he'd sent to himself? Can we prove *anything* we know this fellow did or said or suggested or planned? A single thing, Keats?"

Wallace looked up at Lieutenant Keats of the Hollywood Division with respectful interest.

Keats glared back at him for fully three minutes.

Then the Hollywood detective reached for his hat, jammed it down over his ears, and stamped out.

The front door made a loud, derisive noise.

And Keats's car roared down the hill as if the devil were after it.

Ellery sighed. He began to refill his pipe.

"Damn you, Adam. What am I going to do with you?"

The man reached for another of Ellery's cigarettes.

Smiling his calm, secretive, slightly annoying smile, he said, "You can call me Alfred."

236